Old News

Books by Ed Ifkovic

The Edna Ferber Mysteries
Lone Star
Escape Artist
Make Believe
Downtown Strut
Final Curtain
Café Europa
Cold Morning
Old News

Old News

An Edna Ferber Mystery

Ed Ifkovic

Poisoned Pen Press

Poisoned Pen Press
6962 E. First Ave., Ste. 103
Scottsdale, AZ 85251
www.poisonedpenpress.com
info@poisonedpenpress.com

Printed in the United States of America

For Bob and Ginny

Chapter One

"Murderer! The nerve!"

My mother's icy words startled me. I stopped walking, baffled, as she pinched her face into a tight, hard mask, her dark eyes glassy with fury. Yet she was staring straight ahead, taking in the busy hot July sidewalk. Nearby, in front of a four-story apartment building, a boy in grimy knickers and slough boy cap was batting a baseball with a hickory stick while another boy, crouched down on the opposite sidewalk, yelled to him. "C'mon, Izzy. Learn to hit the ball. C'mon." Hearing my mother's loud voice, the boy with the bat froze, stepped onto a stoop, tucked his bat between his legs, his eyes wide.

"Mother." I reached out and touched her elbow, but she flicked me away. "What?"

She darted ahead. "That brazen woman," she was mumbling. "How dare she!"

For a split second, almost involuntarily, she

turned her head to the left, resting her glacial gaze on the woman tucked into an old Adirondack chair on a shadowy front porch. Throwing back her head in a display of disgust—a gesture I'd long endured—my mother let out a harrumph. I found myself smiling in spite of myself. My little mother, like a fussy yet feisty stepmother out of a child's fairy tale, appeared a stick-figure vaudeville dowager, all indignation and bile.

"*Khutspedik*!" She slipped into Yiddish. "Brazen! Some folks have no shame, Edna."

"What?" I adjusted the package I was carrying.

My mother unfroze her mask, striding ahead so quickly she left me standing there, the bewildered daughter, watching the old woman on that porch.

Suddenly, horribly, our eyes locked.

What I saw in that woman's withered face was a troubling mix of fear and sadness, a woman folded into that big chair. She wrapped her chubby arms around her chest and suddenly dipped her head so that her abundant ivory white hair shielded a haunted face. I gasped, so stark was that fleeting meeting of eyes.

My mother had already climbed the steps of the sprawling Victorian home next door, pausing on the landing to look back and yell out my name—"Edna, really!"

I said again, "What?" She responded with a loud clearing of her throat.

When I looked back at the porch, the old woman had disappeared. A screen door slammed. Then an unseen hand closed the heavy oak door behind it.

I couldn't move.

"Edna, would you become the talk of the street?" my mother hissed. "What is the matter with you?" Her waving became frantic.

I followed her up the steps, but glanced over at the empty front porch. The two houses were similar in style, three-story homes with wraparound porches, floor-to-ceiling windows, though the one we were visiting had ledges with boxes of ivy and phlox. Glorious houses with arabesque trim and gingerbread scalloping. They were anomalies on Monroe Street, now dotted by four-story wood-framed apartment houses, the first floors occupied by storefront dentists, tobacco shops, kosher bakeries, and tailors. The long block began at Maxwell Street, that roaring, cluttered open-air marketplace. My mother and I had stepped off the Jefferson trolley, skirted around pushcart peddlers and hawkers, and headed down Monroe. The soot-blackened apartment houses were ramshackle, unpainted, with faded green asphalt shingles and tarpaper roofs. At the corner little girls played hopscotch, giggling and speaking in broken English. Despite the heat, two bearded men argued in a doorway, both dressed in *kapotes*, those long black coats, and wide-brimmed Russian hats pulled low over shiny foreheads. They spoke rapid-pace Yiddish, pointing at each other, speaking over the other.

Every time we walked along Monroe, my mother grumbled. Today an itinerant scissor-grinder, his rickety contraption braced to his back, had jostled her, and was rewarded with a verbal comeuppance. The same with a shifty young man who pulled up his sleeve to reveal his arm covered with used watches as he whispered of a deal he'd give her. Only look, please.

When she entered the foyer of the home we were visiting for two weeks, she let out a sigh of relief: the grisly gauntlet survived, pesky street rabble avoided, precious refuge won. My mother wasn't happy visiting on Monroe Street.

"I really have no choice," she'd whispered to me when the invitation was offered. "Old friends. My dear Esther. We have no choice."

Now my mother dropped her packages onto a little oak table near the front door, then grasped her throat, a gesture that mimicked someone strangling her—in case I missed the point. She faced me. "I will go to bed knowing a murderer sleeps steps away."

Again, my feeble question. "What?"

"We will be murdered in our beds."

"Mother…"

She lost patience with me. "Lord's sake, Edna. For a writer you certainly have no memory for… important events." She nodded toward the unseen home next door. "Leah Brenner. That dreadful woman stabbed her poor husband Ivan to death. A knife to the neck. A decent man, hard-working, stabbed." She pointed. "Right there in that parlor. Feet from us. Next door." She shivered and walked away. "There is so little justice left in Chicago."

"I remember now," I called after her.

She narrowed her eyes. "I should hope so, Edna. I talked of nothing else for days. Frankly, it was the murder none of us will ever forget."

● ● ● ● ● ●

I did remember, of course, though I'd not thought about the scandal for years. In fact, I never knew Leah Brenner years back, and probably had glimpsed her only a few times. But I did have a vague memory, one time, of seeing an attractive woman standing on that very porch. True, I'd only visited my mother's old friend, Esther, one other time, back in the summer of 1905, another sweltering, heat-wave summer, two blurred weeks when I was nineteen years old and working as a reporter for the *Milwaukee Tribune*. That was eighteen years back now, a lifetime ago. I'd never said a word to Leah Brenner, though I kept that image of a beautiful woman in her forties, out of place on that porch in a dress no one else on Monroe Street would dare to wear, a daffodil-yellow taffeta go-to-meeting dress.

Now one image came back to me: she stood there, immobile, her dark hair covered by a black lace scarf—despite the steamy heat—as she watched the street with a cold stare. It was the coldness that made me notice her. A colorful Goya portrait—a voluptuous woman in yellow and black.

I was a young woman then, impatient with that mandatory visit to my mother's old friends, Esther Newmann and her family. Esther was a kind, overflowing woman, round as a plump hen, someone my mother, Julia, sometimes claimed was a distant cousin. Other times she said Esther was simply an old friend of the family, part of a close-knit neighborhood back in Germany. Kindred spirits, these families, bound with a loyalty to the Old World left behind. But the story shifted every so often.

During that short visit, Leah Brenner stood on her porch dressed in that elegant tea dress and muttered as some errant boys took a shortcut to the next street by running through her yard, slingshots in back pockets and huckleberry grins on their beet-red faces. That was the sole image I held of her—not one of heinous murder.

At that time I had a schoolgirl crush on her son, Jacob—slender Jacob with the shaggy hair and careful moustache and those mooncalf mink-brown eyes in a long, gaunt face—twenty-five or -six, a vagabond poet who once idly flirted with me. I, horrified and sputtering, turned my back on him—not because I was rejecting the handsome man but because I was afraid he'd see me blushing, trembling. He wasn't happy with my cavalier dismissal. His cruel ditty spread up and down the street that week, words that others happily hurled at me as I walked there:

Edna, Edna, sugar and spice,
An orchid locked in frozen ice.
Edna, Edna,
Not nice—

The rhyme did nothing to squelch my foolish ardor. I'd watch him saunter down Monroe, headed to Maxwell Street, whistling, his coal-black hair glistening with oil, black polished high-button shoes, and a rakish cap on his head. He'd wink at the girls, do a half-bow, and his matinee-hero moustache would shift seductively. I dreamed about him, felt my heart flutter when he appeared, but so did my sister, Fannie. So did most of the girls on Monroe Street.

Three years later, another brutally hot Chicago summer, August 2, 1908, his mother plunged a knife into the neck of her ailing husband, Ivan, the local butcher. A marital spat, ferocious, in the family parlor, and then—an impossible act. Or so it was said. The police dragged her in, but she'd seemed in a coma, unresponsive or icy, stoic, so the gossipmongers variously reported. According to my mother, she had to be carried to the Harrison Street Station lockup. She nodded her head at their questions, closed her eyes, and waited. Everyone believed she was guilty because she never fought back. Even, I heard, her children—including my beloved Jacob. Everyone talked about it...that long hot summer in South Chicago, a word-of-mouth court of law, a rag-tag gossip mill of Homeric sweep. Did you hear how Leah Brenner, that beautiful woman, went mad and killed her husband? A pity, such a stunning woman.

My mother had whispered. "And a Jewish mother, can you believe? Such things don't happen." Then, a sigh. "A curse on that family, always."

I hadn't thought of that murder for years, though I still thought, rarely, of Jacob.

We'd all read the sheaf of news clippings Esther sent to us in Appleton, Wisconsin, the blow-by-blow account in the *Chicago Tribune* and the *Herald & Examiner*. My mother devoured them as though reading a yellow-backed potboiler from Bertha M. Clay. Leah Brenner a murderer? It never worked for me: that juxtaposition of the attractive matron in yellow who struck me as so composed, a beautiful woman eyeing the hardscrabble boys slinking past. Then the story disappeared from the press and from our conversations.

My own world was unraveling then—my disaffection with my grueling reporting job in Milwaukee, my sudden and unwelcome nervous breakdown, my sheepish return to Appleton, my… my beloved father dying…

Now, fifteen years after the sensational murder of a simple Jewish butcher by his devoted wife, I was back on Monroe Street for two weeks—and Leah Brenner sat on her front porch. She probably was in her late fifties or early sixties now, but she looked older—the abundant white hair, the tiny body. She startled me. Worse, I'd caught the woman's eye and was immediately enveloped by a stunning loneliness that covered her like a shroud.

The knife-wielding murderer back on her porch, her hands folded decorously into her lap, her woeful stare taking in the helter-skelter street.

Leah Brenner had come home.

Chapter Two

My mother raised her voice and wagged a finger like a hectoring schoolmarm. "For God's sake, why didn't you tell me, Esther?"

Rattled, Esther mumbled an apology.

"We'll be murdered in our beds." My mother pointed to the ceiling, doubtless imagining her unprotected bed at the end of the upstairs hallway. She shivered.

Esther's voice faltered. "Well, Julia, really…I think…you…I didn't think you…" She stopped, helpless. "*Nu*, I'm sorry."

My mother was muttering something.

"What?" I asked.

"That woman was always too pretty. Such women are dangerous. There ought to be a law against…excessive beauty."

I smiled at her. "Mother, hardly a crime."

Her glance was unfriendly. "Thank God we in this family never had to worry about such a problem."

Esther's eyes softened. "It's all right, Julia. Leah is harmless. She's been back for a few years now. No one says anything. Life is…normal now. Nothing bad…"

My mother started to say something, but stopped.

In the steamy, large kitchen, I caught my breath. Sweat dripped into my eyes. My dress stuck to my body. A dreadfully hot day. A loaf of bread was rising in the oven, a pot of water boiled on the stove, and Esther chased after a pesky fly with a swatter. The two women seemed oblivious to the sauna. Instead, they chatted away, merrily, peculiarly content in the room, while I patted my forehead with a handkerchief.

This was the heart of the house, the pulse, safe haven for the women of the home, *di kikh*: cozy, with the tantalizing aromas of a meal in preparation. The heart and soul of the rollicking, loving Jewish family, a room where conversations and confidences among women took place. The thick oak round claw-foot table was covered with stained oilcloth, the walls had been painted too many times—now lush green and white, with traces of old red and black seeping through—and on the walls hung homiletic mottoes encased in glass and blunt black frames, an oversized calendar by the doorway, Hebrew letters advertising Nate's

Delicatessen on Maxwell above a grainy black-and-white photograph of the popular storefront. The air was thick with the battling scents of cinnamon, of vanilla, of diced peppers and onions, of sour cream. Every afternoon the inviting, rich tang of yeast as bread dough swelled in a white enamel bowl on the sink counter, stacks of freshly laundered dish towels covering the top. Comforting as a baby's breath, the heartbeat here took you back to storied villages happily, if mournfully, left behind in the Old Country. *Unsere leite.* Our people. Sit. Please. Make yourself to home. *Kum areyn.* Come in.

Esther had been rolling out dough for strudel, and the wafer-thin dough covered most of the table, even lapping precariously over one edge. Motes of white flour drifted into the air, and a slant of afternoon sunlight streamed in from a side window, illuminating a ghost-like shaft across the room. She'd started to cut the dough, but had paused, knife in hand, as my mother thundered the news of Leah sitting on her own porch. I saw momentary confusion in Esther's face, her eyes blinking, but also something else: a desire that Julia leave the subject alone. Esther liked an even, serene life, daily routines that allowed her peaceful nights of undisturbed rest.

"Well…" she stammered, glancing away.

"Well, nothing, Esther dear."

Sighing, Esther put down the knife and wiped her flour-white hands with a dishtowel. She turned to me with a feeble smile. "Edna, some lemonade. Fresh. For you." She hurried to the icebox and poured me a glass. Icy cold, tart, and robust. I remembered it from eighteen years before. Esther's summertime elixir. A cure-all.

But not today.

Both women stared at each other, a curious standoff, these two childhood friends. Esther sighed, but my mother was not in the mood for peace. A contrast, indeed, these two women, though both were short. Esther, early sixties now, happily round, ringlets of fat around her neck, her middle, even her forearms, her moonlike face unblemished and pink, the old woman beginning to look like the baby she was more than a half-century before. She'd stuffed herself into a flowered housedress that had seen too many washings, the crimson tea roses now bleeding pink; she ignored a burst seam at one hip, the unraveled hem of the dress that sagged at her ankles, these days an old-fashioned look in a post-war decade in which hemlines had begun to shoot upward. A stained white apron, much like a butcher's apron, thick and severe, was tied at the back and dropped to her shins. With her iron-gray hair pulled back from her forehead and sloppily tied with a frayed ribbon, she looked the aged family servant, the Tuesday washerwoman who spoke no English and wept in Yiddish.

A contrast to cosmopolitan Julia Ferber, the same age, born into the same comfortable North Side Chicago neighborhood, this woman who left the rigidity and coziness of the German Jewish home to marry the handsome Hungarian immigrant with dreams and nothing else. Julia, a slender slip of a woman, always in fashionable dress of frilly lace brocade or creamy burgundy silk or summery white linen—Julia, whose narrow, tight face you never forgot because her deep-set eyes held you, shadowy, so much anger there, so much resentment, so much judgment, so much…unforgiveness. A woman who never let her two daughters forget her failed marriage to a quiet, scholarly man who wouldn't fight back. A dynamo, always here, then there, and never happy anywhere. A husband dead now after years of illness and blindness, her life spent six months in New York, six months in Chicago, dependent on a daughter who made bags of money from her popular short stories sold to *Everybody's* and *Good Housekeeping*.

She never thanked me.

Both woman sat down in the hard-backed chairs pulled from the table, and I joined them, all three of us quietly sipping lemonade. Julia faced her friend, waiting.

"Nearly one hundred in the shade today," I commented slowly. "Three days in a row." No one answered me. Beads of sweat glistened on our faces. Another housefly buzzed by, and Esther absently followed its progress. She was too tired to swat it. She sat there without talking.

Avoiding Julia's stare, Esther finally broke the silence, her fingertips playing with the edge of the strudel dough, already turning brown. "You gotta feel sorry for her."

Julia bit her lip and put down the glass with a thud. Flour wafted into the air, a small white cloud. "Esther, you were always the easygoing, soft-hearted sad sack." A thin smile, kind. "I grant you that. A *mensch*, truly. What can I say? A little girl hugging stray cats who always scratched you. Giving away your last piece of candy." Then her voice hardened. "But surely you cannot allow…"

Esther held up her hand. "Allow? Julia, a woman can live in her own house. What say do I have? Any of us? No laws broken…she has children…"

My mother returned the hand gesture, traffic-sign style. "In the name of God, Esther. Do you hear the words that come from you? There are

young children on this street. Families. Respectable folks."

Helpless, Esther turned to me. "Edna, what
do you think?"

I deliberated. "Esther, I have one brief image
of Leah Brenner from eighteen years ago. Before
the murder, of course. She is standing on her
porch dressed for a party in a bright yellow dress.
I remember thinking—what a beautiful woman.
Jacob's mother. That memory—which I know is
not helping here." I drew in my breath. "Well, to
be truthful, today she's a little old lady, harmless,
still an eye-catching woman, I grant you—but
lost-looking, sad."

My mother tapped my wrist with her fingertips, her familiar Morse code that communicated
my failure to grasp even basic human behavior.
"Edna, really. You're always ready to forgive the
worst of humanity."

I narrowed my eyes. "And you sometimes
condemn the best of humanity."

She drew her lips into a thin line. "That makes
no sense, Edna."

I shrugged, imitating her, and spoke to Esther.
"It was so long ago. All I recall are bits of information from the clippings you sent us. I remember
that she was sent away, no? But not to prison, if
I remember correctly. Some home? So now she is

living back at her home? Was she found guilty?"
My mother visited Esther three or four times over
the long span of years, the last perhaps five years
earlier, but she never mentioned Leah to me.

Both women glanced at each other, conspiratorially, as though considering how to shield a pesky
child from grownup indiscretion and scandal. My
mother's crooked mouth suggested disgust—and
disbelief.

Esther peered up at the copper-plated ceiling,
disturbed by a wispy dust web hanging off the
overhead light. She whispered a word. "Guilty." She
shook her head sadly. "The whole story…I mean,
it's the only story that this street cared about. But
there are not many old-timers still living on the
street nowadays. When it happened back then,
she…froze. They found her bending over Ivan's
body, quiet, quiet. Like…dead. She never said a
word…even when they charged her with murder.
The whole time—quiet. Only this moaning from
deep inside her. She wouldn't answer. Like she just
lost her voice."

Julia interrupted. "They never found the knife.
I remember that."

Esther had a faraway look in her eyes. "I never
understood that. They said she probably washed
it off, put it back in the kitchen. You know, there

were knives everywhere. The wife of a butcher." She actually smiled wistfully.

"And they believe she had the presence of mind to do that?" I wondered. "A crime the result of an argument. That strikes me as impossible."

Esther shrugged. "So who knows? What can I say? They took her away. Everything happened so fast."

"She confessed?"

"No. Stony silence. What I know is what Jacob tells my Adolph. They are very close, those two…even afterwards. Especially afterwards. Adolph the jokester can't tolerate nobody talking about that family. Jacob took it real hard. After all, his mama was taken away. So close to his mama, that boy. Always. He's a young man then, a boy really, crying, crying. Some whispered her silence covered her son's guilt. A mother will not let a son be taken away. So who knows? So my Adolph he followed Jacob around, the protector always, even as boys. Everyone pointed at Jacob. So sad, the young boy whose mama slices his father…" She squinted. "And Adolph tells me that Jacob says to the police, 'She didn't kill Papa.' Over and over, like a chant, he says. Jacob almost arrested, fighting the police. He wants to rip his mama from the arms of the police. Yet the police don't believe it.

'Yes,' they say, 'simple story. Wife kills husband. It happens all the time.'"

I interrupted, peeved. "And the whole street believes it."

My mother whispered, "They'd had a big fight that morning, Leah and Ivan. A horrible fight, bloody. Everyone talked about it."

"Married folks fight," I offered.

A slap of sarcasm from my mother. "So how would you know?"

A familiar barb. Me, unmarried at thirty-eight, the spinster novelist who drifted from Chicago to New York, suitcases and mother at her side. My sister, Fannie, happily married now with daughters. Though my mother harped on my unmarried state, I also knew—as she knew, deep down and resolutely—that she demanded this spinster daughter remain so, and stationed at her side.

I pursed my lips. "Because that's all I used to see."

My mother and I both tried to look sorry—a tired skirmish, that one.

"Anyway," Esther went on, "I guess they decided she was crazy, like she'd lost her mind in a fit of anger—she'd have to be, Jacob told Adolph, so the judge or someone put her away. Not jail but…"

Julia burst out, "Not over to Dunning, the asylum for women, but to Jacksonville, an asylum hundreds of miles away from here. A seven-by-eight cell, I heard."

Esther concluded, "The family told everyone she went to stay with cousins in New York. Down Hester Street. We just nodded at them. What could we say?"

"Good God," my mother cried, "a bed in Bedlam for her. A murderer, after all."

"But life went on. You gotta go on. So Jacob and Leah's older sister, Sarah, lived in the house, along with her twins, Ella and Emma. The older son, Herman, got married right away, ordered everybody around. He makes a lot of money and moves away." She shrugged her shoulders. "Rich and more rich, that man. *Gelt geyt tsu gelt.*" Money goes to money. "After a while people stopped talking about Leah Brenner, the butcher's crazy wife. Now and then someone babbled something and Rabbi Kurtz would knock on the door. Silence, please. A little respect. A family shattered. My Adolph, then so religious—the Talmudic scholar, would you believe?—he quotes, 'One shouldn't open his mouth to Satan.' Like evil talk brings the devil into the house. So Adolph shut the gossipers up."

"But now she's back on her porch." My mother pointed through a kitchen wall, her bony finger trembling. "A dreadful reminder. When you

romp with the devil, you infect the neighborhood."
Again, the shudder. "This cannot end well."

Esther shrugged as she moved to refill the
lemonade glasses. "Now you sound like my Adolph
quoting Scripture." She went on. "Around three
years ago we heard she was back. Maybe less. No
one knows exactly when. She was let out for some
reason. I don't know the facts. But one day, casual-
like and without warning, Jacob tells my Adolph
his mother was back at home, but hidden inside.
He seemed…happy, my Adolph said, but he didn't
know how to talk to her. We never seen her, maybe
a fleeting glimpse through a window…if you were
passing by and glanced over there. The summers
went by, and she never came outside. You knew she
was inside that house. Like a shadow on the wall.
It was a little…scary or something."

"What about her family?" I asked.

"You'd see Sarah heading to Maxwell Street
to shop, you'd see some strangers knocking on the
door and disappearing inside, you'd see Herman
in his Chesterfield topcoat and silk hat and cigars
parking the town car at the curb and going inside
to see his mother. But never with his wife and little
children. You never saw Leah outside, gossiping
over the back fence like the old days. Or hoeing
in the vegetable garden like she always liked to
do." She sighed. "Leah and I used to share coffee

at this very table…so many mornings. She was my friend." She touched the strudel dough gingerly. "Then Jacob stopped talking about it. Adolph had nothing to tell me." She stressed, "And I *did* ask. What can I say?"

I ran a finger down the sweaty glass I sipped from, puzzled. "But today she's on her porch. She's outside."

Esther whispered. "Well, maybe she got a little crazy inside that house. Wouldn't you? Like, go crazy? A world outside and you can't go to it. No air to breathe, you know. This hot, hot summer, so brutal. Maybe she got tired of staring at those walls. How many cages do a woman gotta live in? Yes, I've seen her out there one other time, a week ago. It made my heart race. I even nodded at her as I passed to market. She turned away."

My mother was impatient. "Esther, you were always too forgiving."

A surprisingly sharp look from Esther. "Leave the woman in peace, I say. Please, Julia dear. The woman's been through hell."

"She created her…"

Esther stood. "I feel sorry for her."

"She ruined her family, Esther."

For a second Esther closed her eyes, then popped them open. Her eyes were bright. "I sometimes wonder if that's true. We sit in this

kitchen and have all the answers." She grinned
now. "Enough talk, this sadness. A short visit, Julia,
you and dear Edna. After all these years. And Edna
getting real famous, too." She smiled affectionately
at me, a twinkle in her eye. "Who'd have believed
it? The short stories in the magazines that come
in the mail. The novel *The Girls*. Your picture in
the *Tribune*, no less. Everyone talking about the
Ferber girl who is a New York wonder. A writer.
And when I heard you were writing a new book on
Chicago—about the Dutch truck farmers outside
the city, High Prairie, the marketplace Haymarket,
maybe even Maxwell Street, what do you call it?
Selina? Or *So Big*?—I don't know, I remember you
told me, Julia—I says to my Sol that an invitation is
overdue. She can visit the marketplace so close by,
a block away, the peddlers, the hot dog stands…"
She stopped.

A throat cleared, a rheumy grunt. We stared
into the doorway. Esther's mother-in-law, Molly,
unseen, listening from the hallway.

Julia was mumbling, "Dear Esther, we *do*
have rooms being readied in the Windermere at
Hyde Park in a couple weeks—the painting will
be done then. Edna likes to be in Chicago in the
summer—to write. The energy, she says."

"I do *love* it," I added. "To walk to the stores
off the Loop, a block from Lake Michigan with

the soft breezes, up and down State Street, lazing in Jackson Park, the theaters on Randolph and…"

"It ain't this old neighborhood," Esther broke in. "Here"—and now she smiled at me—"you come for atmosphere."

"And your cooking." I laughed and patted her on the wrist. "Your pot roast makes me slobber like a family dog. So succulent, so perfect."

Esther spoke to my mother. "But I don't know how Edna can finish her book in this scorching heat. Is it the hottest Chicago summer ever? Such a life we live here in Chicago. Every day in the nineties."

"I think 1923 will go on record as…"

We stopped, all of us turning. *Tap tap tap.* The loud banging of a cane on the hardwood floor of the hallway, purposely, deliberately, Molly stood there, her wrinkled face set in a censorious glare. While we watched, she emphatically banged the cane. *Tap tap tap.*

"Molly," Esther faltered, "you were napping?"

A quivering voice, laced with iron. "What napping can an old lady do with the three of you yammering out here about stuff you got no business talking of?" She stepped into the room but didn't sit, staring at us.

The tall, thin woman was slightly stooped now, one shoulder lower than the other, the slight hint of a sagging cheek. Molly Newmann, family matriarch, redoubtable, the fierce head of this household, a woman who stymied conversation in a room and then, begrudgingly, would permit it to resume. Molly Newmann, felled by a piddling stroke last year that did nothing to temper her power, save for her reluctant reliance on a thick black walnut cane and too much peach-tinted rouge on that failed cheek. Brilliant white hair maneuvered into an incongruous French pompadour, always impeccable, a face ravaged by wrinkles I didn't remember, the martinet in her late eighties. A face dusted each morning as though flouring a table for strudel. Long, stringy arms, liver-spotted, arthritic in the fingertips, but awesome in their power to demand. Once she'd been famous for her aristocratic mien, the erect spine, the absolute pronouncements, that unyielding stare that made her daughter-in-law quake and sputter; now, crippled, she refused to believe she was mortal.

I'd heard Esther whisper to my mother that she was dying, the doctors warned them, but Esther added that no one, especially Molly the near-nonagenarian, accepted the inevitable. "She'll bury us all."

Molly adored my mother—a kindred dictator—and tolerated me, but was notoriously indifferent to her son, Sol. Yet she doted crazily on her forty-year-old grandson, Adolph, affectionately called Ad by everyone but his mother and grand-mother, unmarried and living upstairs, a gadabout bachelor who spent most of his free time flattering the old woman when he wasn't promising to marry Minna, his adoring girlfriend of ten years. A Jewish patient Griselda, long-suffering.

"Molly," Esther reported, "Leah is on her porch again."

I spoke up. "We were surprised, my mother and I. We'd gone to pick up some things at Marshal Field's and…"

Molly tapped her cane, lethal punctuation. *Tap tap tap.* "So what?"

"I guess the old reporter in me…you know… it's a intriguing story, that murder, filled with…"

Molly drew in her parched cheeks, and the multitude of deep-ground wrinkles shifted like some sudden seismic upheaval of landscape. "We will not discuss that woman in this house. That harridan. Poor Ivan, a good man, stabbed." Her words leaked out of her barely open lips.

"I caught her eye and…" I stopped.

Again, the rhythmic tapping of that cane. Fierce, demanding. *Tap tap tap.* One hand gripped the table, her fingers carelessly squishing the hardening strudel dough. "Old news. That's all it is. Over now. Lord, we lived though it *once*. Next door to reporters and noisy folks and prying idiots and weeping children and pathetic Jacob hiding out upstairs here with Adolph when he wasn't baying at the moon…I'll not have it in my home." Her voice bounced off the ceiling. "I won't."

With that she turned, nearly toppling, stabilized the cane, and left the room.

Esther picked up the knife and gazed at the table. "My God, I've ruined the strudel."

Chapter Three

On Friday night and on Saturday till sundown, Monroe Street was quiet. The reverential shade of Shabbas, the suspended breath and the intoxication of prayer. You could hear the long wail of the Illinois Central trains. Sometimes you could hear the wind off Lake Michigan. You heard the low hum of soft voices as folks strolled to temple, a murmur that lulled me, especially after the roar of New York City on a brilliant Saturday morning. I lingered on the front porch, waved off invitations to attend services, and fiddled with the pad in my lap, sketching out the midnight scene at Chicago's rough-and-tumble Haymarket, my heroine, Selina, loading her vegetables onto a two-horse wagon and venturing with her little boy, Dirk, into man's territory.

It didn't work, that scene—not here, not under a blazing sun and an Old World tableau of black-clad congregants, men with beards and bewigged women, a line of bedraggled children behind them.

A street now home to Russian Jews, devoutly Orthodox, who eyed the old guard worldly Germans with suspicion and sometimes anger. The Newmanns were nominally religious, German Reform, the men and women sitting together and the men without kippahs outside shul. Years back, a previous owner of the Newmann home had nailed mezuzahs on the entrances, though no one in the family ever touched them as they passed in or out. An occasional service, on the High Holy Days, of course, or to hear Rabbi Emil Hirsh speak at Temple Sinai on Grand Boulevard. But everyone went to hear that august man who inspired even the lackadaisical believer.

But on Saturday night Shabbos was over. The street began to percolate, children streaming outdoors, folks gathering on sidewalks, on stoops. And on Sunday morning, early, the sun peeping out, Monroe Street came gloriously alive. I rose at dawn to the distant *who-wah who-wah* of auto horns and excited sidewalk chatter and children yelling. Outside of my second-story bedroom—Mother across the hall, snoring contentedly, with Sol and Esther one door away, quiet—I saw the street bustling and jumping as souls headed to Maxwell Street, baskets over arms, canvas bags slung over shoulders, carts dragged behind them, little children tucked into sides.

Hurriedly, I dressed, intent on being in that swell of people, lost in that robust spirit, believing it would make my Selina come alive, my prose sing. When I came alive, my heroines did, too. A quick cup of strong black coffee in a chipped mug, a chunk of homemade, butter-slathered pumpernickel, a hard-boiled egg, and a glass of fresh-squeezed orange juice—and I was out the door.

Walking by the Brenner household, I noted its shabby respectability, the chalky white paint peeling off the sagging clapboards, a pale green shutter slipping from a hinge, a few missing roof tiles, the untrimmed boxwood hedges lining the cracked walkway. It was a house the inhabitants forgot about, and so different from its twin next door. There, proudly, Sol Newmann manicured the hedges, edged the sidewalk with an artist's eye, slapped on a fresh coat of sunny yellow paint to the clapboards at the end of winter, accented the shutters with a dark green tint. And Esther doubt-less was responsible for the glittering windows, so hard-polished they seemed not even there. Rows of petunias and larkspurs and marigolds banked the sidewalk, a wash of brilliant color. English ivy dripped from boxes positioned on the porch rail-ings. A showplace, really. In front of the Brenner home was a yellowing parched lawn. A large fallen tree limb rested in a clump of evergreens—an ugly remnant from the harsh, icy Chicago winter.

But as I passed by, the front door suddenly opened and for a brief second Leah Brenner stepped out, pushing against the screen door. She was juggling a cup of coffee and a napkin that held pastry or a roll, cradling both to her chest, so she didn't see me gawking there, the pesky intruder on her solitude. Then, spotting me, she backed into the screen door that had closed behind her, turning away, almost frightened.

Apologetically, I yelled, "Good morning, I'm…"

She was gone, scrambling back into the house, the heavy oak front door slamming behind her.

Feeling a little foolish now, I scurried down the block, past the apartment houses, and turned onto storied Maxwell Street. For a moment, breathless, I was overwhelmed by the spectacle before me, this cluttered, frantic Jewish marketplace, a cacophony of whistling and yelling and hectoring—a flow of mangled English, rapid-fire Yiddish, and a Babel of greenhorn Russian, German, Spanish, Polish, what have you. What really hit me were the pungent smells—frying onions, hot dogs boiling in bubbly oil, roasted garlic, overripe apples and pears, hot peanuts, roasting meats sputtering on grills, unwashed bodies, tattered clothing—stale, fetid aromas, both appealing and disgusting, so intense as to make me dizzy. On Sunday this "Poor Jewish Quarter," as the locals called it, at the intersection of Maxwell and Halsted, in the shadow of the Loop, pulsated, thrived, swelled, exploded. From dawn to dusk, an unbroken rhythm. "Jewtown."

Yet, even as I walked through the crowds of shoppers and vendors, Leah's riveting image stayed with me—I couldn't escape that face.

For an hour I wandered, enthralled by the spectacle that made me conjure up old market days in Eastern Europe: pushcarts with squealing wheels lumbered by, vendors hawked notions, old shoes, tobacco, watches, baubles, bits and pieces of jewelry, pocket knives. Women in shawls haggled over the price of tomatoes. Or beans. Or toothbrushes. A rug with the fringe coming undone. Under signs in Hebrew the pullers cajoled, beckoned—the fancy young men, slick and cheeky, who attempted to pull passersby into shops.

The first customer of the day—that needed sale that guaranteed good luck. *For you, sir, a deal. A bargain.* A skirmish between two bearded peddlers. *Mach mores, Judi.* Mind your manners, Jew! People in and out of shops—pawnbrokers, haberdashers, money lenders, kosher meats, bath houses, dry-goods emporiums, tailors, tobacco stands. *Your son, he should go to Izzy the shakhans. A marriage arranged. Easy. Such girls he knows, dutiful daughters.*

Long johns, worn once, almost new. Chickens squawking, then eerily silent. For a kosher home. Look inside. I. Klein. Bremmer Cookie Factory. Nathan's Ice Cream Parlor. Phillipson's Clothes. Wittenberg Matzoh. Nate's Delicatessen. Mackevich's Notions. Magic potions. Jezibel Root.

The streetcar emptied peddlers carrying packed burlap sacks on their backs. Haggle, haggle. *Such a bargain, you wouldn't believe, yes?* Or: *Today only, for you alone, your name on it.* Or: *New today, and only slightly worn, a winter coat from a rich lady.* In the middle of a heat wave, stultifying, the puller draped the wool coat over his shoulders. *A bargain. Today.* Mottled phrases mixed with Yiddish. *Trog Es Gezunterheyd.* Wear it in good health. *Such a hat will make you look like a Hollywood beauty. Five cents. A nickel. Is nothing. Truly. A bargain.*

Who's the big shot, oy? Such a Macher! Bertha's Rummage Store. Myer's Cigars. *A few cents. We're all poor. With God's help, we starved regularly,* the writer says. *Gypsies everywhere today. Watch out!*

Exhilarating madness, though uplifting.

I munched on a salty soft pretzel I bought for a penny, a smear of brown mustard gracing it for free. *For you alone, my dear…*

Fruit ice for you. Cherry. Pineapple. Lemon. An organ grinder. *Roszhinkes mit Mandlen.*

But my mind kept wandering back to that

quick glimpse of Leah Brenner in her doorway—
her hurried retreat. Worse, yesterday's sudden
eye contact: all that naked loneliness there, that
haunted emptiness.

Leah the murderer.

A knife in the neck.

I imagined I saw her on Maxwell Street. On
Twelfth Street. On Halsted Street. The white-haired
woman pushing doilies at me, her small eyes weepy.
Another old woman with a gaunt face—could an
old woman still be that beautiful after all the years?
Like Leah? The gnarled, bent woman, her head
wrapped in a black babushka, dipping her withered
fingers into hot water to extract a hot dog. Her, too.
All the old women. *Mein Yiddische Mame. For you,
my dear, a special treat, the best wiener. Today. The
sun is shining*…Even the beggar on Des Plaines.
The *schnorrer* with the melancholy eyes. Him, too.

Leah Brenner, touching all my moments on
the teeming street. Hand-shaking, back-slapping,
laughter, grunting. The puff of tobacco. *Menshlikh-
keit.* Communion. The Jew in the blood.

Finally, spent, I turned off Maxwell back
onto Monroe and stopped dead. On the corner
was the old kosher butcher shop once owned by
Ivan Brenner and his partner, Morrie Wolfsy. I'd
walked by it before, and often during my visit,
but now considered it. The two old friends ran

Nathan's Meat Market for years, the market named for Morrie's grandfather and Ivan's father, a happy compromise. Both their names still on the shadowy window, though Ivan was long murdered and Morrie had closed up shop a short time after the murder.

An unlikely partnership from the start, ill-fated: Ivan the German Jew who liked to sleep all day Saturday when the shop was closed for *Shabbos*, and Morrie, the craggy Russian Jew who criticized him for it, though he was hardly devout himself. *Ah, my friend Ivan, becoming a goy, he is.* They'd met years before at a bathhouse on Halsted, and became friendly. Each with so little cash. A partnership of shared monies that began to unravel almost at once, though they stayed in business for years and years. The bickering, the name-calling. Threats to leave.

Threats...

And then the murder.

The store sat empty now, not rented because Morrie refused to rent it for reasons no one understood, and the front plate-glass windows were smudged and grimy, ignored. Peering in, I saw empty counters, sagging shelves, thick dark sawdust still covering the floor. A light dangled off a loosened fixture. An abandoned store. Last night Esther told me that Morrie had operated the left side of the store—the meats—and Ivan the right side—the poultry. A line down the middle. Hours spent late on Saturday night and all day Sunday. Morrie hopped the Halsted Street streetcar, headed to the stockyards, returned with a slaughtered cow strapped to his hunched back, the carcass wrapped in waxed paper, staring at the floor as he ignored the other riders. Ivan lined up crates of squawking chickens and other fowl in the back room, where, once chosen by a finicky customer, they were summarily dispatched.

"Such fabulous duck breast, succulent, the lines for it on Sunday," Esther rhapsodized.

That compatible arrangement ended with Ivan's death. Morrie gave up the business.

But I was surprised to see a long table pulled into the center of the room, covered now with heaps of old clothing, bunched rags tied with string, battered shoes, crumpled hats. *Shmatte*. A rag picker's trove. As I stood there, an old man hobbled from a back room and spotted me, my face pressed against the window. I jumped back, embarrassed, but I realized he'd shown no surprise, no interest, not even an iota of curiosity. He simply *looked* at me. An ancient man with an ill-kept yellowish beard and a nearly bald head, dressed in a rumpled black suit with fringed black-and-white *tsitsis* under his black vest, a yarmulke precariously on his head. Then, eyes narrowed, he motioned me away.

I had no idea why I became so rattled, so easily.
I read his lips: Go away. *Oy*. You.
Stunned, I rushed to Esther's house.

Chapter Four

Leah Brenner was sitting on her porch.

I stopped walking. Glancing up, I half raised my arm, a tentative greeting that was awkward—and probably intrusive. I wasn't sure why I did so, but at that moment I flashed to my mother's blatant condemnation, Molly's fierce disapproval, and Esther's kind regard. There was something wrong with that picture, though I had no idea why I felt so. I didn't move, planted on the sidewalk. Heat waves rippled off the pavement. The leaves on the towering maple tree on her front lawn wilted, drooped. The sun hurt my eyes.

Her response took a moment, a swallowed "Hello." As though she'd not spoken in decades and was unsure she had any voice left. And that one muted word exacted an awful toll because she folded into herself, shoulders dropping, arms loose, her head dipping like a bird burying its head into its feathery chest.

"I'm sorry, Mrs. Brenner," I stammered, uncertain. "Do you remember me?"

A pause, then a scratchy voice, metallic. "No, but I know who you are now."

"I'm Edna Ferber, visiting next door. At the Newmanns'."

"I know all about your visit. You're the writer."

"Yes." I squirmed. "How do you know…?"

"Jacob told me you're next door. My son. He tells me the news of the street. Then my daughter mentioned *The Girls*. My daughter, Ella. They were talking about you. You know, I read one of your short stories…once."

"Once?"

"A while back." She leaned forward. "I loved it."

An awkward pause as we watched each other.

"I met Jacob eighteen years ago. One summer. I was here for a week or so. A vacation. My last time here. Visiting. I remember your son."

An unfunny laugh. "Of course. Everyone remembers Jacob. Every *girl* remembers him, I should say. The Yiddishe Romeo, himself." She clicked her tongue. "It's just that he never stopped running long enough for any of them to catch him."

A strange remark, a little bitter.

I raised my voice, glancing toward the Newmann porch. "I remember you standing on this same porch, Mrs. Brenner. One hot afternoon. Just that one time. In a beautiful yellow dress."

"Really? I don't remember that dress." A heartbeat, too long. "That was another lifetime."

I started to walk away, but she spoke quickly. "You arrived a few days ago."

I nodded and took another step. "Yes…"

She rushed her words. "I saw you yesterday." Now she glanced toward the Newmann home. "With your mother. I remember Julia Ferber… from years ago."

Yesterday: the sudden locking of our eyes, that moment when something was communicated in a bizarre flash, and then was gone.

Boldly, surprising myself, I said, "Do you mind if I come up on your porch?"

She hesitated, and then, once again, glanced toward the Newmann house, closed tight again the day's growing heat. She nodded, her hand waving to me slowly, a butterfly's gentle fluttering. As I stepped onto the porch, I imagined my mother peering out the upstairs window, wondering about her overdue daughter, and then, horrified and sputtering, sinking into an unlovely swoon on Esther's oriental carpet.

On the porch, facing me, Mrs. Brenner seemed at a loss.

"Would you like some iced tea?" she asked,

and I nodded. A noise from the street jarred her—
two girls passing, giggling, tickling each other. Her
eyes searched the street. A boy kicked a ball down
the sidewalk. "Inside," she mumbled. "Please."

The air in the parlor was stifling, the windows
sealed tight, heavy dark blue damask curtains
drawn, an overstuffed sofa and two bulky armchairs blocked by scattered tables cluttered with
plaster-of-Paris figurines, gaudily painted cheap
tchotchkes, crystal bells, a porcelain planter with
wilting ivy growing from the body of a garish
French shepherdess. Disquieting, this rummage-
sale collection, though every piece of bric-a-brac
seemed shellacked and spit-polished. A gigantic
menorah on a sideboard dominated the still room.
A dreadful room, airless, a coffin, dimly lit by a
light in the hallway.

Leah saw me eying the cheap carnival collection. "My sister, Sarah." She pointed at a
particularly egregious paperweight—Niagara
Falls at night, painted-on glitter stars, a tourist's
unfortunate souvenir. "She insists that it's art." A
bit of sarcasm in her voice. "I spend most of every
day fighting the dust." A quick smile. "Although I
insist the dust softens the ugliness of the pieces."

"You live with Sarah?"

Steely-eyed, unblinking, she said, "She lives

with me. This is my house. My husband's and mine. Back then."

"I didn't know."

"Because I haven't been here doesn't mean it's not my home."

"True."

She took a step toward the stairwell to the second floor. "Sarah is unhappy that I decided to open the front door and breathe in the fresh air. To sit outside. In front."

I grinned. "It *is* your house."

No humor in her voice. "It is, indeed." She pointed to a chair. "Please sit…Edna." A heavy sigh. "I forget how to invite people into my life." A shrug of her shoulders.

"Frankly, sometimes it's better *not* to."

She ran her tongue over her lower lip. "How cynical you young people are today."

I headed to one of the armchairs. "When you've been a girl reporter in Milwaukee…"

"I hate reporters." She drew back. "Oh, I don't mean…"

"Oh, I don't care…Mrs. Brenner."

"Leah. My name's Leah."

"All right, Leah."

"Let me get you a cold drink. Sit. Please."

She bustled about, bumping into a table, stepped back, deliberated, then swirled around, a maddened dervish, before heading into the kitchen. Unable to settle, frantic to please, her hands fluttered around her face.

I said to her back, "I'm glad you've made it to the front porch."

Gazing straight ahead, she answered, "I watch a street that most days says nothing at all." A pause. "I like it that way."

When she sat back down opposite me after placing a pitcher on the table, she pointed at a glass. "Help yourself. It's not very good."

"A tempting offer, then." I smiled at her.

She drank nothing but watched me quietly.

Finally, breathing in, she began talking in a low voice, almost difficult for me to hear. "When Jacob told me you were next door, I was thrilled. I don't remember you from years ago—no reason to, I suppose, so many young people on the street then—but I did read your short story 'The Homely Heroine' in *Everybody's* when I was away. I realized who it was, who wrote it, I mean—you know, Appleton and all. Your mother visiting next door years ago. We'd talked once or twice. I was so… thrilled. I remember the story because it was so… so sad. One line I memorized: 'Pearlie Schultz used to sit on the front porch summer evenings to watch the couples stroll by, and weep in her heart.' I can't forget that line, Edna. 'Weep in her heart.'

I told myself you understood something about me—about others—like me. And so…I waited to see you walk by. I hoped I'd have the courage to *talk* to you."

A beautiful woman, Leah was, even now at sixty, a face that held you, yet she was a woman who'd seen herself in my homely heroine, the sad Pearlie, fat, unwanted, morose…

"I'm glad you did."

A quizzical look. "Why?"

That jarred. I had no answer. "I don't know. I…"

A wispy smile. "I'm the neighborhood woman with a past. You shouldn't be talking to me."

"I suppose so."

But she was speaking over my swallowed words. "Edna, I was so hungry to get back home. I got sick to my stomach thinking about it. I've been back now for nearly three years…but in solitary confinement. For a woman like me, every place becomes a jail. Every space has four walls. The cage makes you crazy, though." She reached for a glass, then changed her mind. "Yet, I've accepted my place as the town leper. What choice do I have? Madness— or acceptance." She shrugged. "It sort of makes it easy, finally. Others tell you what you are—define you. You know how the world sees you."

"You don't know how I see you."

That surprised her. "Tell me."

I waited a bit, carefully chose my words. "Simply, a woman tired of isolation."

I watched her. Such a small woman, though soft at the edges, a little plump, pale as if sheltered from sunlight, but with dark, flickering nut-brown eyes, a woman who struck me as years older than her sixty or so years, her face drawn, a puffiness around those alert, brilliant eyes. Yet something about her…no homely heroine, this one, truly…a real beauty, exotic, foreign, the forbidden gypsy on the outskirts of town. You could see that she'd once been stunning because, in some way, she still was: the alabaster complexion and the dark eyes, that regal chin with the cupid's-bow mouth. But it was more than simple beauty— her slight movements were the instinctive moves of a sensual woman. A regal Cleopatra sitting with me, the Jewish slave girl on the Nile.

"That's so, I guess." She echoed the word. "Isolation. Yes." Suddenly she locked eyes with me again. "You know what they say I did."

I started. "Yes."

"Tell me what I did."

My throat went dry, my vision blurred. I sputtered, "You stabbed your husband to death."

She watched me carefully, her eyes faraway. "That's what they say I did. But I don't remember *that.* What I do remember is bending over him as he slumped on the sofa and seeing my fingertips dark with blood and wondering where it came from."

My voice was a squeak. "You don't remember a knife?"

She shook her head back and forth slowly, a sleepwalker's rhythm. "No. Nothing. Nothing but my…wonder at that dark blood. Then I forgot how to talk. Strangers were talking at me and I was nodding, nodding, nodding. Staring at them, just staring at them. A moan from deep inside me. I don't remember anything after that, though they tell me they asked me questions. But I simply stared. Nothing. It was like I forgot how to talk—or *couldn't* talk. A blur, all of it, the days that followed. Echoes in my head. They told me that I killed Ivan, washed the knife, hid it back in the kitchen, then stooped over his body on the sofa to make certain he was dead. Over and over they said that to me. They said I kept nodding: yes yes yes yes. And then, I don't know how much later—a blur, everything a blur—some man tells me I'm going away. A home for crazy women, a cell, a cot, food I can't eat. Food I spit out." She stopped talking. Her fingers trembled as she touched her cheek. Her face was flushed.

"But now you've come home."

She was looking over my shoulder. "One day

they tell me—you can go now. I have conversations with the doctor, and he says, 'You can be around people now. You can walk outside. Everything is all right now.' My Herman comes to pick me up in a car that scares me…so far away. Another planet. Herman, the only one who visited but then stopped because I couldn't speak. For years I didn't talk—I stared at people. *Who are you? What do you want me to say?* And then, one day, like that, I found my voice again. Words came tumbling out. I couldn't *stop* talking." She smiled wistfully. "Like now—with you here. I can breathe again—at that moment. And they say, you can go home now."

She stopped talking for a moment.

"Home," I echoed.

She waved her hands around the room. "I wanted to be home. Back here." She shot me a look. "But now that I have my voice back, Sarah tells me to keep still—don't talk to anyone. People will *hurt* me. Be still. Stay inside. People don't want to see you—know that you're back on Monroe Street. She gets nervous when I talk to Jacob, who watches me too closely. To my daughters who are afraid of me. My son, Herman, who thinks I embarrass him. Embarrass! No, a mother who gossips embarrasses her children. A mother who kills…what word is there that fits? 'Quiet,' Sarah tells me. 'Lower your voice. The neighbors!' My biggest sin was opening the screen door and sitting on that porch."

I sat up, spine rigid. "They took your life from you."

She stood and touched a figurine on a side table, held it up to her face. Her fingers squeezed it tightly.

Suddenly, her voice rising, "You don't think I killed Ivan?"

Irrationally, I blurted out, "No, of course not."

A bitter grunt. "Ah, a majority of one." A shrug. "Maybe two. You and me. Who can believe that?" A long sigh as she tilted her head to the side. "*Gey red tsu der vant.*" Go tell it to the wall.

But at that moment I knew, to my soul, that my instincts were true and just. Something was wrong with that faded photograph. "No," I repeated firmly. "When you found your voice again, you would have remembered."

She put down the figurine, too close to the edge of the table, but then walked to the front window, stared into the street. She faced me. "It doesn't matter now. I can't shift the axis of the Earth, right the wind currents, turn back the tides. And, I suppose, I *am* to blame somehow. I *caused* my world to turn upside down."

"What?" This was making little sense.

"I wasn't a good wife." Another bitter smile.

"Ivan and I fought for weeks. My fault, I tell you now, Edna. Yes, Ivan was a cruel, hard man. He could be nasty, controlling. Not at first—not when we first married. They never are, their words lovely and assuring. Then they change. He'd be mean to me—to the children. Especially my Jacob." She shivered. "Such cruelty to that boy. The world's sweetest boy, that one. Impossible—despite my pleading. Of course, the more I defended Jacob, the worse the cruelty."

"But how did *you* hurt him?"

Slowly she left the window and settled into a chair, facing me. "I *hurt* him bad. We hurt him, me and Morrie, his partner. One stupid, idle flirtation, weak and silly, a lapse of judgment on my part, regretted immediately. And confessed at once. I brought shame on Ivan's head—and he rightly accused me. My wife—Jezebel. He *told* everyone. I suppose he had to because he was so mortified, embarrassed—what will folks think of *him*? The proud man with the wanton wife. And I sat on that front porch with a scarlet letter on my chest for the neighbors to gaze at. For Morrie's angry wife to spit on me. For old Molly Newmann, happy to slight me as we passed."

I'd not expected such candid revelation, nor, frankly, wanted it. "Leah, I don't think that I…" I sipped the last of my tea and reached for the pitcher. Her eyes followed my movements.

She spat out her words. "I courted disaster, Edna. Men always watched at me. Lovely, they'd whisper. A beauty, they'd whisper. Look at Ivan, dumpy, a *lumpen*, the fool with the ravishing bride. Men followed me, got silly, said things they never thought they'd ever say to a woman. But Ivan spent long hours in the back room of the butcher shop where the men hung out. The butcher's cave, they called it. They talked about me. He said they found me…I don't know…attractive. So it started to bother him. Pride gave way to fear…to a lack of trust in me. What did I unconsciously tell them when I strutted in? What did those men see when they watched me walk by? Why did it *please* me so?" For a second she closed her eyes and didn't move. "All those times Morrie flirted—frivolous, dumb, a ladies' man behind his wife's back. A reputation, he had, that man. Ivan laughed but I knew it bothered him. He'd married a wife everyone said was beautiful, and that meant trouble. When we got married, it pleased Ivan, me on his arm. You know, Ivan *reveled* in it—at first. Drunk with it. But then he got mean, accused me, shut me out. Screamed at me—made me cry. Never tempted by those dreadful men, I was always faithful. The wolf whistles. The leering." She shuddered. "But

I let myself—once—with Morrie—a hug, a kiss. Stupid, stupid. So…stupid of me. Nothing more. A kiss in a doorway. One minute of a nun's life. I confessed—I had to, because I loved Ivan. But how we fought. And that morning, Ivan home sick and fighting, fighting…"

Here she was now, weary, drawn, but I imagined her years back, a woman in her middle forties, vibrant, those dancing eyes, the Rubenesque flesh, the sinuous flow of a woman's body that drew men closer, Circe's siren song. Some magic other women couldn't understand, only sense, but men couldn't resist. Leah, the impossible temptress, all the more lethal because she did nothing to foster it—indeed, didn't *want* it.

"Leah, I don't know what to say."

Suddenly she leaned forward, poured tea into a glass, and drank half of it. When she put the glass down, her hand trembled. "I brought about Ivan's death. I believe that. That night I let Morrie touch me. That opened the door to all the chaos to follow."

"But you didn't kill him."

She shrugged and interlaced her fingers, spreading them before her face. Only those brilliant eyes were visible. "What can I say?"

A shrill voice erupted from the hallway. "Leah, who are you talking to?"

A woman stepped into the room, a frightened look on her face. She actually pointed at me.

"Sarah, this is Edna. We talked of her staying next door with Esther Newmann. Edna Ferber. Ella gave you her book and…"

A phony laugh that became a cackle. "We really are not ready for guests, Leah."

She stood with her arms folded across her chest, a humorless schoolmarm momentarily taken off guard.

Leah said in a soft voice, "We're just talking, the two of us." She pointed to the pitcher of iced tea. "A cold glass of…" She stopped.

Sarah pivoted on her heels, glanced toward the kitchen, unsure of her next move. From the back of her throat came a slippery rasp that reminded me of a baby's sudden regurgitation. "That may be…" she began, but stopped, indecisive. Her eyes caught the figurine Leah had picked up. Nervously she moved it—positioned it next to another. She scowled at Leah.

Like a failed negative of her sister, Sarah had a similar small face, narrow chin, high forehead, with the same abundant white hair, but there the comparisons ceased: Sarah was skinny, wiry, the bird on the wire, twittering, while the alluring songbird luxuriated nearby. Brittle arms, breakable. Her eyes were not Leah's vibrant, deep brown that hinted at the voluptuous siren of days gone by—rather, Sarah's were dull, the washed-out eyes of a woman who had lost all interest in life—who, in fact, was indifferent to a world she'd never cared for.

That revelation bothered me because her attitude toward Leah made it clear she found Leah's return home a nuisance. Routines shifted, the workings of a household realigned—plaster-of-Paris figurines in regimented positions—nothing demanded from Leah but nonetheless her presence monumentally annoying. The spinster forced to share her coveted space.

She spoke to her sister as though I weren't there. "Jacob didn't come home last night—again."

Quietly. "I know."

A darting glance at me, lips pursed. "Is that why you were sitting on the porch? Waiting?"

"I was sitting on the porch because these rooms are a prison."

Sarah glanced back at me and shook her head slowly, letting out a tinny laugh. "The years away have allowed dear Leah to cultivate sarcasm."

Leah clicked her tongue. "Not sarcasm. Realism."

"No matter." She turned away, but at that moment the front door opened.

Jacob Brenner strolled in, pausing in the

entrance, one hand balancing himself against the doorjamb. "What?" he stammered.

"Jacob," his mother said. "I was worried."

A slight, wistful smile covered his face. "My mother loves me."

"Really, now," Sarah barked.

Jacob was nearly forty but still resembled some romantic hero on a vaudeville stage, the aging juvenile, though one now tarnished and a bit dissolute. With those dark brown eyes, half-closed, and that shock of coal-black hair in need of a trim, he struck me as a Semite Heathcliff—dangerous because of his beauty and brooding. He'd inherited his mother's once-in-a-lifetime beauty. Eighteen years back, at twenty or so, he was dashing and smooth. I would watch him move down the sidewalk—that casual saunter or strut, the shoulders high, the head rocking as though to a tune only he heard. He owned the street, that boy—the pavement seemed to dance underneath him. Now, sadly, the long face with the square Leyendecker jaw and the elegant Roman nose seemed puffy, loose, but when he turned to stare into my face I still saw the young, erstwhile matinee heartthrob, the man who gave me sleepless nights.

"A fellow gotta have some fun."

His mother nodded toward me. "Jacob, do

you remember Edna Ferber? We talked about her visiting the Newmanns. The novelist."

He smiled, trying to charm me, the old instincts taking over. Turning, his foot slipped. "A pleasure."

I didn't know how much pleasure he was having at the moment—his Aunt Sarah frumpy and grunting beside him—but he half-bowed and reached for my hand. I refused to offer it.

Edna, not sugar and spice.

Edna, not nice—

For a second, in a practiced, uncalculated manner, he stared into my face, wooing, trying to claim my attention. But I was invisible—me, the dowdy, unloved thirtyish spinster with the bushel-barrel hair and the sallow complexion.

"You don't remember me?" I asked pointedly, really too sharply.

In his boozy state he tried to focus. A man not skilled at lying. "Of course. I do. I…" He stammered and, of course, he said the wrong thing. "I remember every girl I ever met."

Sarah grumbled. "For God's sake, Jacob."

Jacob, confused, turned away with that chivalrous half-bow, and left the room. I could hear his sloppy footfall on the stairs.

Leah burst out laughing, a little out of control. Sarah watched her, as did I, but Sarah's look was harsh and spiteful, mixed with nervousness. I was filled with wonder. Leah's laugh sounded rusty, jagged, The musical instrument you haven't played since high school.

Leah sputtered, "Lovely, Edna. Lovely. My Jacob doesn't listen to himself." Then, through her girlish giggles, "You know, I haven't laughed in fifteen years. I haven't…laughed. Really." She was observing me with affection, and I realized how much I liked the woman. A ripple in her voice, the laughter rose again.

Then, like a slammed door, she stopped, her face closed up. It was as though she'd been slapped in the face. She trembled. I thought she'd cry because her lips quivered, but she said in a cool, deliberate voice, "I won't allow myself to cry… ever again."

She looked lost, helpless.

I stood up. "I need to leave. I'm expected back."

Neither sister moved as I stood up. As I opened the front door, sighing deeply, I heard the rush of clipped steps behind me. Suddenly, Leah stood near me—too near, almost on top of me—as if, because of those horrible, confined years, she'd forgotten about the civility of space. Her face so close to mine, eyes moist, nose running. she was still smiling. Impulsively, she reached out, not to grab my hand, but simply to touch my shoulder.

So sudden a gesture, so charged. Like a numbing shock from an electric current.

"Thank you, Edna."

She backed away.

Outside, stumbling down the wooden steps, I realized I was crying.

Chapter Five

My mother lay on the sofa with a cold compress plastered to her forehead. Sarah Bernhardt, rehearsing. As I walked past her, headed upstairs to my room, she let out the choked death rattle she'd employed many times, always with me, the errant daughter. A moan, a whimper, an alley cat's meow. This was the plaintive anthem of aggrieved Jewish motherhood, doubtless carried over to America in an immigrant's heart and soul, in the red blood, the one precious item not declared at Ellis Island.

"My own daughter!"

I stopped walking because I knew my part in this seasoned melodrama.

"What?" I asked with little patience.

My mother struggled to sit, letting the compress slip into her lap, unnoticed. Her face was ashen. "My nosy daughter...of course, you talk to the one person *no one* talks to. You choose..." She fell back into the cushions.

"Ah, spies in the house of Newmann."

Sitting up, smoothing her dress, my mother leaned in to me, confidentially. "Molly is a snoop, truth to tell. That old woman doesn't miss a trick. A real *kokhlefel*." A busybody. "She may be an old lady hobbling around with that noisy cane, but her eagle eye covers the street. She can out-walk me to Maxwell, amazingly." But then, remembering my misdeed and the reason for her taking to the couch, she whispered, "I was in the kitchen with Esther, the two of us sipping lemonade and chatting of… of…nothing, you know, the way old friends talk of nothing. And Molly yells from the back of the house, 'Your Edna is walking up the steps of the Brenner porch.' I was flabbergasted."

"Mother, it's no big deal. A conversation."

Leah's voice echoed in my head. *Thank you, Edna.*

My tears as I stumbled on the sidewalk.

A conversation.

Slowly, my mother stood up. Huffing, she walked by me, close enough so I could see the pain in her eyes, though she ignored me. In the kitchen, in seconds, I heard the overlapping titter of excited voices—a strident Molly, a hesitant Esther, and the tumultuous Julia Ferber, who apologized for my behavior. "What can I say?" said Julia, fatalistically. "A mother does her best." My mind slid maliciously from the idea of the Three Fates—mythic and magnificent—to the dour witches of Macbeth stirring a pot of chicken soup (with just the right amount of black pepper, really) and cursing the heavens that allowed the dutiful daughter her unfortunate lapse in common sense.

Furious, I made a decision. I stood in the doorway, arms folded across my chest, and glowered. All three women paused—all three had been speaking at once, a waterfall of babble—and waited.

"Leah Brenner did not kill her husband, Ivan, fifteen years ago."

That wonderful line echoed off the copperplate ceiling.

My mother gasped, grabbed for her throat, though she probably wished it were mine she reached for. "Edna, really. We are *guests* here."

I repeated the line, louder now, spacing out the words, adding, "I believe she's been railroaded."

A good exit line, worthy of Ethel Barrymore as the curtain fell. I turned and began walking upstairs, although I missed the first step, banging into the wall, a clumsy move that somehow diminished the impact of my purposeful declaration.

Silence in the kitchen, and then, as expected, a thunderous roar of indignation, disbelief, and shock.

"Julia, what in the world…?" From Esther.

"Craziness, this child of yours. *Meshuga.*"
From Molly. *Tap tap tap.*

• • ● • •

That evening, headed downstairs for the Newmann Sunday supper, I dreaded what awaited me.
Throughout the afternoon I fiddled with my notes
for my novel, even pecking away on my typewriter,
a *click click click click ping* that battled with the *tap
tap tap* of Molly's cane in the hallway. My mother
had purposely avoided me, except for a guttural
grunt as she passed my room. Our first Sunday
supper at the Newmanns', an anticipated one:
Esther Newmann's suppers were legendary. This
night's, especially, due to my mother's prodigal visit
after so many years, my own return after eighteen
years—me, the feted novelist, a matter of pride,
that invitation. Right now, however, I expected
silence, recrimination—I expected a collective cold
shoulder or marrow-deep wail.

What I found was a drifting conversation that
skirted the taboo subject of neighborhood murder.
Instead, the chatter was of food: the first course of
soup, hearty beef barley soup with marrow balls,
with hand-rolled hair-fine noodles, served in a
tureen so ornate it seemed a relic from a Roman
bacchanal. Esther's roast chicken, a gigantic bird
glistening brown, juices running, the aroma of

generous paprika and bay leaf. A stuffing of chestnuts and apples and a hint of red onion, a nutty confection that made my mouth water. Mashed potatoes so fluffy, laced with diced parsley, they seemed cotton candy at the fair, pats of sweet butter melting in the white canyons. A salad of tart brine-soaked dandelion greens mixed with bits of sliced oranges and sugared strawberries, and slathered with a vinegar glaze that seemed lit by fire. A robust feast, a triumph, and my mother discussed all parts of it, a culinary autopsy, praising, celebrating, worshipping. And rightly so, because I relished Esther's domestic art, her magic touch, that deft reach of spice and invention and love.

We sat around the heavy mahogany dining room table on chairs covered in deep-crimson plush fabric. I faced a fireplace fronted with a fire screen of vaguely oriental design—hummingbirds flitting on bamboo stems. An antique grandfather clock stood across from a built-in china cabinet. Over the mantel was a spread of family photographs in black-walnut frames, sepia-tinted—a formal wedding photograph of Esther and Sol, young and slender, unsmiling, he in an ill-fitting suit with a boutonniere (a sprig of lilac) and she in lace, with wraparound filigreed train, a bouquet of calla lilies held tightly.

So animated was the conversation about food,

so heady and almost comical, such a purposeful skirting of what occupied our minds: darling little Edna's mammoth transgression. Each time I began to say something, one of the women spoke over me. "Such a copper pickle you find at Lyon's Delicatessen," Molly blurted out. "I mean, it looks painted green. I swear."

"A blouse I found on the bargain table at Goldblatt's—only a small tear I can fix." From Esther.

I didn't care.

I wanted to talk about Leah Brenner.

Once, opening my mouth to mention something about my morning stroll through the Maxwell Street marketplace, old Molly, bent over her plate, brightened and shared an anecdote that had no end. In fact, it really had neither beginning nor middle, some ramble about a greenhorn peasant trying to buy a *shiffcart,* a steamship ticket, at a drug store off Union. It was blather—and welcomed at the table. We waited for a punch line, but none came. Molly was upbeat and sparkling, yet it was forced and deliberate. It tickled me, I had to admit, that chaotic story, because I liked the old woman. She believed it was her job to give direction to her undemonstrative family. Esther, a soft-focus sentimentalist, beamed over her food, and her husband, Sol, a generous man who cultivated serenity, often struck me as asleep when you spoke to him. A little balding man with a scaly scalp and bushy white eyebrows on a blotchy face, he responded to most questions by checking first with his much-adored wife, as though begging her to answer for him. They were as wonderful a couple as God chose to send to this Earth. Old Molly, ancient now and opinionated and fiery, was the bandleader of that family.

"Where's Adolph?" my mother asked.

Esther pointed to the grandfather clock. "He's late. That job at Feinstein's Hardware, I suppose. Some afternoons he works, some mornings…" She waved her hand in the air. "Who knows? He's picking up Minna."

Molly addressed me. "Adolph's intended. A lovely girl, a grade-school teacher."

Sol spoke up. "Yeah, he's been *intending* for ten years now." He stressed the word, but with affection. "I keep telling him—a little bungalow like they're building now. Come May One I'll borrow Sy's truck." The first of May, when all of Chicago chose to move, whether they planned to or not.

Molly smiled at her son. "Now, now, Sol. He's just a boy."

Sol grunted. "He's forty, for God's sake. He hasn't been a boy since I had hair." He touched the top of his bald head. "A *batten*." A lazy boy.

No one laughed.

Sol was perplexed. "I seen him up on Clark.

At Bob's Quick Lunch. Early this afternoon. He was walking out of there with Jacob. They…" He stopped. "What?"

Apologetically, Esther explained to Molly, "They *are* old friends, you know."

Molly wasn't happy with the direction the talk was going. "A bad influence, that Jacob."

"Two drifters," Sol added.

Molly turned to me. "A drinker at the taxi-dance halls, that Jacob, I tell you. People tell me things. Adolph tells me but makes excuses for him." She smirked. "Jacob calls himself a poet. What kind of money can a poet make?"

"A poet?" I asked.

"Yes, Jacob Brenner, the idler, he tells everyone he's a poet. A…wastrel, he is." Molly raised her voice.

Esther's voice was hurried. "Jacob is always so polite to me."

"Only to women," Molly grumbled.

I cleared my throat. "Not *every* woman."

"Edna, really," my mother sniped.

Esther was chuckling. "Our Monroe Street Romeo without a balcony."

Sol muttered, "And his sidekick is our Ad. The two running off to the movies at the Biograph. I seen them. Even at the Tivoli on College Grove, fancy-spancy, one dollar a ticket. Crazy. Throwing away money neither one got."

Molly breathed in. "Now you leave Adolph alone, Sol. A good boy with a big heart."

"Two playboys with polished shoes and flashy spats," Sol added. "Ad and Jacob. The Katzenjammer Kids up there on the stage. One jumps left, the other jumps right."

A vaudeville cue, it seemed, because the front door opened and Adolph strolled in, unhurried, trailed by a wisp of a woman, a nervous grin on her face.

"I'm late, I know," Ad said with no apology in his voice, a wide grin on his face. "It's Minna's fault." He bowed toward the woman, still grinning but now red-faced.

"Don't believe him," she said softly.

"We never do," Sol said.

"C'mon, Papa." Ad swirled around clumsily, the loose-jawed clown.

He'd changed since my fleeting acquaintance with him eighteen years before. Then he was a gangling young man, early twenties, prominent Adam's apple and cowlick, though attractive in a farm boy way—an ah-shucks goofiness. Of course, he was no dashing Jacob, his next-door buddy and ne'er-do-well wanderer in the streets. But Ad Newmann had a shyness that made you like him, smile at him—as though he was genuinely surprised when someone noticed him and—*liked* him. I liked him because of his breezy manner, the way he seemed tickled to find himself drifting somewhere in the solar system. When Jacob said something vaguely risqué, though out of earshot of his parents, Ad blushed. He was Sir Galahad, a shining knight that no one needed.

He grabbed his father from behind and squeezed him. "You love me, Papa."

"Only on rainy days."

Everyone laughed.

"You know I'm your favorite son, Papa."

"Ah, clever—my only son."

Ad had added flesh to those long stringy bones, and the effect was pleasing: a hail-fare-thee-well soul, a little beefy but still appealing, if slick and smooth in his rumpled summer linen suit. Another perennial bachelor, Esther insisted, though his endless engagement to the doe-eyed Minna Pittman, a teacher out in Lawndale, occupied much of the suppertime talk when Ad was absent. Ad once played with the notion of becoming a rabbi, caught up in Talmudic studies for what seemed a wasted year—his family holding its breath—but since then he'd had too many jobs. He worked as a puller on Maxwell Street, wooing customers into Wittenberg's Clothiers; but, painfully honest, he pointed out the faulty seams in the pants he peddled. So he did this, then did that, and nothing for very long.

The atmosphere of the dining room shifted when Ad and Minna sat down. Ad's smart-aleck affection for his family caused Esther to *tsk tsk* at his rolling nonsense and Sol to betray his impatience with the son who liked to stay in bed most mornings. But everyone seemed to *relax*. Because, most times, the conversation of the dowager Molly and her son and daughter-in-law, though friendly, was peculiarly formal. Ad was the yeast that bubbled the surface of things. He even got my mother to smile when he described his battle with a peddler on Maxwell.

"So he says to me, '*Gay avek, nudnik,*' and I say back, 'You're *a gantser kener,*' and he says, 'You call that English?'"

I struggled a little with the translation. *Get out of here, you pest. You're a know-it-all.*

Minna Pittman said little and seemed thrilled with Ad's performance. The Ben Franklin eyeglasses on the small, tight oval face gave her face a pinched look, with a worrywart's nervous habit of darting eyes and twitching nose. She was dressed in a prim summer smock with too many girlish blue periwinkles dotting the fabric, the woeful look of an older maiden aunt, one good for darning one's socks and embroidering a frilly parlor antimacassar.

A mean-spirited depiction, I admit, but Minna Pittman kept staring at Ad Newmann with the unadulterated adoration of a frenzied girl gaping at a Saturday-afternoon matinee idol. A little disconcerting, and wholly delusional.

Ad monopolized the supper, as I suspected he often did—a rollicking, if insipid, spiel of zany stories from the marketplace. At one point he began an anecdote about a friend and his battle with chopped liver—"So a pan of *gehakte leber* slips into her lap and…and…and the man says"—which suddenly veered dangerously into the risqué, though, I realized, Ad was oblivious of the double entendre he was executing, which made it all the more delightful. But his father, rolling his eyes, grumbled, "This from the sad rabbinical student."

That failed vocation was a sore spot with his father. Ad, I knew from his mother's long in-kitchen catalogue of her son's occupations, had especially disappointed his father when he'd abandoned his studies. Ad's yearlong fevered fascination with a religion he'd paid scant attention to most of his life had resulted from an old man who sat for hours at the butcher shop, the cracker-box Talmudist in the back room. Ad lingered there with Jacob, a scoffer at the strictures of his own religion. But not so Ad, enthralled by the old man's devotion to storytelling…the ancient and mysterious lore of Judaism. Jacob had little patience with Ad's new passion.

The result, unfortunately, was that Ad reinforced his image among the men as a moralistic prig, tinged now with a bit of the mystical medieval Jew, a scholarly diversion at odds with his fly-by-the-seat-of-his-pants life. When that ended, Ad worked as a handyman, a pushcart vendor of hot dogs, a helper at Nathan's Meat Market after Morrie Wolfsy went it alone for a few months after Ivan's murder. "That was so short a time," Esther told me. "The spine-chilling squawk of a chicken beheaded sent him out the door." An encyclopedia salesman, a shoe salesman, a pretzel maker, and now, a jack-of-all-trades gadabout at Feinstein's Hardware up on Halsted.

Perhaps Sol was resigned to his son's wanderlust, though his impatience seeped through his love for his son. But the cult of adoration was not the sole province of Minna, at that moment picking gingerly at a chicken wing. No, the charter member of that familial club was old Molly herself. Severe and crotchety though she might be, and a magpie of neighborhood gossip, she doted on her only grandson.

"She always has," Esther told my mother and me earlier. "Her special boy. She blames Jacob

Brenner for Ad's lack of…of focus, you can say. She doesn't *like* Jacob."

Sol and Esther's other child, a younger daughter named Harriet, lost in the shadows created by Ad's sunshine, married young and retreated to Cleveland with a husband and three children, returning only for the High Holy Days. And only sometimes, at that.

Molly left the room for something, beating that cane on the hardwood floor, *tap tap tap*, forcing us to stop talking, and, as she passed Ad's chair, her gnarled fingertips caressed the back of his neck. He smiled up at her, a little boy's grateful glance. It was, frankly, a loving gesture that communicated to the rest of us that there should only be two people at the dining room table. I caught my mother's eye. Her glance said, emphatically, *This is how devotion is supposed to look. Pay attention, Edna.*

I supposed it was hard to dislike the scattered Ad because, well, we tend naturally to *like* children.

I'd been watching him, lost in thought, enjoying his schoolboy banter, so I'd missed something. I wasn't paying attention to what was said, but the air in the room got heavy. Sudden stillness at the table, every head turned to Ad. Molly, returning to the room, had stopped walking, teetering there on her cane. No *tap tap tap* now. She swayed, then fell into a chair, her face grim.

"What?" Ad asked, puzzled. "You all crazy? All I said was that we met Jacob sitting on his porch as we were walking here tonight. He told us Edna stopped in to see his mother earlier today." He glanced at me. "They had iced tea or…or something. And…" His voice trailed off.

"This afternoon," Minna finished. "I think."

Now every eye centered on me. At that moment I realized—how had I not?—that my visit to Leah Brenner, which had devastated my mother and infuriated Molly, the unspoken topic of conversation at supper—had surfaced. The lethal river sloughing under our pleasantries and bonhomie had burst to the surface. Edna, the trespasser in the Garden of Eden.

Esther sighed. "Adolph, we know all about that."

Ad was perplexed. "Well, what's the problem? Jacob was downright *happy* about it. He…he was happy. And Jacob ain't happy very often. It's strange, that household. His mother hides away, and nobody knows what to do with her. I stop in, but I know I shouldn't. I gotta meet Jacob… elsewhere. Jacob said Edna, here"—he nodded at me, smiling—"Edna, here, made his mother…you know…"—fumbling, fumbling—"happy."

Molly smiled without any humor. "This is not suppertime conversation, Adolph dear."

Helpless, faltering, with a trace of anger, he replied, "She is our neighbor."

"I know who is my neighbor," Molly snarled.

Baffled, he spoke to his father. "Papa?" But Sol was focused on his plate.

Of course, it was the only topic I was interested in, and so I began. "How is Jacob dealing with his mother, Ad? I'm sure, after the years away, and now back at home, he…"

My mother's scream broke in. "Edna, really!"

"You must admit it's an interesting household. A woman accused, sent away, deemed mad, returned, a killing that remains a mystery."

Ad was watching me, a hint of a smile on his lips. "Edna, we don't talk about Leah Brenner in this house. Or Ivan. Or that horrible day. The dark blot on the street."

His grandmother sighed. "Adolph, dear, we're not monsters. The way you paint us. It's just best to bury the past. Such sadness then…that woman…"

I spoke up. "But clearly you haven't buried anything. That wound is still open, frankly, if it's a taboo subject here and the merest mention raises everything to the level of high drama."

"Edna." My mother barely squawked out the word. Only Julia Ferber could make my drab, unlovely name seem a curse. "Edna!" She'd been cutting a piece of chicken and she held the knife in mid-air as we all stared at it.

Ad answered my question. "He says his mother is quiet. Lonely. By herself. Waiting for visits from her children. He skirts around her because he doesn't understand what's going on. There are days he's real depressed...like he doesn't know what to do. You can't talk to him those days."

"So he hasn't made peace with her return."

Ad nodded. "She's his mother but, you know..."

Molly hissed, "She killed a good man."

"A mean man. Rotten." But then Ad was sorry for the remark. Molly frowned at him.

I went on. "Does Jacob believe his mother killed his father?"

My mother rose, dropped her napkin to the floor. She still held out the knife, menacingly, but, spotting it gripped in her fingers, let it drop onto her plate. It clanged and slid onto the lace tablecloth. At that moment the grandfather clock chimed the hour and she yelped, like a shaken child. "My Lord, Edna, are there no boundaries?"

Ad was enjoying this, the smile still there. "He's happy she can talk to someone like you. A writer like you. She likes you. He's glad." A glance at his grandmother and then at his mother. "I'm glad, too. The Talmud says"—he winked at his father—"if I can remember from my scholarly days, 'It is fitting for a great God to forgive a great sinner.' Maybe we should obey."

"Obey!" thundered Molly. "We're not God, sorry to say." A wry smile. "The Talmud also says, 'Let yourself be killed but do not kill.'" She banged the table. "All right, enough. Let's clear the dishes. Esther made strudel to die for."

Minna, who'd been swiveling her head back and forth, panicked, jumped up and grabbed a platter. "Shhh, Ad," she whispered to him. "*Sha*! Quiet! You know how this will end up."

I laughed nervously. "It's the reporter in me, I suppose. A curiosity. Back in Appleton the great Houdini and I solved a murder, the two of us a team. I covered a gruesome murder and trial in Milwaukee and…" I stopped.

My mother's look was venomous. "An unmarried girl on the streets of that beer-besotted hellhole. Thank God for Prohibition." She faltered a bit, observing the bottle of Manischewitz on the sideboard. "My daughter, the *alte moyd*." The old maid.

I would have none of it. "I'm sorry. I don't believe Leah Brenner killed her husband. Not one bit. Where was the knife? A dazed woman wouldn't plan…" Again I stopped.

An explosion in the room. Sol let out an unintended belch, immediately frowned upon by a decorous Minna standing near him, still holding that platter. My mother, uncertain, sat down and then stood back up, though she never took her eyes off the ponderous grandfather clock, as though she coveted the power to turn back time. Molly gasped for breath as Esther reached for her glass of lemonade, an involuntary sob coming from the back of her throat.

I was growing nervous now, aware of my impolite behavior and suspect talk. After all, I *was* a guest—at least for the remainder of the next week. Short story writer for the national weeklies be damned: I was simply the pushy daughter of an old friend, and not a nice one at that. Edna Ferber, ace reporter, once again ruining one more suppertime. I thought of Jacob's cruel doggerel. *Edna Edna not nice…*

But still…"She seems so…lost. A dark Rebecca on that porch, watching…" I breathed in. "I kept thinking of the beautiful woman in a Walter Scott romance…*Ivanhoe*, you know…And what evidence? Really! You know, they never found the knife. Not in that room. Not in the kitchen. Not in the body. Wouldn't the knife be in the body? In the neck? Strange, no? Given her paralyzed stare when they found her, leaning over the body, speechless, and for years afterwards, how could she have had the presence of mind to…?" I stopped. Enough.

Esther was sobbing quietly. "Ever since she got back—like three years ago now—we *avoid* her. We don't see her, but we know she's there in that house. It's like a huge boulder fell onto the street. It's ruined everything. Leah was a friend of mine. We shopped together. We visited in each other's kitchens, had coffee. Picked *kirshen* from the tree out back…cherries for pie. Yes, she was a little… different. I don't know what word to use…"

"I do," said Molly, her ragged voice breaking. "A Jezebel. A harlot. A temptress. Take your pick."

"Mama," Sol began. "Not again. Please."

She silenced him with a ferocious glare. "That…that sickening moment with Morrie, that horrid butcher. Yeah. The men always gaping at her, joking, the improper wink. What kind of decent Jewish mother, that woman?" She turned to Ad, who avoided her face. "You remember how the men talked about her, sitting in that grimy back room of Nathan's, that *fleyshmark*, the meat market I never went into, refused to, those groups of strange men, tongues out, yammering on and on. That dark hole. And she loved it, don't tell me she didn't, I could see—the attention of stupid, stupid men. Ivan was a hard-working slob with a wife who moved like a courtesan. Yeah, the man could be hard. How could he not be?" A rasp from the back of her throat. "She brought Sodom and Gomorrah onto this quiet street."

Esther sobbed into her plate and Sol gently touched her shoulder, let his fingers rest there. It was, I thought, as loving a gesture as any old married couple could share.

"I'm sorry to ruffle everyone's feathers," I went on. "But"—a nod at Ad—"what does Scripture say about love? Ah—'God wants the heart.' Right? Doesn't Leah deserve *that*?"

Ad was still smiling, but a quiet, mischievous boy's smile. Though I liked him, it dawned on me then that Ad thought me a frivolous woman, a silly meddler, one not to be taken seriously. I was a rabble-rouser who at the moment was amusing him. That rankled, surely, and I wondered how shallow he really was. His knee-jerk sympathy for the marooned—and maybe railroaded—Leah had the depth of oilcloth. Maybe I shouldn't like him so much.

Molly was trying to stand, grasping the edge of the table and gripping her cane. Her voice trembled. "A supper ruined." Eyeing me sharply, she stepped away from the table.

"I'm sorry," I said, though I wasn't.

My mother spoke to the clock. "A lifetime of 'I'm sorry' from a daughter who digs the hole for my early grave."

"I'm…" I began again, penitent, but stopped. I wasn't sorry.

Molly began her slow move away from the table, *tap tap tap*, but she paused, and I watched her teeth chatter in the hot, hot room. She faced me. "A lifetime lived here," she whispered, "and that woman changed everything." She slammed the floor with her cane.

She turned to her son, Sol, who seemed baffled by her fierce stare. Then, quietly, she repeated her awful line: "That woman changed everything."

Now her eyes were on me.

Chapter Six

The next morning I hailed a taxi on Halsted and headed downtown toward the Loop, and finally, refreshed with coffee at Moe's, walked into the *Chicago Tribune* building. Using the name of an old friend, Tim Boyden, a features editor now living in New York—and employing my own current celebrity—I managed to get hold of a small stack of clippings in a manila folder at the *Tribune* morgue. The meagerness of the file surprised me because I'd expected a wealth of newsprint spilling out. After all, this was a Chicago murder story, one that happened in the safe and quiet Jewish neighborhood off Maxwell—not like the recent whoop-it-up gangland murders Chicago was beginning to wrestle with since Prohibition became the law of the land.

But there was so little information, and contradictory at that, most facts repeated day after day, then spottily, until a month later a small paragraph buried deep in the paper chronicled Leah's quiet removal to an asylum. Hardly splashy news, this domestic murder, not newsworthy. A woman—with a rumored sub-rosa reputation, wink wink wink—kills her loyal and faithful husband in a blind rage after a violent argument, then sinks into silence and solitude, and is finally defined as mad. What amazed me was the cavalier tone of the reportage—Leah cattily recalled by neighborhood women and even some men as notoriously flirtatious, sometimes irreverent, non-observant, this Jewish mother—a woman with a flippant remark, a reckless laugh. A woman already talked about, and not nicely.

So little about the actual murder.

Such a paucity of facts. The investigative detectives located no knife, no bloodied clothing, and there was no confession. A man slumped over, a cruel gash on the right side of his neck, dead from choking on his own blood. Nothing, save a woman paralyzed over the dead form of her husband. Her fingertips smeared with his blood. Blood splattered on his shirt collar, on the sofa cushions, on the floor.

The very first news account accused her. As the first patrolman on the scene noted, "She looked like she did it."

That said it all. Case closed. Hang her. Stone her.

I raced through the clippings, my fury growing. A glib, skewered portrait of a woman with questionable character. Innuendo, suspicion. One cagey reporter shared cigars with a bunch of men gathered in the back room of Nathan's Meat Market, cracker-barrel philosophers all, the wisdom of Solomon at the ready, men who praised Ivan as sweet and friendly and Leah as—a vamp.

"She never fit into the neighborhood," one man told the reporter.

Murder in a fit of anger, a burst of sudden madness, a marrow-deep depression, and a slow descent into the dark corners of the irrational mind.

Leah, by all accounts glass-eyed and frightened, said nothing, a piece of beautiful clay moved from one spot to the next. The Chicago House of Corrections. The Cook County Hospital. She answered no questions.

The judge quietly signed papers to commit her.

No one, I realized, got her to talk about what happened.

When Detective Tom O'Reilly was asked by a noisome reporter about the whereabouts of the knife, he blithely remarked, "A butcher's wife's kitchen. Come on. *Her* kitchen."

Not really an answer at all.

So my morning at the news morgue did little to answer my questions, though the hour there firmed up my initial sense of Leah's innocence. Detectives entertained no other suspects. The case had been simply too *easy* to wrap up, to file away. The same way Leah was conveniently filed away in a small cell far from home, like Hester Prynne with her nagging inner thoughts and mournful reflection. A woman sat alone, forgotten, until one day she decided she'd had enough of silence and found her voice again.

She came home.

• • ● • •

I left the *Chicago Tribune* and wandered, window shopping, making the mistake of boarding the slow-moving, jam-packed streetcar on Indiana Avenue, hopping off, buying ice cream, but finally ended up back on Halsted Street, that long, long street everyone ended up on sooner or later. Tired, my mind back at the news morgue, I ambled down Maynard, off Maxwell, a poor stretch of wooden shanties, soot-blackened tenements, dark basement apartments without baths or light. The world of sweatshops, rows of skinny boys in black-brimmed caps and *tzitzis* hunched over tables, boys who never saw daylight.

Here on this bright afternoon the East European *shtetl* emptied out into tenements that once housed German Jews, who were now abandoning the area for the green lawns and pristine boulevards of West Chicago. And yet—not everyone. Esther and Sol and Molly, and Leah and Ivan—they stayed on, wanting the old neighborhood. The children left, but they remained. I wondered why.

Once again, turning toward the Newmanns' house, I stood in front of Nathan's Meat Market, that touchstone to the past. Empty now, abandoned, the interior dark.

"Edna." A sweet voice from behind.

Jacob Brenner stood near me, a loaf of bread cradled to his chest.

"Jacob, you startled me."

"You seemed lost in thought." He pointed at the butcher shop. "The only kosher butcher on this block. *Der kosherer katser*. You know, Morrie Wolfsy kept it going for half a year after Papa died, though he seemed to lose interest. He'd forget to open some days."

"It sits empty?"

Both of us peered through the dark front window. Someone had left a light on in the back room.

"He owns the building. He keeps an apartment upstairs, but his wife hates the neighborhood, sticks up her nose at it. Too *poor* now. They got a grand house out in Lawndale, a la-di-dah place with a concrete fountain in front like it's Versailles, but

Morrie wanders back here, stays in his old apartment upstairs or sits in his back room where all the guys used to spend useless hours. Me included. The boys' club. Forbidden poker. French postcards even. Craps. Sometimes." He laughed. "Chickens beheaded and the politics of America argued over and over."

"You'd think he'd rent the store."

"He won't. Won't give a reason. But he owns a couple of the apartment houses on Monroe. He comes back here once a month to collect the rents. He lives on that money now—the butcher shop is history. He runs his rental properties from the upstairs apartment. That's the only time we see him in the neighborhood. He's old, tired. Hey, Morrie's not a bad sort. Sometimes, back then, a spell of religion would overtake him—the result of old Levi the ragpicker thumping his fist at the infidels—and Morrie'd boot us all out. When Papa died, some folks blamed him."

He stared into my eyes. "There was even a rumor that he killed Papa. No one believed *that*, even though they didn't get along. But afterwards, though, he just went through the motions at work. Like his soul died. Like his heart was pierced. He stopped being friendly, snubbed folks. Customers drifted away."

"Did you think he murdered your father?" I asked bluntly.

Jacob didn't flinch at my words. Nor did he answer me. He shrugged as if I were discussing the ongoing heat spell.

"Wanna look inside?"

He stepped to the front door and turned the knob. It opened.

"Morrie never locks it. Nothing inside of value anymore, really." He lowered his voice. "I think he hopes the old gang will stop back in, especially those times he's upstairs counting his money. But there is no old gang left. He knows I sit by myself here at night. Alone." Then he grinned. "I used to slip in to write my poetry at night—when I did that sort of thing. Waiting for inspiration that never arrived. It's quiet here."

He stepped inside but I didn't follow him into the shadowy dark room. "No, Jacob. No." A violation, I felt, trespassing. I walked away from the shop but glanced back at Jacob in the doorway, as he shut the door.

He joined me. "You shouldn't ask me that question, Edna. I still have…nightmares. I still…" Then, a helpless shrug. "Well, I guess everyone was a suspect." A hint of a smile. "Even me. I was upstairs that day."

He started to move away. "Jacob," I called to him, and he stopped.

His melodious voice, always so cooing and seductive, suddenly got brittle, harsh. "I don't want to talk about *that*. Not anymore."

"I'm sorry."

He stepped back, in his eyes a flash of—not anger, but pain. "No, you're not, Edna. I can see this...that horrible event fascinates you."

I nodded. "True, but I don't want to *hurt* you—or your mother."

A sad smile. "Me—you can't hurt. At least *most* days. I don't care about most things these days. I get morbid, curl up inside. Too many years have passed me by. After the murder, I got depressed. Before that, I was the rah-rah playboy of the neighborhood. Me and Ad all night at the Booster Club on the roof of the Morrison Hotel. Everyone wanted me *there*. Bert Kelly's band struck up a song when I walked in. I was *popular* then. The girls circled me like I was gold in the street. I thought I'd be young forever. Lord, Edna, I'm gonna be forty years old this year. I make my money running numbers in a speakeasy on Clark Street."

"But you're a poet."

Now he laughed long and hard. "Edna, Edna, I don't think you realize how funny you can be." He got a faraway look in his eyes. "I do wish I could remember you from…what? Eighteen years ago, right?"

"Why?"

"Because, after all these years, I think you still like me." A sheepish grin.

"And others don't?"

He frowned, his eyes darkening. "When everyone wants to be around you 'cause you're good-looking, you keep waiting for them to get tired of begging for your attention. You end up…" He trailed off.

"You end up feeling sorry for yourself." I paused. "Or despising yourself."

He chuckled. "God, you don't let a soul get away with anything, Edna."

"No reason to."

Suddenly he put his face close to mine. "I don't want my mother hurt."

I waited a heartbeat. "Jacob, I think your mother has found her own way. Maybe, like you, she can't be hurt anymore. She's found a peace she can live with." I paused. "But I don't know if I believe you. I think you *can* be hurt. You lie to the world, Jacob. You've been hurt—badly so."

He sidestepped that. "You know, I'm real glad you talked to Mama. Maybe you're right—she's made her peace with the world, but it doesn't help that the other women on the street shun her."

"I know. Molly Newmann, for one."

A fake shiver. "An unforgiving woman, that one. But she didn't like Mama from the start. When I was real small, I remember she snubbed her—gossiped. Mama was just too...pretty." But then he sighed. "Esther was the only one who was friendly. I mean, Esther invited Mama into her kitchen for coffee. They went shopping." He frowned. "The women of Monroe Street have made a devil's pact to make certain my mother never is happy again."

"Horrible,"

"You're not like that."

"Jacob, I don't think your mother murdered your father."

That statement stopped him cold, and for a second he flinched, turned his head away as though afraid our talk might be heard by eavesdroppers. Sweat covered his brow. Finally, he said, "I think you're wrong, but, as I say, I don't care anymore. Papa was a tough man, brutal."

I was indignant. "I can't believe you'd say that. You'd accuse your mother?"

He tried to look apologetic. "Look, Edna. It's got nothing to do with my love for Mama. That's *there*. Always. She and I...always close. We had—have—a special bond, the two of us. But...who *else*? The police told me..."

"I wish I knew." Then, turning my head, "Yes, the police had all the answers."

He walked away but turned back. "Please don't, Edna. Don't make things messy again. That was an awful time for all of us. Let sleeping dogs lie."

"Yes, especially for your mother."

"C'mon, Edna. Really."

I fumed. "Jacob, you're not very attractive when you're so…callow."

His eyes popped. "You think I don't know that?" A bow. "I gotta go. Get back to the old fortress."

"The fortress?"

"Me and my buddy, Ad, the two bumble brothers, each barricaded in our bedroom caves in the old homestead, fending off the Amazon women warriors. Me—my Aunt Sarah, who hates me 'cause I'm still there. Ad, smothered to death by a *bubbe* who wanted him to be the golden child, the revered rabbi, the heir to the covenant of the ark…" Another bow. "Hey, we hide away and dream of being little boys all over again. Goodbye, dear Edna from eighteen years ago."

But then he changed his mind, circling around me like a bratty child.

"What?"

"I just remembered something. Speaking of women warriors, you may have heard of my twin sisters, Ella and Emma." He laughed. "Or is it Emma and Ella? I can never tell them apart." I glared at him, and he fumbled. "It's an old joke. I never tire of it."

"Perhaps you should. I already have. Yes, I know you have two younger sisters. In fact, I have a dim memory of two wide, startled faces peering out a second-story window as I stood on the sidewalk—this, of course, eighteen years ago. They had to be seventeen or eighteen back then."

"Four years younger, unmarried, spinsters now, identical except for one important fact."

"And that is?"

"One won't visit our mother nowadays, the other one does, grudgingly."

"Interesting. And they have what to do with me?"

He chuckled. "Ella—the bossy one who visits once a month like clockwork, the one with the hickory stick, the one who orders meek and trembling Emma around like a dumb house servant—gave my mother your novel *The Girls* when she heard you were visiting next door. She loved it—three generations of women in Chicago or, as I overheard her tell Mama, a story of how insufferable dominating mothers can be." His eyes flashed wide. "A message to Mama, perhaps?"

I laughed. "Not *quite*, that storyline." But of course it *was*—a fact that my own mother pointed out and fussed over. "Have you read it?" I asked Jacob now.

He rolled his eyes, purposely exaggerating the gesture. "A book about unmarried women? Spinsters? You don't know much about me, do you, Edna?"

Wryly, my tongue in the corner of my mouth: "What I know is actually too much. Men—young men in particular—spend their time winning battles in wars no one else has heard of."

"What does that mean?"

"Men love to walk in their own victory parades down imaginary streets."

He grinned. "You lose me, lovely Edna. Anyway, Ella and Emma—or is it Emma and Ella?—lived with me and Sadistic Sarah all the years of Mama's absence. Our own prison sentence. Once Mama returned, Ella and Emma skedaddled, though I'm not sure why. My brother, Herman, who pays all the bills and keeps us all out of debtor's prison, thought it was a good idea. Clear out. Vamoose. Get out of Dodge. Especially Emma, who was *afraid* to be there."

"Afraid of what?"

"Dunno." A heartbeat. "Maybe the nightmares will return—the ones that made her wake up screaming. So Ella won't allow Emma to visit now. Afraid she'll upset Mama."

"And your point is what, Jacob? You do trot around a story."

"They want to meet you. I told Ella how close you and I once were…"

I walked away. "Good day."

He got serious, ran after me and touched my elbow. "No, no, wait. Please, Edna. I'm a fool. They want me to bring you to tea some afternoon. They share a room—genteel as all get out, them being unmarried and possibly prey to ne'er-do-wells and bounders—the other side of Maxwell on Canal, a rooming house run by Mrs. Goldberg, as scary a woman as God decided to send to torment other souls on Earth. For single women only, guard dogs at the front entrance." He turned his head to one side, coyly. "Please. I promised them."

"Only if you read my novel, Jacob."

"I promise."

"You are lying to me again."

A hiccough. "Yes, I am. I lie to all women. They *expect* it."

"You're…impossible." I paused. "But all right. You arrange it."

• • ● • •

That night, meeting Ad in the hallway, he whispered to me that Jacob would meet me on the sidewalk the following afternoon at half-past two.

"Be discreet." He leaned in, a goofy smile on his face. "Hide behind the hedges."

"Ad, what?"

"Jacob, though my best friend, is not welcome here since his mother came home and soured the peaceful life of Monroe Street." He gazed over my shoulder. "If he telephones here, asking for me, he's told no one is home. Even, I suppose, the person answering the telephone."

"And you allow that?"

He bit the tip of a fingernail. "Does it look like I set the rules here, Edna?"

The next afternoon, dressed in a light cerise polka-dot sundress with a brimmed straw summer hat with paper roses, I met Jacob, who was planted dramatically and conspicuously in front of the Newmann house. As always, he greeted me with the gentlemanly half-bow, and off he sailed, two or three jaunty paces ahead of me.

I rushed to keep up with his long strides. "Are we in a foot race, Jacob?"

He slowed down. "I just assumed you'd naturally fall in at my side."

"And I just assumed you had some common courtesy."

"I guess we were both wrong." A wide grin, infectious.

From Maxwell, we turned down Canal, and

stopped before a four-story brick building, squat and ugly, soot-blackened red brick and unpainted wrought-iron fence. A small sign said: "Mrs. Goldberg's Rooms. Single Women Only." And then in some bowdlerized German or Yiddish or God-knows-what: *Hier wir the Englisch sprech.* In sloppy black paint, some passing wag had added the words "Only If" at the end of that sentence, perhaps a bit of sarcasm.

We met the two sisters in the stuffy parlor at the front of the house. They stood side by side, bodies touching, arms hanging stiffly at their sides, both with ridiculous red bows in their hair. Introduced first to an obese Mrs. Goldberg in a black Victorian smock, obviously the moral sentry and resident custodian of maidenly virtue, we then stood in the cramped, overstuffed room among the velveteen-covered armchairs and tuffed settees covered with intricate antimacassars. Embroidered quotations from Scripture hung haphazardly on faded rose-printed wallpaper. Mrs. Goldberg seemed unimpressed by my local celebrity, barely suppressed a belch when one of the twins gushed about *The Girls* and my picture (with interview) last year in the *Chicago Tribune*, and then led us to the small dining area at the back of the house, off the kitchen, where a table covered in slick oilcloth held a dangerously lopsided chocolate cake and bargain teacups from Marshall Field's basement sale. I thought I'd been bizarrely ushered into a failed rehearsal for *Alice in Wonderland*. No matter: seated, tea poured decorously by one of the twins, cake sliced but vaguely moldy on a plate, the twins began to speak at the same time, their voices over-lapping as in an echo chamber. They sang of the delight—the wonder, thrill, pleasure, surprise, fear, panic—of actually meeting me again.

"Again?" I managed to get out.

They laughed. "Not *again*," one said, in a solo performance now. "We do remember you and your sister, Fannie, following Jacob down the sidewalk…"

"Please," Jacob broke in, "I'm blushing."

"I never did such a thing," I lied. Outright. I refused to look at Jacob.

Ella and Emma giggled like schoolgirls on holiday.

So the minutes passed in inane blather. Yet, perversely, the more we spoke of Chicago and child-hood and Maxwell Street and the World's Fair of 1893—which neither of the twins went to, though Jacob said he and Ad had seen Buffalo Bill's Wild West Show there, and, an improper wink, exotic Little Egypt—the more my mind kept darting back to their mother's arrest for murder. That was my only interest here. Yet Emma and Ella seemed not to have a care in the world, save the collection of tourist postcards from Europe that one of them (Ella?) babbled about and the watercolor landscapes the other (Emma?) threatened to show me.

Both were tiny, pencil-thin women with parchment complexions and spit-curl hairdos from another century, though the huge red bows struck me as affectations borrowed from a children's storybook. Both were wearing heavy black patent-leather shoes, square-toed, that I associated with nurses in military hospitals. Both leaned back and forth, bumping into each other like elastic bands that kept snapping back into place. They had the maddening habit of talking as one or, worse, finishing each other's sentences. It was evident, finally, that one of them—Ella—controlled the other by severe looks, by abrupt words, by touching her sleeve when it was time for her sister to shut up. Emma was the meek one, though she never seemed to shut up. Ella ordered her around ("Emma, pour more tea, please" or "Emma, sit back, you're blocking my view of Edna"), and Emma complied, tittering nervously.

"When Ad told Jacob you and your mother were..."

"...visiting, we said, it's hard to..."

"...believe. After..."

"...all these years."

They were Dickensian parlor maids, dithering and bleating.

But I wasn't ready to leave. The one story never touched on—Leah Brenner back in her old kitchen—kept me still.

"It's amazing how much Jacob looks like your mother," I began, staring past everyone at a faded chromolithograph hanging crookedly on the wall.

A moment of silence, palpable, but one woman managed, "Jacob got the good looks, you know."

More silence, awkward now. Ella fingered the crumbs on her plate.

Jacob cleared his throat. "Ella, Mama wondered why you skipped Thursday. You said you would come to visit but…"

No one paid attention to me, Jacob purposely shifting his body away.

"I forgot the time. We were shopping and the time passed. You know how it is." She arched her shoulders and sat back. "Cake," she mumbled, directing my attention to the table.

"I enjoyed visiting your mother," I said to her. "She told me she looks forward to your visits." I was making that up but felt safe fabricating the line. After all, I assumed Leah *did* want visits from Ella.

Jacob leaned forward. "You know, Emma, you need to visit Mama, too."

Emma turned away from us, facing the door.

For a moment her face closed up, eyes half-shut. The color rose in her neck, a muscle throbbed. A hand trembled.

Ella fussed but said loudly, "I won't allow Emma to go." A sickly smile. "You *know* that, Jacob."

"What?" From me, stupefied.

She spoke in a clipped, artificial voice, "She'll get too emotional and say the wrong thing. I've forgiven Mama, of course, but she won't. She *can't*. It'll be awkward."

Emma was on the verge of tears.

Jacob spoke again, "She misses you, Emma."

What she said next stunned me. "She murdered Papa."

So bold the line, said so innocently, a throwaway comment as if about the heat of the day or the price of butter at a market stall.

Ella nodded, a half smile on her face. "See what I mean?" she said to no one in particular. Then, a sidelong glance at me, "She doesn't have a forgiving heart."

Emma was ready to say something, perhaps to counter that notion, but she shook her head and looked down into her lap.

Jacob, flustered, nodded at me. "Edna, do you see how this matching set of humanity has found one subject to disagree on?"

Ella spoke up, nonplussed. "We don't talk about it, Jacob. Emma has her own views."

Which, I thought, you so emphatically reinforce. Emma, browbeaten, servile. Her story squelched.

Yet Ella was smiling at her brother, and even Emma assumed an adoring look as she gazed at him. They loved him dearly, I realized, doted on the gadabout wag, loving his teasing—even, I supposed, his indifference.

"I found your mother delightful," I forced myself to say again. The teacup rattled in my hand. And then, with cool deliberation, I added, "A woman wronged, frankly. I don't believe she killed your father."

Emma yelped and said too loudly, "The police told us…"

I interrupted, "A peculiar case, uninvestigated, a belief that your mother's silence and fright constituted confession. Frankly, that was the conclusion of some vainglorious police sergeant or detective who never thought of what your mother was going through."

Emma was anxious. "But the captain told me…" She breathed in. "He said…definitely…"

"And you listened." I answered in a biting tone. "Men tell me things all the time, and I ignore most of it." Quietly, I sipped lukewarm tea and sat back.

"You're confusing me." Emma was nearly in tears.

"I don't mean to. But, truthfully, all of you were willing conspirators in the easy condemnation of your mother."

Ella cleared her throat. "Well, I never believed it. She just never seemed *capable* of it. I mean, she always ran away from fights with Papa. But the police…" A helpless shrug. "We had to listen to someone. We were all…drifting."

Jacob was squirming in his seat, uncomfortable, mumbling about leaving. "I have to be somewhere."

I eyed him cautiously. "No, you don't."

Startled, he grinned. "Yeah, that's true, but this place gives me the willies."

Yet the visit was an opportunity I'd not have again, so setting down my teacup and pushing away my untouched slab of congealed cake, I said, "You were all there that day. In the house. Didn't you *see* anything?"

Silence, heads turned toward the doorway. Finally Ella whispered, "Emma and I were up in the room we shared. Papa was home sick that day." She squinted, ignoring Emma's short audible breaths. "In the morning he and Mama fought, yelling so loud it scared us. We hid behind our closed door." Her voice was mournful. "We've told this story over and over. I mean—years ago we did. I went to the attic to get some fabric and when I stepped into the hallway, I heard Aunt Sarah screaming in the parlor. Emma rushed out of the room, white as a ghost, and the two of us ran downstairs. Papa was slumped on the sofa, bent to the side. He…"

Emma finished. "His head was back. All the blood on his neck, his shirt. Mama was bent in front of him, quiet, you know, stunned by her bloody fingers."

Ella went on, "Aunt Sarah screamed and screamed. We didn't know what to do."

Jacob added, "I had just fallen into bed, ready for a nap, half asleep, and the screaming jarred me. When I ran downstairs, it was—like pandemonium."

"You'd just come home?" I asked.

He squirmed as he tried to remember. "Yeah, maybe a little while before."

"Did you walk through the parlor?"

He was uncomfortable. "In the hallway, yes. Not *into* the parlor but in the doorway."

"Your father was there?"

"I saw him on the sofa. I thought he was sleeping."

"Slumped over?"

He flinched, nervous. "I glanced in, I think. I can't remember. Sometimes he napped there. I knew he was home sick from the butcher shop. I didn't say anything. I went upstairs, washed my face, lay on my bed."

I waited a beat. "Jacob, you didn't tell the police that you saw your father on the sofa."

He sputtered. "Well, of course, I did. I *saw* him…"

"No," I said firmly, "I've read the newspaper accounts"—that surprised the three of them—"and I remember the police were quoted as saying you hadn't seen your father since breakfast—and you said you had been napping for an hour—that you'd been in your room since lunch."

"I don't think…"

But I knew what I'd read in the news clippings. Jacob specifically said he'd heard his parents quarreling earlier and he'd hidden in his room, emerging only after hearing Sarah's wailing.

Now he sputtered, "Maybe I'm remembering wrong." He snickered, "It was fifteen years ago, for God's sake. You know, a person can forget things. It was a bad time—I wanted to block out some things. I don't remember *what* I told the police." Now there was an edge to his voice. "C'mon, Edna, you expect me to remember stuff like that. Maybe I'm thinking of another day. You know, Papa slept on the sofa a lot. A lot of times I walked by, and he was there."

"But not during the day. He was usually working at the store."

"Sick that day, yes. I don't know…" His voice broke at the end.

Emma spoke up in a clipped voice. "Jacob never had a memory for things."

Ella shot her a cautionary look, nodding furiously. "He can't remember what he did *yesterday*."

Emma agreed, echoing, "Yesterday."

"Jacob is always a little boy."

"A boy," Emma echoed. She was smiling at her sister.

Jacob's eyes dipped into his lap, his lips quivering. "It's all a jumble in my head. So long ago…"

Ella spoke loudly. "You know he's a poet, Edna."

"I've heard that," I answered. "But what does that have to do with his memory?"

"Nothing, but you can't expect a man like him…to…he's a wonderful writer, Edna."

"Brilliant," Emma said.

"You know *Poetry*, the magazine here in Chicago? Real prestigious."

I admitted I did. In fact, I knew Harriet Monroe, though faintly. A friend of Lillian Adler, my friend who ran the Maxwell Street Settlement House. I'd watched her teach dancing to awkward Polish and Russian and Jewish girls.

"They published his poem."

Jacob interrupted, "Emma, that was five years ago. One poem." He smiled sadly. "About our grandmother who'd died when we were all very small. My Bubbe."

And then, as though auditioning to be the best student in elocution class, Emma stood, prompted by Ella. "Now, Emma, now. Yes, now." Still holding her teacup, Emma recited in an oddly stentorian voice that doubtless carried out into the street and gave Mrs. Goldberg an immediate heart palpitation:

> *My grandmother*
> *Was supposed to live till ninety*
> *Though she had no legs*
> *(We'd wheel her around*
> *Until the flowers were dust)*
> *She died at eighty-one*
> *Not quite making it.*
> *When I was small*
> *She made old-country challah*
> *Covered herself with eggs flour salt*
> *Until the bread rose in the oven*
> *Like evening in her eyes*
> *And the smell took us both back*
> *To a land I never saw*
> *She'd never see again.*

When she finished, Ella applauded, and I followed suit, though self-consciously. Jacob was pleased, though he pooh-poohed the whole performance.

Emma bowed and sat down.

Jacob stood up. "Edna, it's time we left."

Both twins immediately began clearing the dishes. Neither one looked at me.

Chapter Seven

The next morning, lying in bed but wide awake, I delayed going downstairs for breakfast. Though my door was closed, I could hear muffled voices—Esther's high soprano laugh and my mother's deep rumble—bits and pieces of their discussion of a theater performance they'd seen five years ago at Glickman's Yiddish Theater. An absurd rendering of King Lear. *Der Yiddisher Kainag Lear.* My mother kept saying it was too melodramatic and far-fetched; Esther insisted it was so sad she cried just thinking about it.

"Esther," my mother laughed, "you cry when the first flower blooms in spring."

Cracking my door slightly, I heard my mother telling Esther that lamentably, we'd not stay the full two weeks—another cousin insisted we visit in Evanston for two or three days. Blather and nonsense, of course, simply an excuse to secret her wayward daughter from the explosive household.

Yet another reason kept me in my room, tucked into a chair by the window and staring out at the leaves of the sugar maple tree wilting under the unrelieved heat. An awful reason: the visit with Jacob to Emma and Ella's rooming house. Jacob's careless dissembling, that slip about what he saw on the day his father was murdered. Perhaps meaningless, perhaps not—but curious. And Ella and Emma's spirited defense of his memory—and that curious sleight-of-hand maneuver of having Emma recite his poem, a preamble to my being shooed out the door. It bothered me, his failed memory. You'd remember every step you took on such an awful day, no? Stunned at that moment, of course, dazed, but later, recollecting in the painful days to follow, you'd order your thoughts, check off the moments in your head. But maybe not the helter-skelter Jacob—and his two bizarre sisters, his hip-hip-hurrah cheering team, panicky in their defense of a much-loved brother.

What to make of it all?

I waited until I heard Molly, Esther, and my mother leave the house, headed to the markets, then went downstairs into the kitchen for coffee and Esther's butter-slathered rye rolls. But the house was not empty after all. Ad was munching on toast, his face buried in the morning newspaper. He yawned and smiled. He was wearing a crisp white cotton shirt, unbuttoned at the neck to reveal a sunburned neck.

"Good morning, Ad."

"You hiding, Edna?"

"I thought everyone was gone."

"They've gone shopping." He chuckled. "I guess you were not invited. Papa's at the cigar store, of course. Only Lazy Ad stays home to masquerade as the leisure class. Lawn tennis at noon with Mrs. Potter Palmer, then a spin around the Loop in her ritzy fliv." He smiled. "Actually I'm leaving now. I've been helping Old Man Feinstein in his hardware store—he pays me practically nothing, but it keeps the folks from exiling me from the castle." He started to fold the newspaper. "Jacob told me you visited Ella and Emma yesterday at Mrs. Goldberg's. That woman scares me. The twins scare me. Ah, Edna, you and your acts of courage."

"Why? I found them delightful."

He narrowed his eyes as he smirked. "Yeah, sure, Edna. Convince me of that, can you? The silly Siamese twins. Ella giving marching oom-pa-pah orders to her sobbing sister. You probably didn't witness Ella screaming for hours at poor Emma, 'You don't have the brains you were born with.' It ain't pretty, let me tell you. Even though they put on a great act for the world to see, they don't *like* each other. That's clear. And yet they share a small, cramped room. Talk about your prison sentences. They hide from the world—they squeal if I say hello to them. They're so…scattered, those two. Yet, I suppose, harmless."

Ad's face got tight. Standing, he placed his cup in the sink and tucked his folded newspaper under his arm. "Jacob was *bothered* by what you said, Edna."

"What did I say?" I poured myself coffee, sat down, watching as he faced the outside window.

He hesitated, as though debating what to say to me. "I don't know exactly. Jacob only tells me just this much." He held up a thumb and index finger and punctuated the *this*. "He *avoids* sensitive talk, you know. Stuff about his mother. He thinks you've been asking a lot of questions about what folks remember." His hand flew to the air, a dismissive gesture. "He says you badgered Ella and Emma."

"I badgered *him*."

That startled. "Why?"

"He contradicts his own story."

A quizzical look. "So what? Why now? What does it matter?"

I munched on a bit of the delicious bread, moist, warm, scented with chewy caraway seeds, crispy outside, creamy inside. "Because now he suspects his mother is *innocent* of murder."

Ad started to cough, doubled over. When he

leaned back, rubbing his cheek, he wore a quizzical smile. "He didn't tell me that you said *that*. That news must have stopped him cold in his tracks. Good God, Edna. You are something else. I can see why Jacob got depressed."

"Depressed?"

"He got moody. Maybe not real depressed. Sometimes he gets down in the dumps. There's no being with him those times. I back away. It's like this wave of melancholy drowns him."

"Maybe it's time someone in that family paid some attention."

Ad pulled a chair out, swiveled it around, straddled it. The newspaper slipped to the linoleum floor. Nervously, he lit a cigarette. "You don't think Jacob did it, do you?" Breathless, staring into my face.

"I don't know."

Ad didn't expect that answer and thumped the table with his fist. "Lord, Edna, do you hear yourself? This is Jacob. Sweet Jacob. He *loves* his mother. He never wanted his mother to be the one accused. But that's the way it happened. Problems with his father, everybody did, but he wouldn't *kill* him."

"He wouldn't be the first son to kill a father." I stared into his troubled face. "Sometimes those who love find themselves killing. That's the way it is. Because of the *love*, Ad. In a rage. A momentary fit.

Passion. I read the articles in the Chicago *Tribune* about the murder, Ad. All of them…"

"What? Why?"

"I'm a reporter. It's in my blood."

"But it's so…long ago."

I bit my lip. "Yes, I know. Old news. Your grandmother so aptly dismissed it that way. That's the sentiment of the whole neighborhood. The only problem is that Leah has come back home. That's a wrinkle no one counted on."

He wagged a finger at me as though I'd said something amusing. He thought me one more nosy neighbor.

"You know, Edna, I just realized—you want a different ending. Leah Brenner fooled you, too. God, even now she can seduce, you know, entice. How many men fell under her spell and now…"

I cut him off. "You're missing the point, Ad. She didn't kill Ivan."

Ad's face got hard, his eyes dark and hooded. "Let me tell you something about Jacob." He counted a beat and then went on. "You gotta know this. When his father was murdered, Jacob got… miserable—crying jags, blubbering, sad, hiding in his room all day and night. Everything shut down inside him. It was horrible to watch. He fell apart, my best friend. Everyone but his sisters left him alone because they didn't know what to do.

No mother, no father, and an aunt who didn't like him. His brother, Herman, kept saying that he should shape up and be a man, and 'What the hell is wrong with you?' His sisters baked him too many pies, like they piled up on the kitchen counter, insane. They gave him books of poetry by…by Ella Wheeler Wilcox, you know. 'Laugh and the world laughs with you, weep and you weep alone.' That kind of stuff. They'd read it *at* him. His Uncle Ezra mocked him. Ezra, his father's brother, a nasty man who was never around. Jacob cried all the time—I didn't know what to do with him. I thought he'd kill himself, so bad it was. He was a lost boy, really. I got scared of him. For him." Ad brought his face close to mine. "He ain't a strong guy, Edna."

I stood up. "Don't worry, Ad."

"I *am* worried. Don't make this into a game."

"I would never…"

With a sharp wave of his hand he left the kitchen. I sipped my coffee. It was cold.

• • ● • •

Upstairs in my bedroom, restless, I dabbled with my notes, reviewing some typed sheets, drawing a line here or there, striking out a paragraph, bored. Again, determined, I planned on a midnight run to the Haymarket, the South Water Street market-place. I wanted to witness those dedicated Dutch truck farmers from outside Chicago bringing in their produce in the deep of night—the pivotal scene in my novel *Selina* or *So Big*—I couldn't decide which title I liked— Selina in her ramshackle wagon with her sleepy little boy Dirk nestled in blankets. But, again, that dirt farm grubbing world was far removed from the gritty pushcart world of Maxwell Street. The rich soil of New Holland had nothing to do with the tar and asphalt of Jewtown and Yiddish gab. Herring snacks on black pumpernickel. No—it wouldn't work for me. Not yet. I'd have to get away from Monroe Street.

Leah's story nagged at me like an old dog at my heel.

Downstairs, standing in the kitchen doorway, peering out the screen door, I could hear tinny music wafting across the yards. Someone in Leah's home was playing the radio loudly—fragmented words of that ridiculous popular song, "No No Nora" by Eddie Cantor. I find most popular ditties tedious. Eddie Cantor with that *wazza wazza* crooning drove me to distraction. That adenoidal screeching. A house of noise—Sarah's booming music and Jacob's banging his way through the rooms. And Leah sat quietly by herself. But I lingered there, listening—and wondered: What had anyone in the Newmann household heard that morning years ago? Yes, they'd heard screaming. I knew that. Leah and Ivan's battle royal. But what else? What was said? The wailing of Ivan when he was knifed? The screams and weeping of Sarah and the children? Who heard what?

Had the police even talked to the Newmanns about it? I doubted that. After all, they scarcely talked to Leah.

Within minutes, standing on the sidewalk in front of Leah's home, I could hear the radio playing, but muted now. Impulsively, I climbed the stairs and knocked on the front door. Someone pulled back a curtain in a side window and then, finally, the door opened. Leah smiled at me. "I couldn't imagine who was here. Family always comes to the kitchen door." She pointed behind her. "Or through the back screen porch."

"I heard the music."

Leah raised her eyebrows and shook her head. The razzle-dazzle music was coming from an upstairs room, but at that moment the volume swelled so loudly that Leah and I had to raise our voices. Someone was fiddling with the knobs, searching for a station perhaps. A needle under the skin, that dissonant, staticky noise. *I wish I could shimmy like my sister Kate.* Claptrap music, utter novelty for a world of dancing fools in a speakeasy tavern.

"Sarah is telling me something," she yelled. "Ever since I got back home, she has discovered the volume control. Paul Whiteman thrills her—and he enters my nightmares. I tell her, beg her, but she goes against my wishes. Jacob pleads with her, but then he runs off. What can I do?" A weary shrug.

A sudden break in the music, a run of static as Sarah shifted the dial. But another crash of noise—stomping, a foot drummed on the floorboards, a fist slamming a wall. *Bam bam bam.*

"What?" I caught Leah's face.

She raised her eyes to the ceiling. "My Jacob."

"I don't understand…"

"A battlefield, Edna. Jacob staggers home and, like a restless boy, he thrashes around his room."

"A protest against Sarah's musical taste?" I joked.

She frowned. "The stomping around—a caged animal—even when Sarah is at the market."

"How can you bear the noise?"

She shrugged. "I have no choice." Again, the glance upward. "Jacob watches me too closely the last few days." She bit her lip. "His eyes accuse Sarah as she puts supper on the table."

Someone upstairs yelled, the music soared, the crash of a boot against the floorboards.

I motioned toward the Newmann house. "Join me for coffee."

She started. "Oh no. I—not there—Molly—"

Stepping close to the staircase, I raised my voice over the din. "No one is home, Leah. Molly and the others are out shopping. They're lost on Maxwell till afternoon. They'll linger at Nathan's Ice Cream Parlor. Trust me. I've been shopping with them. A sale at Louis Gabel's Clothing, and the hours go by. Come. There's coffee on the stove. Please. This noise is...impossible." I touched her elbow, though she backed away. "Please."

Numbly, almost mechanically, she stepped out onto the porch, shutting the door behind her. But her slow walk alongside me was a prisoner's plodding death march: short shuffling steps, a baby's tentative exploration. Once she sat opposite me in the Newmann kitchen, she sighed, relaxed in the chair, and folded her arms across her chest. "I haven't been in Esther's kitchen for—years."

"Did you come here often?"

She thought about her response, as if impossible to answer. "We were *friendly*. I *liked* her. She liked me, I knew. But she was always nervous *here*."

I smiled. "The shadow of Molly."

A slight wistful smile. "Molly didn't like me. Never liked me. Didn't trust me." A pause. "A *makhasheyfe*, she called me." A witch.

"I know."

Suddenly she stood, and I thought she'd flee.

Instead, her hands fluttering, she walked to the sink and stared out the window toward her own house. Her back to me, she spoke quietly. "We moved here exactly one year after the Newmanns bought their place. May Day. May first. I mean, Sol and Esther, with Molly in tow, had already settled in, knew people, the rabbi." She turned her head, and I stared at her profile. "More than forty years back, a real neighborhood of greenhorns and off-the-boat boarders…and on windy days the sickening smells from the stockyards, sometimes from the I. C. trains. Our first home. Sol and Esther, new married. Me and Ivan, new married. Our home a wedding gift from his parents."

Now she faced me. Her eyes swept the kitchen as she ran her fingers across the counter, letting them rest on a cutting board. Her eyes took in the white-painted cabinets. "Nothing has changed here. Nothing. I used to sit in Esther's kitchen, here, friendly, you know. And then Ivan and Sol sat with cigars in the basement, arguing about something in *Forwards*, maybe. Molly made believe friendly, you know. But somehow—one day, maybe—Molly caught her Sol, a young man then, smiling at me a little too long. I was talking of something, and he laughed a little too long. Maybe."

Her face tightened. "It ain't my fault, Edna. Well—that day it wasn't. I was always blessed—or cursed—with the looks, you know. My mother warned me. Trouble, my little Leah. Trouble for you. My Papa said if we was Catholic I would be hidden away in a nunnery for good."

She shook her head back and forth slowly and dreamily. "A curse I didn't see coming, Edna. So Molly spotted Sol that day, real innocent it was… you know Sol, a nice guy always—you know him, such an innocent man—but Molly yells at him, and then at me as I sat there with a red face, and the rumors start."

For a moment she turned her face away, her lips trembling.

I stood up, touched the coffee pot on the stove to see if it was still warm, took the milk pitcher from the icebox, then lifted cups from the cabinet. She took one from my hands. Her fingers cradled it, turning it, and she whispered, "Nothing has changed."

Quietly, she poured coffee for herself, then took my cup from my hand. "I used to pour Esther's coffee while she chatted. Like sisters. It was…" A sigh. "Then she'd listen for Molly's step." We sat back down, but she jumped up to put the milk pitcher back into the icebox.

I waited until she sat back at the table. "Rumors."

A nod. "The fingers wagging. Coldness to me.

At shul the whispers. People don't nod at me in the street. The families were very religious then, the first years in the neighborhood, always to temple, morning prayers, food. Esther didn't know how to handle it—she's just so…sweet and *good*. But Molly—I guess she was in her forties then—was cranky, sarcastic always, a gossipmonger. She had the rabbi knock on my door. The poor man, embarrassed, babbling, Molly's reluctant messenger. But it made my Ivan angry and he stayed away from shul."

I sipped my coffee but watched her eyes. "She wouldn't talk to you?"

Solemn, eyes locked with mine. "No. Forty years now, maybe."

I clicked my tongue. "She hasn't changed much, though the unforgiving part has become set in stone. Even with the stroke she has…a tongue on her."

Leah shook her head. She ran her fingertip around the rim of the coffee cup. "She got a tough life, Molly does—so Esther told me. The old village in Germany near the Polish border, Jews beaten, stones thrown, her home destroyed at Passover when the *goyim* accused a cousin of blood libel, killing a Christian child for blood to bake matzoh, horrible, horrible." She breathed in. "Then the long days in steerage, poor, a husband dying young and her alone with little Sol. A seamstress for years. In a sweatshop on Canal Street in New York. A grubby life till Sol grows and works in a cigar-making factory." Leah grinned. "Her biography is told over and over like a legend in that family. Struggle."

"As well it should be."

She stared into her cup. "So you can sort of see how the hardness takes over a person—gets in the blood. America saved her. Made her *safe*—allowed her dreams. So she thought I was a home-wrecker, maybe. So much to lose. I had no eye for Sol, of course. Believe me. A quiet, mind-your-own-business guy. Slap-on-the-back kind of guy. 'Come in, come in. My Esther gives you hot tea.' I had my own Ivan, a good man before he got mean. Molly badmouthed me and told the women to watch their husbands. That started my loneliness."

That last word jarred her. Standing, she walked to the doorway, peeked around the corner, then moved back to the sink. Again, she stared across the yards to her home as though somehow, in the minutes passed, it had vanished. Her eyes caught a framed piece of Esther's embroidery on the wall—a bucolic landscape of English cottage and trellised roses. Her fingertips traced the roses as she mumbled, "Esther's romantic world." A loving touch, lingering.

I raised my voice. "Well, you're still a beautiful

woman, and you don't have to apologize for what God saw fit to give you. A gift."

She ignored that. "I confess something to you, though. I let the attention of the men go to my head. You know, Ivan and Morrie got the butcher shop together, but the real life of the shop was the friends who met there to socialize. Morrie didn't care for selling, really. He wanted the friends around him. That's all. Lord, you could walk into the back room there and you got six or seven men lounging around, a glass of beer or wine and a stack of cheese sandwiches—you know, like a second breakfast, *Zweite Früstück* they calls it—cigar smoke like a cloud you can't get through. Storytelling, laughing, bragging, arguing politics all day long. A club, you know. And when I went there for something, their...eyes, you know."

"I don't know."

She sat back down, facing me, her hand pushing her coffee cup away. "See, Edna, I married Ivan. I *loved* Ivan, sloppy fool that he was. That maybe *I* was. No one understood *us*—the quiet laughter, the—" She stopped. "The early days was good—always laughing. We joked about the looks given to me. Ivan was dumpy, always with mismatched buttons on the vest, his hair shaggy. I think it made him *proud* to have a pretty wife, but a *good* wife. One who kept a kosher kitchen back then. The proper Shabbas. Always. A good mother to his children. But sometimes I felt like a doll he showed off. That kind of…loving wears off."

"He changed?"

"He got suspicious, and for no reason. The silence in the house like a blanket thrown over your head. Stupidly, I let that fool Morrie touch me. A moment, and then it stopped, praise God. But Morrie brags about it to the boys in the back room—and to Ivan. By then, they fight all the time in the shop—hate each other."

I drank the rest of my coffee, and Leah, noticing, moved to the stove. As I started to stand, she held up her hand. "Let me." She opened the icebox and took out the milk pitcher, placed it on the table. But she didn't sit back down—as though she desired other tasks to perform. The rhythm of a mother in her kitchen, comfortable, sure, efficient.

I counted a beat. "Tell me about the fight you had that morning."

Her words low, hesitant. "We never fought like that. Yes, the little spats, yes. It started over Jacob and the way his papa treated him. He *hated* the *softness* of my boy. But the screaming, cursing that morning. And him being sick on top of it. He couldn't stop the yelling. Jacob, yes, but then Morrie, the rumors. All the ugliness of the—the indiscretion with Morrie. It was like someone broke…his doll. I cried and cried."

"Still, one moment shouldn't condemn you to a life of…"

She held up her hand. "Edna, I started *liking* the attentions of the men. I'm—what was I?—I was forty-four then, getting a little chubby, lines in my face, but the men still joked—whistled. Downtown even the *goyim*, the wolf whistles. How the old bearded men walking from shul yelled at me, accusing, watching, praying at me. I used to think I encouraged it—helpless to stop it, not *wanting* it to stop. One time Jacob and Ad were there in the back room, young men then, boys really, and someone made a remark. Not bad but…*wrong*. You don't mention another man's wife—or mother. Like *that*. You don't. I'd just walked in and overheard it. About me. I didn't know where to look. Everyone laughed but not Jacob. Of course, not Jacob, my son. But Ad laughed too long, trying to be one of the men. He ribbed Jacob, and Jacob struck out and hit Ad in the face. They didn't talk for a month. Ad was doing what all the men did, but Jacob wanted something better from his friend. Ad later apologized, I remember. He apologized to *me*—that was hard for a young boy to do, no? When Ad was a shy little boy, I teased him. How I could make him blush! This was before he got—religious."

She threw back her head and laughed. "That was when he gave Jacob long lectures about such things. Quoting the Talmud. Jacob ran away from him."

"But Ivan knew you were loyal."

"Men have doubts. God knows what was said in that awful back room. And then Ivan's brother, Ezra, moved back from Philadelphia. The college brother, the swanky lawyer, the older brother, widowed now, childless, with gold in his pockets."

"So what?"

"I courted *him* first, Edna, when they were young men. The families chose *him* for me. Back then families told their children who to marry. And he wanted to marry me. He was a slick man, phony, too smooth. *Nu.* You know, a *gantser kener.*" A know-it-all. "Ivan was down-to-earth, sweet then. I liked Ivan. Ezra didn't talk to Ivan for years after I chose Ivan. I fought my parents. Let me marry Ivan. Please. They had no choice, my family. Ezra, furious, missed the wedding. A huge slight back then in the close-knit Jewish family. Brother stopped talking to brother. Then Ezra came back, scooting around in a newfangled automobile, tossing coins at everyone, and Ivan got nervous. No reason to. I don't like Ezra. He makes my skin crawl. But he comes around then and befriends my Jacob. He sits in my parlor and waits for me to walk through."

"Lord," I commented, "the curse of beauty, magnified."

Leah squinted. "What?" She rustled in her seat. "I have to go." She half-rose, and her hand hit the coffee cup. It slid to the edge of the table. We both reached for it, and our hands collided. For a second I held her fingers—cold, clammy in the hot kitchen.

I wasn't through. Hurried, "Your Jacob looks just like you."

She laughed. "I know, though a skinnier version these days. His own curse—the playboy of Maxwell Street. A matinee boy from the magazines in his soft slough cap worn at an angle, just so—the brogans, the pressed London coat, the ear-to-ear grin. He hops off the El and the girls bump into one another."

"I confess, Leah. I had a crush on him way back when."

"Sooner or later everyone does."

"A charmer."

She rolled her tongue into the corner of a cheek. "And look where it got him, Edna. Nowhere. A poet who stopped writing poetry years ago. A drifter. Pennies here, there. For one week sweeping the floor of the barber shop in the Palmer House, then he can't get out of bed."

"Ella—or was it Emma?—recited by heart his poem from *Poetry*."

She chuckled. "I know about that. They *love* him to death." Her face got somber. "Edna, I heard all about your visit there. The twins were thrilled. You, the author of *The Girls*. I even told Ella to go to the public library to read that short story that meant so much to me, but she can't understand *why* it means so much to me. 'The Homely Heroine.' Of course, she never did. But Edna, Jacob wasn't happy with the visit. Your conversation made him a little crazy." She glanced toward the window and her hand pointed in the direction of her home. "So he comes home and the banging on the walls starts. The nervous pacing on the floor. Slammed doors. He sighs out loud. We don't *discuss* that day, Edna." Now a sliver of a smile, sad. "You've become drawn to it, he told me. The reporter. The moth to the flame."

"Well, I think you've been wronged."

"Jacob and the twins don't want to think about that day again. It's too horrible. I'm home. They want to believe that life is normal again. You're giving Jacob the idea that everybody got everything *wrong* back then. Everything they were told by the police to believe is false…"

"It *is* false."

"Edna, Edna."

Impatient, I stood up. I moved to the window. The Brenner home was quiet, the shades on the windows pulled down. I swung back to face her. "Leah, don't you want the truth to come out?"

She refused to look at me. A long silence, then she spoke in a soft, frightened voice. "No."

"This whole business smells."

She joined me at the window and grasped my wrist. "Edna, you come out of a different world. Yes, your feet are planted in the same Chicago neighborhoods—we all were—but you were built different from other folks. Your brain buzzing, your feet running up the street. Words humming in your head. What's out *there*? *Let me see.* That's who you are. You didn't want *this*." Her hand swept around the tidy kitchen. On the counter a red-and-white enamel bowl of rising bread, covered with dishtowels. A jar of ginger snap cookies, never empty. Flowered curtains laundered twice a week, faithfully. A black-and-white tiled floor, scrubbed daily. A pot on the gas stove, diced potatoes in cold water. A similar kitchen up and down Monroe Street. Look in the backyards or on back porches of the apartment houses and you'd spot clotheslines of flapping laundry. A garden bed of mint and chives and parsley surrounded by Sweet William and mignonette. The same. Always the same.

A decent life, but not one I wanted.

"That's true."

"Of course, it is. Your picture in the *Chicago Tribune*. In the *Bookman*, clipped out by Ella and tacked to a wall."

"But I'm still the same little Jewish girl, almost forty, traipsing after a termagant mother who tells me how to behave."

Leah nodded, her face close to mine. "Some things will never change. Your widowed mother will never set you free, the unmarried daughter." She glanced over her shoulder. "It's a Jewish commandment that only women understand. The cord cannot be cut. Don't even try."

"I'll see about that."

We started to laugh, a little crazily, enjoying the moment. Leah's eyes got moist and her nose ran. Idly, she removed the dishtowels covering the enamel bowl, peered in at the rising dough. She clicked her tongue. "Esther put the bowl where too much sun hits it." She ran her fingers under the cold-water faucet, then sprinkled drops onto the rising bread. Her fingers rubbed the surface. Satisfied, smiling to herself, she replaced the stack of dishtowels, but slid the bowl out of the shaft of sunlight. "There," she said to herself. "All right."

When we sat back down, she held my eye, dead on. "I don't want my children hurt, Edna."

I gasped. "I have no intention…"

"My son, Herman, called from across town. Jacob spoke to him about your visit to Ella and Emma's. He's a…fussy man, a little pompous, my Herman, he likes the gold coins in his pocket, jingling them. Lord, he should have been Uncle Ezra's son." That thought made her smile. "Which probably explains why they hate each other. Anyway, he wanted to know what was going on. What you're up to. 'I couldn't make much sense of Jacob's rambling talk,' he says to me. 'What is this reporter up to? Why doesn't she stay at the Newmanns' where she belongs?'" Leah chuckled. "Finally, the last solution we all run to. 'Do we have to have the rabbi talk to her?'"

"What?" I stormed, indignant, my shoulders hunched.

"I know, I know. I told him, 'I don't think that would work, Herman. Rabbi Kurtz ain't no match for Edna Ferber. Edna is her own woman.' He grumbled and hung up the phone, but not before he mumbled something about a call to you from him."

I rolled my eyes. "Ah, something to look forward to."

Leah's eyes clouded. "But I don't want my children hurt, Edna. They've been through enough."

"I promise you."

"I can't believe you, Edna. I like you—very much—but I don't know if I can trust you."

"You can trust me to do the right thing."

"That's what I'm afraid of." She watched me out of the corner of her eye. "The right thing ain't always the right thing."

The kitchen door swung open and my mother walked in, her arms filled with packages. She was glancing behind her at Esther and Molly as she complained about the need to haggle with a boorish peddler over some wilted cabbages. "You'd think he was offering gold leaf to…to Michelangelo, such treasures…"

She stopped short, and Esther, also loaded down with packages, collided into her back. Molly, still standing on the top step, grunted, "Am I expected to stand here with the sun beating down on me?"

Then, standing in a straight line, shoulders touching, backs against the kitchen counter, the three women stared from me to Leah, who'd jumped up so quickly she'd knocked her coffee cup to the floor. It smashed into little pieces and, confused, she bent to pick up the shards, then changed her mind.

"We're having coffee," I announced calmly.

Esther stepped forward, dropping her purchases on the table. "No matter, Leah. It's…

it's an old cup." She smiled thinly. "It's nothing at all. I mean, really." She glanced nervously at Molly, frozen against the counter, with her cane suspended in the air, pointing. Bravely Esther extended her hand. Hesitantly, shyly, Leah took it, and Esther gripped the other woman's fingers. "Leah, welcome."

It was, I thought, as exquisite and touching a gesture as I'd ever seen—so quiet and…so right.

But that moment was shattered by my mother's consumptive rasp and her storming out of the room, bumping into a chair and toppling it over. Molly, bent and dependent on her cane, maneuvered her treacherous way around the broken cup and toppled chair. *Tap tap tap*. She paused in the doorway and eyed Esther.

"Esther, you need to clean up this mess. You never were the best housekeeper." With that, she turned and disappeared into the hallway. Angry whispers drifted back into the kitchen, punctuated by that infernal *tap tap tap*. Then silence.

Leah's face drained of color, sagging, drawn. She kept nodding at me and then at Esther, like a mechanical toy, though I noticed her look lingered on Esther, who was trembling. The two women stared at each other, and I marveled at the sudden and awesome transformation. Because, in that lightning-brief exchange, in that immaculate kitchen, Esther was the distraught woman, the shunned woman—and Leah, starting to move toward the door, was calm and sure, her hand gently touching Esther's quivering cheek. Her voice sweet and sure. "All right. It's all right."

Chapter Eight

Herman Brenner was inordinately proud of his new automobile. A *knaker*, he was, a big shot, happy to be one. Parked in front of the Newmann home, a deliberate act of defiance, he stood by the passenger door, his hand resting on the gleaming latch, waiting as I stepped from the porch. He spat into a handkerchief, and with the attention of a mother powdering a newborn, painstakingly rubbed off a spot on the ice-blue glossy surface.

When I approached, he stopped, half-bowed, very Prussian, greeting me. "Two days old, this masterpiece. A top-notch Roamer Auto made by Barley Motor Cars, built right here in Illinois, over to Streator. An exquisite auto, I must say." He bowed to it. It was glittery, long and spiffy, with sparking aquamarine paint, spitfire black tires, and monstrous headlights, its top down, grandly. A chariot of the gods—for one who saw himself as deserving of God's bounty.

"So pleased to meet you, Herman," I said in my friendliest voice.

He pursed his brow. "Have we met before? Jacob said you were here...." He was puzzled.

"Oh, no, I'd remember. I don't think we ever spoke. But I do recall seeing you walk by on the sidewalk."

"We didn't talk?"

"No reason to." I stepped toward the car.

That baffled him, but he opened the door and I slid onto the coffee-colored leather seat. So many gadgets on the dashboard—this was some Jules Verne futuristic vehicle, inherently dangerous. Ralph Waldo Emerson's better mousetrap.

Herman Brenner had called last night after supper. Esther handed me the telephone, her face a mixture of question and horror. He'd been speaking to Jacob, he told me. And Jacob had a lot to say about me. That lad did talk quite a bit, I concluded—Jacob as some kind of Semite town crier, indeed. Herman also understood his mother was fashioning a friendship with me. "Although," he went on, "I understand you'll be leaving shortly." I could detect relief in that last remark.

"A short visit, yes, as Jacob probably told you. My mother is an old friend of Esther and..."

He'd cut me off. "Suddenly you have taken on *our* family business."

"Meaning?"

A curt tone: "Edna, perhaps dinner tomorrow night with me and my wife. You'll like her. You'll meet the children."

I'd waited for an invitation for my mother, which was proper, but none was forthcoming. I'd nudged him. "My mother and I have obligations here." I'd repeated, "My mother…she…"

He would have none of it. "We need to discuss my mother's situation—and what you're up to."

"Up to?" I'd echoed.

"I'm not a fool, Edna."

"I never thought you were."

"I'll pick you up at six-thirty. In front of the Newmanns'." Click. The sound of a dial tone. I'd hung on the line, stupidly, until the operator came on and peevishly told me to end the call.

Which was why, at precisely six-thirty, I was gliding through the city streets, heading to the west side of town, to Lawndale, where Herman and his family lived. We drove past the railroad tracks, past the soot-blackened factories, until we came upon the smart-looking two-flat brick-and-stone homes surrounded by leafy parks. "Chicago Jerusalem," Herman told me, pointing proudly. Across Roosevelt, down Douglas. The automobile knew the way.

Instinctively, I'd dressed for a formal summer supper: a navy blue linen dress with a spray of red paper roses on the bodice, a pale rose-colored wrap over my shoulders. A tiny box hat, trimmed with lace. Annoyingly, I now realized that I'd inadvertently dressed in a way that seemed to accent the automobile—I was a Florodora girl in a back-page glossy advertisement in *Collier's*. "An automobile for the girl in your life."

Herman drove like a man expecting a bearded Russian anarchist, lit bomb at the ready, to step suddenly into his path. His gloved hands gripped the steering wheel, his face was grim, his body hunched forward, spine rigid. An automobile pulled in front of us, and he slammed on the brakes, hurling me to the dashboard. *"A brokh tsu dir!"* he screamed, A curse on you! Then, in English, "Damnation!" Again the slammed brakes as my body banged against the door. There was no apology.

This burly man was portly, pot-bellied, pompous, with a wide pancake face, iron-gray smallish eyes too far apart so that he seemed vacant, a little dumb, with large black spectacles shielding those pebble eyes, making the face almost clown-like. Yet despite that vacuous look I saw a flinty hardness in the eyes, and a stare that would not break. The round fleshy face, a simpleton's glance, was forgotten when his mouth moved—one moment a wide grin, all teeth, almost feral; the next moment a razor-thin line of disapproval. Despite the oppressive summer heat, even at that hour, he was dressed in a severe black broadcloth vested suit, with gold watch fob, a Rotary Club pin on a lapel, and a sensible black derby atop his slicked-back hair. A formidable man, this Herman Brenner, who, unlike his brother, had inherited none of his mother's delicate and wonderful beauty. No, it was as though, born with a physiognomy so distancing, he chose power and fierceness as traits to be cultivated. Frankly, he scared me, this man who oozed authority that I sensed he'd won by utter determination—paying a price for such victory.

"The purpose of this visit is what?" I began.

I knew I'd have to wait for the answer. This was a man who planned his strategies. A day calculated in half-hour blocks, regimented. Intrusive, smart-aleck young women had best cool their heels. He measured out his information in small doses.

So I waited.

We barely talked, but what feeble conversation we had dealt with my visit ("Such wonderful family, the Newmanns") or my burgeoning fame for *The Girls* ("Your picture in the photogravure some time ago was much talked of"). Finally, as though we'd sloughed through a barren desert, we drifted into uncomfortable silence.

When we arrived at his home in Lawndale, he purposely slowed down the automobile, inching its way on the long driveway, nodding toward the house. I was expected to *ooh* and *aah*, but those exclamations were difficult for me. So I sat there in stony silence, which annoyed him. He kept glancing at me, his brow wrinkly.

The house was a sprawling Tudor with sufficient windowed turrets to provide haven for damsels in distress or to warn of approaching infidels with spears and mace. Set back on a parched yellow lawn, with wilting nasturtiums and petunias in long green window boxes, the house appeared unoccupied—shades drawn, lead-glass windows shut tight despite the dreadful heat—and one of the two lamps left and right of the front door flickered madly.

He frowned at that. "What the hell!" Imperfections on the medieval canvas.

Parked under a manicured sycamore tree, we sat in the hot car for a minute, and he said in a gravelly voice, "The only argument my father and I consistently had was about moving to Lawndale. You know, the night before he died, we had a knockdown drag-out battle. My Papa was a stubborn man, difficult."

"About what?" Now I was curious.

"Come now, you've seen the old neighborhood. The old crowd is moving away, the old German Jewish folks, the Reform—the young ones, ambitious, they move here, or out to the suburbs. Lake View. Morton Park. For twenty or thirty years now, that migration. Things changed. Russian Jews streamed in to Maxwell Street with their burlap sacks and cardboard suitcases. Up and down Halsted. They look at us and say—*goy*. A dislike for us, the old-timers." He waved his hand at the landscape. "Deutschland, they call this place. They're our people, of course, but you've seen them."

"We're all Jewish."

"They're not rushing to become Americans like our families."

This was not the conversation I wanted. "You wanted your parents to move here?"

He nodded. "Of course. A good life here. But Papa wanted to stay on Monroe Street. He had that failed butcher shop. He and Morrie always fighting. Morrie'd lost interest. The back room was a den of…iniquity. A place to play poker and argue about politics. Everything grimy and messy. I couldn't budge Papa."

"What did your mother want?"

"She said it didn't matter. She'd be happy there—whatever Papa wanted. But the old customers started to go somewhere else. Morrie indifferent, Papa tired of it all. Nathan's not *kashrut* enough, they worry, the old ladies. Strictly kosher." Suddenly he shut up. "I don't know why I'm telling you this."

"I suppose because you just came from there. Your boyhood neighborhood. Those streets."

"Maybe. I don't *like* it there. You can't breathe there."

But the short conversation—this surprising revelation, so out of character with his stuffy demeanor—abruptly ended. He sucked in his cheeks, reached for a cigarette, and lit it. "Papa was a poor businessman. Morrie, too. Talkers, they were. Oh, they made money, sure, in the early days. Morrie lives in a big house now, away from there. He collects rents for the old buildings he owns on Monroe. A landlord who doesn't fix the broken pipes. But Papa had no head for business." He preened. "I do."

"I understand you own a factory?"

He swelled up. "Brenner's Suits." He tugged at the lapel of the suit jacket he wore. "The best." He opened the door, rushed around to open mine, but then walked on ahead, leaving me to follow. I lacked a requisite basket of rose petals to strew in his path.

A man easy to dislike. All it took was a breezy ride in a hotsy-totsy convertible across town. From the peasant's hovel to the lord's castle.

"This is my wife, Naomi."

We approached a woman waiting in the doorway. She glanced at her husband and then shook my hand, immediately turning away, disappearing into a hallway. Herman acted flustered before motioning me into a parlor where two children stood at attention.

"Henry." A fifteen-year-old boy nodded, a freckled, gawky lad in knickers he'd outgrown, all stringy arms and close-cropped hair, a disarming smile, sweet. "Martha." A young girl, ten or eleven, dressed in a checkered gingham dress, an enormous bow atop her cascading ringlets, quietly turned away, shy. They both bowed, and I noticed that the boy sneaked a glance at his sister, the slightest trace of an impish smile on his face. I said hello, and we stood there, statues, the children helpless in this mandated audience. Children were difficult because they had their own language and customs, unfathomable. A kinship of sticky fingers and warm-milk breath. Of secret codes and schoolyard loyalties. Finally, Herman dismissed them, and, gleeful, they scooted up the stairwell, the boy fairly whooping at the top of the landing, as if to say he'd narrowly escaped the wicked spinster.

We sat at an oak dining table, Herman, Naomi, and the tremulous dinner guest in a room with glass cabinets of porcelain knickknacks and gaudy bric-a-brac and silver-plated bowls, served a dinner of apple chestnut salad, followed by a prairie chicken glazed with honey and mint, currant jelly, with pureed carrots and creamed onions the color of stagnant water. All passable, even the salad, but dismissible. The servant girl, a slip of a thing in a uniform, spoke in a thick Russian accent, but successfully ignored Naomi's clipped, abrupt orders.

"You have delightful children," I lied, which they expected.

Neither said thank you because both didn't believe what I was saying.

We talked of Chicago childhoods, of bitter winters with brutal wind off Lake Michigan (recalled fondly), of the recent heat wave (record-setting and unbearable), of their love of music (a Mel-O-Dee player piano occupied a wall in the parlor—if I wanted, they could play me Paul Whiteman, a favorite), until Herman, clearing his throat and watching the servant girl disappear with an empty platter, whispered to me, "Neither of my children knows *anything* about what my mother did."

A horrendous line, hurled into the quiet small talk. I stammered, "I won't say a word."

"We've *lied* to them," Herman frowned. "It's best. We are always afraid Jacob will slip up. He's not good with…lying."

I thought of an old Yiddish line. *A ligmer darf*

hoben a guten zikoren. A liar needs to have a good memory.

"Someday they'll hear of it."

Herman rushed his words. "Not if I have anything to say about it."

"But people talk…"

"You talk, Edna. *You!*"

"I…" I stopped talking.

The servant girl reappeared. Silence.

Naomi had said perhaps ten words to me, none memorable. A cold woman in that hot room, a woman who never laughed. A white rose pinned to her white dress, a blue ribbon cinched at the narrow waist. Decorous, to a fault. She kept eyeing Herman, who did the evening's rehearsed narration, following his cues, supplying nods and at times a quiet "Yes" or "No," as needed.

The servant girl buzzed around us, deferential, seamlessly moving plates away, and our conversation was purposely circumspect in her earshot. I waited. Afterwards, the girl dismissed, the three of us sat in the parlor with coffee and a poppy-seed apple roll, and I waited. Herman offered me a cigarette, which I took. That seemed to surprise and annoy him. He seemed unhappy striking a match to light my Lucky Strike.

Obviously, not so lucky a strike.

"Ah, you're a modern woman, Edna," he said. "The New Woman I read about in *Everybody's*."

"What can I say?" I ran my tongue over my upper lip. "Give a girl a reporter's pad and the dusty streets of Milwaukee, and hell and damnation come knocking on my door."

"What?" From Naomi, puzzled.

Herman waved his hand. "I've been talking to Jacob about your visits to my mother. You've been—become—prominent in our family, Edna."

"I like your mother."

"And Jacob?"

"Jacob is sweet…"

His hand flew up into my face. "Jacob is a ne'er-do-well, Edna. Let's be frank. A man who plays at his life. He's a Loop hound, nights traveling the El. He and that Ad at Dreamland, dancing with the Italian girls. He thinks every day is a…farce."

"You're very different people, you two brothers."

"Most definitely." Herman snubbed out his cigarette in an ashtray. He was tempted to reach for another, actually tapping the pack in his breast pocket, but decided against it.

Naomi spoke up. "My husband is the only success story in that family. He's held his family *together*."

I was tempted to remark on the very obvious unraveling of the Brenners but bit my tongue.

Something was being told to me here, and I wanted to hear it.

"I'm glad you support your mother," I said into the silence.

That surprised him. "I've never stopped talking to her. I visited her at that…place, though the first years were hard. She stared at the walls and muttered back at me. Nonsensical syllables. Gibberish. But I would talk to her…telling her about Jacob and Ella and Emma. I didn't know what else to talk about." He squinted. "Then, one day, they told me she was talking."

Naomi faced me. "Herman came back a changed man."

Herman sighed, settling back into his seat, comfortable as a satisfied cat. Had he come to believe that he'd wrought that transformation in Leah with his chitchat? Yet I had to admire his loyalty to his mother—all those visits. That did say something positive about the man.

Herman watched me closely. "Her voice came back." A smile that was hard to read. "But there was too much silence. She often refused to see me."

Naomi made a *tsk*ing sound.

"What could I do? I still had to visit, no? She's my mother." A sigh. "No matter what."

I stared at him, perplexed. Had my initial dismissal of him as a self-important fool been premature? Usually my first impressions were on target, especially with smug and cocky men, certainly with moneybags rich men who took themselves too seriously. Yet Herman may have had a soul beneath that suit he conceived, manufactured, and sold to himself. Or not. He was a hard man to read.

"She startled me when she asked about Ella and Emma."

"Why?"

"Because I expected her to ask about Jacob, always her favorite. The boy who had to be taken care of, coddled. The darling boy, the little prince who wrote poems for her birthday and stuck them on her mirror." He smirked. "I was the doorstop that held the door open. It was, 'Tell me about Emma and Ella.' Very strange. Ella and Emma, bookcases without books in them."

An odd image, needlessly derogatory, but I left it alone.

Naomi spoke quietly to her husband. "Before I forget, Herman—while you were gone, Ella telephoned me. I meant to tell you. She said Emma insists on taking a job at Hull House on Halsted with that Jane Addams woman. Some sort of settlement work with poor Russian girls. Ella said you needed to do something about it—she wants you to stop it. She isn't happy. Emma hadn't told her she'd gone there."

Herman harrumphed. "Good for her. Ella should do the same." A sickly smile. "This doesn't sound like Emma, though. I never thought Emma'd have the courage to disobey Ella." Then a pronouncement: "Unmarried women find value in settlement work."

I drew in my cheeks and arched my neck. "We old maids are good for something."

There was no apology in his response. "I meant no…offense."

"That's not how it sounded, Herman."

He eyed me. "You don't know how to read a man like me, Edna."

"I'll leave that chore to your wife."

Naomi, who'd been following the exchange with her head swinging back and forth, made a clucking sound, very barnyard, and Herman frowned her into silence.

He withdrew a cigarette, tapped it on the arm of the chair, and lit it. A puff of smoke, followed by a clearing of his throat. He punched the air. "Jacob tells me you don't believe Mama killed our father." Flat, out there, blunt. He waited, his eyes narrowed, his head lost in wispy smoke.

"No, I don't."

"Based on what, my dear?"

"Instinct, for one." He scoffed at that, and sucked on the cigarette. "And," I added, "the fact that there was no knife found—and so little blood on her. A neck stabbing, a vein punctured, blood all over his shirt, and just a smattering on her fingertips? Really. Given her mental state when discovered, it seems to me she'd not have had the presence of mind to tidy up, hide bloodied clothing, scrub the knife…"

"Folderol!" he blurted out, and I jumped. Naomi bit a fingernail. "You are, indeed, the writer of fiction, Edna."

"I am that. But I was first a reporter."

"And you feel the need to solve a crime already solved?"

I hadn't thought of it that way, but—"As a matter of fact, yes."

"I believe Mama has told you she's content now—made her peace with it all—wants only to live a quiet life."

"In which, I gather, she cannot see her grandchildren."

"So…"

"And she lives with the knowledge that her own children believe her guilty."

"The police…"

"Did a shoddy, perfunctory investigation. No investigation, really. I'm tired of hearing what the police *told* you and the others. A cop observed a paralyzed, frightened woman, he notes blood on her hands—she probably reached out to her husband, disbelieving what she saw, a loving wife's panic—and he thought it was a simple case of husband-wife murder. After all, they'd had that nasty row in the morning."

"Still and all, Edna." He shot a look at his wife. "Please. Your voice." He pointed at the ceiling. "The children."

Frankly, had I been his fifteen-year-old son, I'd have spent the evening tying sheets together to lower myself out the upper-story window. A freight train to California, my belongings tied in a bundle on a stick.

I spoke with quiet fury. "No, listen to me. Let me be frank here. Your mother was—is—a beautiful woman. Men usually forgive such women *anything*. But those same men also happily and romantically condemn beautiful women when they kill in a fit of—passion or a heated fight or some frenzy. They know too many melodramas. They saw your mother as a woman who asked for trouble because, as neighbors happily told the police, your mother flirted, though innocently—and liked the attention she got. A lonely woman, hungry. She was found guilty not of murder but of being a loose woman—a violation of motherhood. Or womanhood. The obedient Jewish mother. Think about it. Men wink at such women but are ready to throw the first stones."

Herman was fuming, restless in his seat. "That's a lovely speech, Edna. Such talk comes of giving women the right to vote. Three years ago. Preposterous. This country sliding to perdition."

I laughed out loud. "I'll never win any arguments with you, Herman."

"I didn't think we were arguing. I've listened to you give me a long-winded essay on human misunderstanding."

"Edna, Herman, please." From Naomi, wide-eyed.

"So you believe your mother is a murderer. All those years you visited her when she was away."

"In my soul I believe she's guilty."

"And you still visit her, this woman who murdered your father. Jacob believes it, too, and he lives there."

"She's my mother."

"So like others—you both threw stones."

He shuddered. "A little extreme, no?"

"No other suspects?" I waited.

He exchanged looks with his wife. "Of course, back then—we *hoped* the police would find someone else—you know—but who? Some thought—Morrie? Jacob? Sarah? Aunt Sarah resented everything and everybody. Still does. The twins? For heaven's sake, Edna. They're afraid of their own shadows. The police even questioned me."

"Why?"

"I stopped by that morning to see Papa. I knew he was home sick. I drove there." He shook his head vigorously. "A brief visit, running in and out. People saw me talking to him on the front porch as I left. We'd raised our voices. Ridiculous." He drummed his fingers on the table. "I did *not* kill my father."

"No, you believe your mother did."

"I can't help what I believe."

He peeked at the clock on the mantel, and I suspected my visit was ending.

Naomi had become agitated when her husband mentioned his being questioned by the police. For the first time the cold, expressionless face cracked, and she hissed, "*Ezra.*"

"For God's sake, Naomi," he yelled.

"I'm sorry. We *did* talk about it then, you know."

"Ezra?" I asked. "Your father's brother. The lawyer…"

"Who'd moved back to Chicago from Philly around then."

"Naomi, tell me why you mention him."

She spoke through clenched teeth, a flat speech that sounded rehearsed. "He hated the butcher.

He'd thought he was going to marry Leah, but she chose Ivan, the nebbish butcher with the bloody apron and the loud snoring, the dull man who fell asleep at the supper table. Not Ezra, the dapper lawyer with the Stutz Bearcat and the Chesterfield coat and the French cigarettes. A greedy, sneaky man, moving back after his wife died, stopping in all the time, grinning and teasing Leah."

Herman was fussing with the cuff of his shirt. "Now, Naomi, I know you like to believe…" He didn't finish.

She went on, louder now. "And he always hated you, Herman. And you hated him. He mocked all the children. Jacob, the wastrel. Ella and Emma, the wallpaper in the nursery, he called them. Now he befriends poor Jacob. Ever since Leah is back home, he's a…*presence* again. Edna," she held my eye, "Jacob and Ezra spend a lot of time together. Jacob relies on him, the shifty, treacherous…fop."

Herman added, "Jacob is so lost he can't tell a good sort from a bad one."

"And you're a good sort?" I asked.

"Yes, I am." He stood now, pointed to his watch. "It's getting late."

I remained seated a moment longer. "Why do you bother, Herman?"

"Let me tell you, Edna. All sorts of shenanigans were happening then—because of Ezra. Even because of Morrie, who wanted to end the partnership. Morrie had that cheap moment with my mother. I didn't trust anyone. I still don't trust Ezra. That house is in my name, as well as my mother's. *I'm* in control. Before Papa died, we talked about it. He was afraid if anything happened—well, Jacob and the twins would be clay in Ezra's hands. Even Sarah, flattered by Ezra into imbecility, though she once spat in his face. So we agreed that I would take over. My name on the deed. I'm a businessman. After his death, I sold the family share of the butcher shop to Morrie—for a pittance, true. To get *rid* of it—and him. I pay all the bills now while Jacob and Sarah rock on the porch and drink lemonade. Through Ezra, Jacob started going to the gambling houses on Clark Street. To drink at Magnum's, off the Loop. Can you imagine what would have happened if *he* had a share in anything?"

I turned to Naomi. "And you believe Ezra killed his brother?"

She wore a blank look. "Back then—maybe. I don't know now. No—I don't know."

"Why back then?"

She waved at her husband, helpless. "He still loved his brother's wife. He refused to accept her decision. Read the Bible. The blueprint is there, I believe. Coveting—and all that."

Herman headed to the door, still talking. "My father knew I'd protect the family. And I will."

He opened the front door and stood too close to me. His breath on my neck: a hit of cinnamon from the apple cake. A hint of garlic, noxious, hot and dry. "Remember that, my dear. I will fight for my family. Even against you, Edna Ferber."

Chapter Nine

Ezra Brenner. The name stayed with me. In the past two days his name had popped into the conversations, first with Jacob and Leah, and then with Herman. The uncle who was the first suitor of the lovely Leah.

One afternoon, staring out the kitchen window, I'd spotted a sleek ebony Ford roadster convertible idling in front of the Brenner home, a man sitting at the wheel, arm half-slung out of the window, a cigarette ash flicked to the sidewalk. Called by my mother into the parlor, I'd not waited to see who was visiting the home. But on Tuesday morning, after my unsettling supper with Herman and Naomi, I sat on the front porch with coffee and a newspaper, instead of staying with my mother and Esther in the kitchen debating the merits of the smoked goose breast Molly had bought at Lyon's Delicatessen on Jefferson during her morning walk. So maddening their trivial preoccupation—"You figure the smoked chub is good, so why not? You'd think so, yes?"—that I escaped the hot room to the hot porch, though I sheltered myself in the shade of the overhanging roof.

Again, that sleek, expensive motorcar, a compact two-seater runabout, with a purposely noisy exhaust system and, occasionally, the driver's rude leaning on a horn that seemed a circus chime. *Wooza wooza wooza.* A boy with a new toy.

Finally, after the flourish of one more annoying horn blast, the driver stepped out and peered up at the house. The door opened and a disheveled Jacob, buttoning a cuff as he ran, yelled, "Hold on, Uncle Ezra."

I paid attention.

Uncle Ezra reminded me of one of those Broadway johnnies I spotted at stage doors in Manhattan: tall, rail thin, long angular face, bronzed, dressed in a white summer cotton suit with oversized gold buttons, a silver-blue silk cravat, a diamond tie pin that caught the morning sunlight, and a flash of lilac handkerchief in a breast pocket. On his feet black-and-white country-club shoes, his long legs encased in expensive on-the-town spats. A dapper Dan dropped incongruously onto proletarian Monroe Street, the smooth operator who took the wrong turn in town.

Ezra shook his head at the errant Jacob, who

rushed by him and jumped into the passenger seat. Uncle Ezra, unhappy, didn't move—he simply stood there, finished the cigarette he was smoking and then ground the stub out under his feet. A trace of a smile as he whistled loudly, a dissonant shrill sound that carried up to me on the porch. Within seconds, he slid into the automobile and sped quickly from the curb, the tires spitting up pebbles and dust. In the open convertible Ezra threw back his head, laughing. But Jacob, I noted, hugged the door, sinking into the seat. He appeared to me—although some distance away—unhappy to be there.

So this was the older brother who escaped smoke-blackened Chicago, went to Columbia University in New York, became a lawyer in Philadelphia, married, buried a wife, and came back a few months before his brother died. A man who never relinquished his love for Leah.

I stood at the balustrade facing the Brenner household, as Esther and Ad walked out from behind me.

"Edna, what are you doing?" Esther asked.

I flicked my head to the street. "Uncle Ezra."

Ad bristled. "Did Jacob go off with him?"

I nodded. "In a jazzy roadster.

Ad grumbled, "Not good."

"Why not?"

"I don't like him. Never did. Never will." He caught his mother's eye. "He had no business coming back years ago and—and stopping in there, bothering Jacob and his mother. Especially his mother. He comes back, Ivan dies, and Ezra sits on the front porch. And now, suddenly, he's around even more these days."

"Because Leah is back home?"

He didn't answer, but his mother did. "He sort of disappeared again after they sent Leah away. But three years ago she's home and…"

"He's back," Ad finished.

"It's unseemly. It's—it's like he thinks he can start all over, like before Ivan, before the murder. Back to school days when they were all young." Esther's voice was hollow.

That surprised me. "So he's bothering Leah? How does she deal with him?"

Ad spoke up. "She ignores him, so Jacob tells me. She won't be alone in the same room with him. He stops in, she leaves—hides away. So it's— 'C'mon, Jacob. You and me, let's go get a sandwich and coffee at the one-arm lunch room on Clinton.' Jacob nods. He always agrees because he doesn't know how to say no. Ezra is real…slimy."

"A snake," I said.

Ad grinned. "In the grass, Edna. In the grass."

Esther said she and Ad were going to lunch,

though my mother and Molly were staying home. "Come with us," Esther pleaded. "A walk. You haven't been around much the last couple of days."

So the three of us walked down the block toward Maxwell in a comfortable silence. The heat of the day was rising, and Ad said, almost mournfully, "The paper says this'll be Chicago's hottest summer. Brutal."

Esther smiled at him. "You sound like your Papa, Adolph. That's his favorite topic—the heat. Every day he begins with the weather."

"I spend each summer in Chicago," I told them. "New York in the winter—for Broadway, my publisher, walks in Central Park. But I need Chicago in the summer—Jackson Park, Hyde Park near the water, picnics in the woods south of the city. The Point. Lake Michigan. The Marshall Field's on State Street. The…"

"The heat from a blast furnace," Ad finished for me. "The red glow from the steel mills. The stink of slaughtered pigs." Ad wrapped his arm around his mother's shoulder. "It'll kill us, Mama."

"What will kill me is your father telling me the same story every day."

I changed the subject. "Ad, Jacob didn't look too happy getting into Ezra's automobile. He pushed himself against the door, huddled there like a reprimanded child."

He shook his head vigorously. "Yes and no, I suppose. He does like his Uncle Ezra, who dotes on him, flatters, spends time and money. Stuffs dollar bills into his pocket. Ezra is nearly seventy now, the fashionable gentleman with the fancy clothes. Jacob probably looks at his uncle and understands how *he'll* look as an old man. The same good looks. Not like his father Ivan—Herman is that—but like a romantic lead in a burlesque review."

"Really, Adolph," his mother chided. "You're exaggerating."

"No, I'm not," Ad protested. "Jacob is my best friend, but he's—he's a weak man. You can lead him anywhere. And Ezra does. A foolish man. I mean— Jacob. All Ezra talks about is Jacob's mother. 'Leah this, Leah that.' Jacob gets…uncomfortable. That's what he tells me over and over. Ezra calls and Jacob rushes out. Driving around the city—Jackson Park to the Midway, to Washington Park, to Garfield. Driving, driving, driving. Quail dinners with apple pie at the Palmer House. Tickets to the White Sox games at Comiskey Park. Every day is a holiday. It's intoxicating. He won't listen to me."

"You don't go with them?"

A pause. "I ain't invited."

"Thank the Lord," Esther said.

"But," Ad went on, sneaking a glance at me, "to answer your question, no, Jacob being miserable's got nothing to do with Uncle Ezra." He lowered his voice. "And I think you know why?"

"Why?" From Esther, doe-eyed.

"The comments I made?" I asked.

Ad's head bobbed up and down. "Jacob doesn't like it when things get confused for him. He doesn't like it when he has to…" Ad stopped short. "You rattled him, Edna." A quick glance at his mother, but he spoke to me. "You made him *doubt* the police."

I took a step ahead. "Good."

"Hey, I don't know if it's a good thing." He rushed to catch up with me.

"Of course, it's good."

At the corner at Maxwell, I noticed the front door of Nathan's Meat Market was propped open. Standing inside the doorway, facing out, was the old man I'd spotted there before, bent over, intent on adjusting an armload of wrinkled old clothing. A pair of tiny eyeglasses rested on the bridge of his nose. A black yarmulke on his head.

Ad saw me staring. "Levi Pinsky."

"And just who is he?"

"A junk man. A ragpicker. An old friend of Morrie. Maybe ninety years old now, maybe more, Orthodox you know, from a shtetl in Poland, and he'll tell you all about it. Once a *shochet*, a ritual meat-slaughterer. That's how he got to know Morrie way back when. A hanger-on from the old days, he lives in the Hebrew Home for the Aged off of Maxwell. Morrie lets him sort out the used clothing he scrounges up on the unused tables now, store his stuff, wander in and out at will, nap in back, then on Sunday he hauls it out to Maxwell. Pennies and nickels and dimes."

Ad waved to the old man who squinted, pushed back his eyeglasses. "Yes?"

"It's me, Adolph Newmann."

"I thought so," Levi said in a creaky voice. He stepped back into the room and dropped a pile of clothing onto the counter that once held butchered and trussed chickens.

Ad and Esther continued walking, but deliberately I turned into the doorway.

"Edna?" Esther called.

"I'd like to see the inside of the old butcher shop."

Esther frowned. "Why?"

Ad tugged at my elbow, but I resisted.

Levi backed up and leaned again the counter.

"I'm Edna Ferber. I'm visiting the Newmanns. I'm…"

He turned his back on me, pushing his arms into a pile of clothing, but then faced me.

A small wizened man, stooped, his nearly bald head covered with a yarmulke, *tzitzit* from his waist. Dull black pants, a tear at the back of one knee.

A scraggly white beard, spotty. Splotchy, old-man skin, pale with dull red patches, bony arthritic fingers, and broken yellowed fingernails.

"So?" A word said without interest.

I surveyed the abandoned butcher shop, heavy trails of sawdust covering the floor. The rancid scent of dried blood and old wood, the whiff of decay and sweat, although the heaps of used clothing accounted for much of that. Used shoes stacked in a corner, laces hanging out like tangled eyes from old potatoes. Abandoned, this store—mouse droppings on the counters, the stink of old pulp newspapers piled in an uneven stack, yellowed now and sickly sweet with flakiness.

Old Levi watched Ad and scratched his head. "I remember you, lad. You're Adolph. The rabbinical student."

Ad grinned. "One of my many failures. Yes."

The old man narrowed his eyes. "No, one of *my* many failures." He shook his head back and forth, a look of disgust on his face. "The old days. Before Morrie lost interest. You and Ivan's boys. Herman and—Jacob." A deep sigh. "That Jacob."

"What about him?" I asked.

"Those were bad days here, you know." He arched his back, stretched out his withered limbs. "We sit in the back room"—he pointed behind him—"and I'd smoke my cigar while the fools carried on."

"The fools?"

"They were *all* fools." He leaned into Ad. "You remember, Adolph. You were a fool, but a boy. So maybe you I can forgive. You and silly Jacob and even Herman with his nose up in the air, sitting with the old fools who waited till Ivan left the room and then smirked and giggled about that beautiful woman. A mother, she was. Godless, them all."

Ad spoke up, "That was a long time ago, Levi. A lot of nonsense. Yeah, it was wrong, all that."

Levi spat out of the side of his mouth. "Respect for the womens, yes?" He wagged a bony finger. "I cursed at that Jacob—'This is the way you let the mens talk of your mama? Shame, boy, shame on you. You, Adolph, you was being a rabbi, yes?—you alone shut up, turned away. I seen your red face."

Ad was flustered, unhappy with the horrible conversation. "I told Jacob to say something. I didn't *like* that—it was about his mama."

"Yet you smiled. You was nervous."

"What could I do?" Helpless, his hand waving in the air.

He yelled out in a shaky voice. "You curse them. What I did. That's what you do. I yelled at Morrie, the others. This is a married womans, the wife of your partner."

Ad, helpless, glanced at his mother. "Ivan seemed to find it…funny."

Levi exploded. "You simple boy. A man hears his wife talked of that way, and he likes it? A boy, you are. Listen to me. Such a rabbi you would have been, a fool."

A shrug. "That was a long time ago."

Levi narrowed his eyes. "It was yesterday, Adolph. Yesterday because the wife walks in and you can see she likes the way the mens looking. Eve in garden, temptress. And what happened? The worm in the soul. The spider in the web. A man dies. A knife. A good man." Angry, spitting out of the side of his mouth.

Ad was fidgeting, anxious to flee, stepping from one foot to the other. "Yeah, I told Jacob to ignore the talk."

A cackle, ragged and phlegmatic. "What? You the knight in shining armor? I sat with you, helping with the studies, read the holy words, talking, talking to you. How to behave." He touched his temple. "But behave is not *idea*—but action."

Esther spoke up. "Levi, what could Adolph do? A young man, involved with his Talmudic studies then, loyal to a friend."

"Jacob has a dark spot on his soul," Levi said. "He smirked with the rest."

Ad had moved to the front of the store.

Sarcastically, he muttered, "A pleasure seeing you, Levi. You haven't changed. You're still the angel of no mercy."

Levi's eyes became slits. "I am the voice crying in the wilderness, and you and Jacob were little girls picking daisies in the field. Bah on you, boy."

At that moment footsteps sounded on the stairwell in a back corner and a small, squirrelly man, hurrying down, stopped in his tracks. He sucked in his breath, a nasally whistle, and turned, ready to flee back upstairs.

"Morrie," Adolph yelled. "You here today?" He smiled. *"Vi geyt bay dir?"* How's by you?

"I heard noise. Levi, yelling."

Levi frowned. "No yell. I'm talking. You remember Adolph the almost rabbi, his mama, and…"

No matter the introduction here because Morrie disappeared up the stairs and out of sight.

Esther turned to me. "Ivan's partner, Edna. He keeps the upstairs apartment, which his wife won't come to. I guess he likes the old neighborhood…"

"But not the people in it," Ad added. "A couple nights a week he's upstairs heating soup by himself."

"Yet he lets the store stay empty—unrented?"

Ad shrugged. "He hasn't been happy since that horrible day."

So that was Morrie Wolfsy, the man who'd had

that pathetic indiscretion with Leah, immediately regretted, who saw himself as a catalyst of the awful death. Or maybe not. Yet a man frightened out of living the life he had built for himself, stumbling, hiding out, yet still on the street. He interested me, this Morrie Wolfsy—what part did he have in that calamitous afternoon?

On the sidewalk Esther tucked her hand into Ad's elbow, protectively. "I never liked that Levi, Adolph."

He glanced back over his shoulder. "Nobody likes that man." Then he added, "He made Jacob nervous. The talk about his mother, wagging his finger at him."

We met Minna Pittman for a bowl of soup at Katz Dairy Restaurant off Halsted, Ad's intended grabbing a lunch break from her job. A grade-school teacher during the fall and winter, she worked a summer job as a seamstress. She had an hour break for lunch and was waiting when we arrived.

Ad was out of sorts, rattled by Levi's accusations. So scattered were his monosyllabic responses that Minna, a twitchy woman to begin with, became all jerky angles and jutting head. She kept asking, "You all right, Ad?" Over and over, a tinny question said too often, and never answered by Ad.

A curious couple, these two, with their epoch engagement, Minna's abiding trust that she'd be

Mrs. Adolph Newmann someday. Esther had told me she'd bought her white lace gown after the engagement announcement a decade back, taking it in periodically as she lost weight. But Ad was in no hurry to commit to anything. He liked his unstructured, desultory life, the jack-of-all-trades, master of none.

They struck me as a couple who'd been married for decades, comfortably so, happily so, an old man and an old woman who knew the little things about the other: no strawberry jam on the rye toast, never bring roses or carnations, don't mention the crying jag five years ago in that restaurant on Des Plaines. That sort of picayune trivia—the stuff of a long but durable marriage. What was lacking was romance. No touching of hands, no fluttering eyes—no talk of moonlit nights. No picnicking in the park. No whispers as they watched the salmon-pink sunset over Lake Michigan. They were dependable, stalwart, loyal, dedicated. They simply *were*.

I asked Ad about Levi's comments, though I could tell the topic rankled him. "Why *did* Jacob sit by when the men said those things about his mother?"

Ad squirmed. "You know how it is, Edna. Or maybe you don't. It was easier to smile than to say something. Thinking back on it now, it seems like speaking out would have been easy to do. But we were young men sitting with older men. We wanted to be a part of things. That back room was the place to be. Our—hideout. Everybody talking at once—politics, baseball." He smirked. "Even religion, when old Levi had the floor and deemed us all sinners. These older men let us stay—that meant something then. Me and Jacob. Not Herman so much. Three or four times and he stayed away."

"Levi says you were quiet."

He cast a sidelong glance at Minna. "I was the holy of holies then. A make-believe rabbinical student kneeling before a wisdom-spouting Levi Pinsky. I was a moral prig, I admit. I didn't like the teasing. I *liked* Jacob's mama. She made me welcome at her home. Ivan didn't. At suppertime I had to leave their house. His rule—only family sitting at the table—and silence."

"He had his rules," Esther said. "The children could not talk during the meal. Imagine that."

Ad nodded at Minna. "Yeah, I thought his mama was beautiful. Everyone did. She was like… like Lillian Russell on the vaudeville stage. I was giddy when she smiled at me. One time I even said so to Jacob in earshot of his papa, Ivan the Terrible. 'Jacob, your mama looks like Lillian Gish,' I said. Or some star like that. I can't remember now. But Ivan told me I was an ass. And I was. But Jacob said nothing—it tickled him in some way to have a beautiful mother. Well, *he* was beautiful—like her. Mirror images. He liked that. When you talked about her, you were also saying something about *him*. But I was the one they all made fun of—too serious that year, too much the one who didn't fit in. The prude. I was Levi's special project, the old religious Jew mentoring me, giving me direction, choosing me. Jacob was the only one who liked me."

"Why?"

"Because I was the one who told him what he wanted to hear."

"You never discussed the nasty stuff about his mother? The two of you when you were alone? You must have."

"Yeah." He sighed. "But after a while I never mentioned it. I could tell Jacob got uncomfortable. It wasn't my business."

"But then Ivan was murdered."

Ad shivered. "Then everyone got serious—not only me. Everyone blamed everyone else."

Minna sipped her soup. "All we do lately is talk of Leah Brenner and the murder." She pouted.

I narrowed my eyes. "It seems to me that the event still colors Monroe Street."

She grunted and stirred her soup with a spoon. "I know. It's such a...sad street."

The line seemed a mournful benediction, so we rose, Ad heading off for his afternoon job of stocking shelves at the hardware store, Minna returning to alter the hem of a dress. Esther and I walked to the markets.

Esther whispered, "I felt Levi was attacking my Adolph for being *good*."

"He was."

"I never liked that man. Religion made him— horrible. He's sour."

"He's old and poor."

"Being old and poor shouldn't make you bitter."

"Sometimes you don't have a choice, Esther dear."

• • ● • •

Late afternoon, idling on the front porch with a book on Dutch immigration to Chicago, scribbling notes into a pad, I spotted Ezra's roadster speed-ing up the street, slamming to a stop in front of the Brenner home. Jacob jumped out but seemed reluctant to say goodbye to his uncle, standing on the sidewalk, his body leaning against the door.

I realized why: Aunt Sarah, arms folded, was perched on the top step, her body rigid, her steely eyes locked on Ezra, who'd switched off the igni-tion. Finally the man got out of the automobile. His intention, it struck me then, had been to visit Leah, who was nowhere in sight. But the sight of the indomitable Sarah, the hound of hell, stayed his movement. He stood sheepishly, ignored by Jacob, who didn't know what to do.

I tottered off the porch and called to Jacob. "Jacob, a minute?"

Alarmed, he was ready to flee, eyes darting in a continuous sweep from me to Ezra, even up to Sarah.

"Edna." A rasp, unhappy.

"So this is Edna Ferber." Ezra bowed, too grand a gesture, overly dramatic, mocking. "Jacob has done nothing but talk about you." Nothing friendly in his tone.

Shielding his eyes from the sun, Jacob hunched his shoulders, his head tilted away. A beaten child.

"Jacob, hello." I smiled at him.

With that, he fled into the house, bumbling up the steps, brushing past Sarah who never turned to watch him. No, she kept that unforgiving look at Uncle Ezra. Her dislike of her sister's brother-in-law was obvious. A dangerous man, her look conveyed. And probably rightly so.

"Uncle Ezra," I said to him.

"Charmed." Again the Prussian bowing from the hip.

The sun glinted off the diamond in his stick-pin, making it seem a blinding sunburst.

"Jacob seems troubled."

His eyes searched the porch. Sarah had disappeared into the house and Jacob was nowhere in sight.

"We should talk, Edna Ferber." Ezra's voice dipped an octave, some of his words muffled. His voice had a natural high ring to it, fake laughter undercutting the spaced-out words. A glib man, practiced and imperfect, much as I remembered the gigolos from my post-war sojourn in Paris, those men *voulez-vou*-ing me in the night cafés.

"About Jacob?"

"About a lot of things."

He opened the passenger door and I slipped in. As we pulled away from the curb, I shifted in my seat and spotted Sarah peering out the front window, half-hidden by a curtain. And then, glancing up, I saw Jacob in a second-story window, his face pressed against the panes. I'd become, as my mother had warned, the neighborhood scourge. An indiscreet one, as well.

At Clark's Confectionary I drank a small chocolate egg cream with Ezra downing cup after cup of black coffee, which he declared vile. Each sip elicited a grimace from him, as though he were ingesting foul medicine.

"Don't drink it," I told him.

He ignored that and took another sip. "Jacob

told me about your…nosiness about the death of my brother."

I smiled disingenuously. "I've come to like Leah. A melancholy woman, and—a wronged woman."

The soft features hardened. "So I hear. Do you really think your probing is prudent?"

I wiped a smear of chocolate from my lips. "When I was a reporter in Milwaukee, I covered the Schmattie murder trial there—a rich family, brewery people, scandalous, man's utter ugliness toward his fellow man. I learned that there is often a hefty price you pay for justice."

"And you're that instrument?"

A slight smile. "Possibly."

"Edna, the case was closed years ago. Fifteen years—a lifetime. Life has moved on. You are only stirring up old resentments, opening old wounds."

"Old news?" I tossed out Molly's glib summation.

His eyes got wide. "Exactly. Well said."

"Nonsense, Ezra. Nonsense. False accusations cannot remain…old."

"But Leah is home at last—and content."

"Content? Do you hear yourself?"

"Yes, I do." His voice dipped, harsh. "Would you have the street talk of this all over again? The busybodies of Monroe Street? The smirks, the pointing, the cruelty. Leave Leah to be…content."

"I don't think she's content."

"I know her better than you do." He stared into my eyes, unblinking.

"You're bothered about Jacob." My tone was blunt.

He sat back, breathed in. "Well, yes, I am. A gentle lad, breezy, carefree—at least he was. But now he's withdrawn, moody, quick to flare up. He *snaps* at me. That's your doing, Edna."

"He was convinced his mother was a murderer. Everyone told him that, the police…"

He interrupted me. "And now he isn't sure. You put doubt in him. You know what he said to me? 'Edna asked me where was the knife? Wouldn't it have been there? Wouldn't my mother be holding it in her hand?' He expects me to have an answer. I don't."

"Doubt, maybe some guilt."

He was seething now, though he tried to hide it. When he went to light a cigarette, he dropped the match. "How dare you, young lady? Tell me—guilt about what?"

"Hold on. I don't mean he's a murderer. I would never accuse him. I have no proof of that—"

"Yet?" he broke in, snidely. "Is that what you mean?"

"He's guilty of keeping his eyes closed. He allowed injustice to prevail."

"Are you aware of how his behavior has changed?"

"Yes. And the question is—why? Why so sudden this… moodiness? What does he know?"

He blew smoke across the table into my face. "He knows what the rest of us know—poor Leah, perhaps in a panic, killed my brother."

"And you believe that?"

A long pause. "Yes."

"And yet I understand your visits have increased to the house these past three years. You… squiring Jacob here and there. You knock on their door. You once loved Leah. You wanted to marry her—it was expected by the families. Before she chose your brother."

He actually grinned. "I'll never understand that misguided decision by Leah. Ivan the plodding, the overweight dullard."

"And you? The sleek expensive animal."

He laughed out loud, enjoying the description. "Good God, Edna, how you do go on. I'm not a beast. Yes, I love beautiful women. And Leah, to this day, still has about her that… exotic aura, that dark-skinned Rebecca out of a romantic novel."

I winced, recalling my own description of

Leah as that memorable heroine out of a Walter Scott novel. "Anyway…"

"She's almost sixty and…you've seen her. I thought we'd marry someday, but Ivan stole her from me. I never knew how."

"Perhaps Leah was hoping for something beside a glossy finish."

He pulled in his cheeks. "Ah, a cruel and easy barb, my dear. The slings and arrows of the outrageous Jewess. And unworthy of you. Ivan had a secret weapon, which I discovered too late."

"And what was that?"

"He didn't talk about himself."

"And you did?"

He chortled, choked on the cigarette smoke. "All the time. I was trying to impress."

"It never works that way."

A light laugh. "So I ran away. I refused to go to the wedding—to the horror of my devout family. I buried myself at school, then in a marriage I paid no attention to. A wife who died too young in childbirth, though it was a convenient way for her to leave an unhappy husband. I practiced law in Philadelphia, and then drifted back here—just in time for the horrors that happened in that house. Bad timing, wouldn't you say?"

"Yes, especially for Ivan."

"I didn't mean *that*."

"You weren't close to Ivan?"

"Well, we spoke. We argued. He thought I'd come back to steal Leah away."

"Had you?"

He bit his lip and leaned in. "You want to know something? She was foolishly, annoyingly in love with my brother. He'd become a harsh man, terrible to Jacob, even worse to Leah who fought him over Jacob, but she still was loyal to him. But Ivan didn't want me around, he said. I supposed I oogled his wife too much." He tapped the table with a fingertip. "To this day, a whole part of me refuses to believe she killed him. It seems impossible. You've met her. Impossible. But sometimes I think—why not? A nasty man with a cruel tongue. There were times I wanted to kill him." He waited a heartbeat. "But I didn't. Don't pursue me, Edna Ferber, with your pack of sniffing bloodhounds. There are times I blame her—too seductive, too *unconsciously* the siren, you know—though that added to my ardor. The *naturalness* of her attractiveness. Do you understand that? Yeah, she knew she drew me in, but she never understood how… how compelling was her power." Still the tapping on the table, rhythmic. "We were school sweethearts. Once you love Leah, you don't ever stop." A faraway look in his eyes. "Even now when she is an old lady."

"But she didn't kill Ivan."

"You keep saying that—without proof. You actually stunned poor Jacob, knocked him for a loop. Do you plan on spreading that venomous rumor far and wide?"

"Yes. Until someone tells me something."

"A dangerous pursuit, Edna Ferber."

"How so?"

He didn't answer.

He took a dollar from his wallet and placed it under a cup. "Even if Leah killed Ivan, I'd still marry her today." He winked. "This afternoon—if she'd have me."

I waited. "Is that your plan?"

"I don't have a plan." He went to put his wallet back into his vest pocket, but deliberated. He withdrew a small photograph mounted on hard cardboard, like a nineteenth-century *carte de visite*. He slid it across the table. I saw Ezra and Leah, youngsters, laughing into the camera. Perhaps they were seventeen or eighteen. Younger. He was dashing and handsome, dressed in some sports outfit—billowing pants tucked into black boots, a cotton jersey that said, quaintly, Maxwell Street Bengals, a cap on his head. Football? I had no idea. Leah stood there in a flowing wraparound sports skirt, a velvet bow in her hair, her dark hair resting on her shoulders. The ivory cast of her skin and those jet black brows. She was exotic, fire in her eyes, head tilted up, and, above all, a stunning face that held you, mesmerized. Circe and her awful powers. The whispering siren who wrecked ships that dared approach.

"A beautiful woman," I commented.

"She's still beautiful."

"You still love her?"

He sighed. "Yes, even though she now has a past."

"So do you," I said glibly. "But yours is harder to understand."

Chapter Ten

Sarah opened the front door but said nothing. She watched me closely, and for a second I thought she'd slam the door in my face. But she stepped back, frowned, and said in a low growling voice, "Leah is napping. I don't suppose you've come to visit me."

"I could."

She scoffed. "I saw that miscreant Ezra dropping you off. How could you get in that rattletrap machine with such a man?"

"You don't like Ezra?"

"He's not an easy man to like, Edna."

"True," I conceded, "but he's become a presence again in this house these past few years."

She clicked her tongue. "He's up to no good, of course. Whatever he's whispering in Jacob's ear is making him irritable and plain difficult. He's not a delight in the best of worlds with his breezy, bumbling manner. A fool staggering home from a speakeasy—such a nice Jewish boy. Add morbidity to that mix and these rooms are an undertaker's front room." She laughed at her own humor, though I didn't.

She motioned me into the room.

"I wanted to see Leah."

She drew in her cheeks. "My, my, my." She made a face.

What was there about her that intrigued me? Was it the calculated, blasé attitude she created? Her whole demeanor suggested indifference, a quick shrug of her shoulders and a cavalier rolling of her eyes. I could respect that in a woman—a curious defense against a world that routinely ignored her, this unmarried woman dependent on others for shelter and companionship. She did not strike me as a chronic whiner nor a gummidging soul. In a world she couldn't forgive, she'd found a way to survive.

"She's napping," she repeated.

"Then I'll…"

"Follow me."

She led me into a back sunroom filled with potted ivies lining a window ledge, yellow bamboo blinds shielding the room from the afternoon sun. A door led to a screened sleeping porch built to catch the wind from the prairies and breezes from the lake. Wicker chairs with sloppy red cushions and glass-topped wicker tables, magazines everywhere. *Good Housekeeping. Collier's. The Saturday*

Evening Post. Everybody's. Piled high, well-read, the corners dog-eared. A novel on a table, its pages spread open.

"This is my room, really," she commented. "I hide out here. I even sleep on this porch these last scorching nights. Jacob avoids it because I'm usually found here. He's afraid of me—my acid tongue. And Leah is afraid of sunshine. She got used to shadows and clouds."

"That's sad, no?" I sat down in an old chair, sank deep into the cushions.

"Not really. At least she knows where she can be…I was going to say 'be happy' but that's not a word I use with Leah."

"Are you happy she's back?"

She poured me iced tea from a pitcher.

She debated her response. "I don't care one way or the other. My life goes on, boring and uneventful. It's just that someone else is in my line of view these days. And we do talk, although I never can remember what we've talked about the minute she leaves the room."

"But you lived here so long without her. You and the twins and Jacob…"

"What can I say? Ella and Emma nodded at me, like they were surprised I was still alive. Jacob, as I say, hides."

"But why?"

"I'm not the mother he missed." She sipped tea. "Edna, you have to realize—I don't *care*."

I locked eyes with hers. "I don't know if I believe you."

A phony laugh. "Well, that's your problem. When Ivan was alive, I was the drone who swept the hallways. The charity case in the closet. The dressmaker's dummy, stuck with pins. Leah was his life. He barely paid attention to the twins, and only liked Emma because she was quiet, thought Ella was pushy, didn't trust Herman, and found Jacob intolerable and weak. The happy-go-lucky swell who staggered home drunk on Shabbas. No kaddish for Papa. So much for the next generation of Americans."

She laughed at her own words, searching for something cynical to hurl at me, but finally, shaking her head, sat back, summing up. "I am the calendar on the kitchen wall, always one month behind."

I compared Sarah with her sister, the differences startling. Yes, both similar, attractive women, though Leah had inherited looks that necessitated words like *stunning* and *ravishing*. Radiant. Dreadful words: the carnival language of besotted or smitten stockyard boys or fawning drummers. Both were dark complected, with deep-set eyes, oval faces with Roman noses over cupid's-bow mouths, a Mary Pickford-cum-Theda Bara marriage. Yet there the comparison stopped. Sarah had none of Leah's sensuality, so elusive it was hard to define—that wave of an arm, that lifting of a finger, that tilt of a head that suggested rarity that made Antony stumble blindly off Cleopatra's drifting barge. No, Sarah was brittle, angular, refusing soft edges, a woman hell-bent on scaring you away. With her hair skewed into a utilitarian knob secured with a long tortoise-shell hairpin, she struck me as the dreaded schoolmarm. The stepmother with the broom, the maiden with the midnight cackle.

"You're so different from Leah."

"Thank God. Men always trailed her like alley cats in heat. Me, they handed their school tablets so I could write their essays for them."

I laughed. "I don't believe you're so…blasé."

"Believe what you want." She drew in her cheeks. "Who is Sarah, who is she, that all the men deplore her?" Then, abruptly, she sobered. "You *are* determined to find the real murderer, assuming Leah didn't kill Ivan."

"Sarah—what?"

She watched me carefully. "Edna, you're hardly questioning and probing in a vacuum, my dear. We're not simpletons. You, a novelist, a journalist, your picture in the paper, here asking questions, displaying more chutzpah than a good Jewish girl is allowed to, trailing Jacob like he's the twenty-year-old handsome lad you followed a hundred years ago."

I started to protest, but didn't. Here I'd thought my schoolgirl crush a secret back then. "What have you heard?"

"Sitting on my porch, I heard your own mother sitting on the Newmann porch and loudly labeling you the town snoop. 'We always had a problem with her, back to Appleton days. How the townsfolk *talked*. She never changes.'" Sarah burst out laughing, but, again, a quick locking of eyes with mine. "You're a dangerous young woman."

I breathed in. "What?"

Rapid-fire words now. "Somebody already died, Edna. Long ago. In this house. And life went on. Now it's like it happened *yesterday*. That makes everything scary all over again. Don't you see?" She leaned forward in her chair, grasping her knees with her interlaced fingers. "You *have* to see the trouble you're stirring up."

"I don't think your sister killed Ivan."

She rolled her eyes, her voice assuming the world-weary laziness. "I know, I know. We all know your thinking."

"Do you think Leah did it?"

She counted a beat. "Do you think *I* did it?"

"I don't know."

"I could have, you know. Ivan was a hard man,

truly, but kind to me. We never said a cross word to each other. But I was in his way, the starved pullet sister-in-law, not aging as beautifully as his centerpiece wife, who reminded him that I would always be here, stuck like a piece of linoleum to the kitchen floor."

I held her eye. "A good reason to kill him, no?"

"If you say so." Sarah now was tired of the conversation, glancing over my shoulder, stifling a yawn. She'd had her fun with me, an afternoon's light entertainment over a glass of tepid iced tea. Now, spent, she'd rather I'd be gone.

"You could have moved out," I offered.

Unwittingly, she betrayed a flash of anger, her dark eyes blinking. "Do you remember that brief, glorious war we orchestrated for the world's amusement—the Spanish-American War, back in 1893? America stretching its raw-boned limbs like a spoiled child—Hey there, old tired Europe, look at me. I'm grown up. Anyway, there was a boy who loved me, drifting after me down the streets, handing me wilted roses. My father spotted him, and that was the end of *that*." A melancholic smile, genuine. "His name was Tim Mahoney. Timmy Mahoney. Freckled and red-haired and speaking with an accent that sounded alarmingly vaudevil-lian. But not a boy you'd invite to Friday night Seder, if you know what I mean. Thank God he got killed in the Philippines. It saved everyone a lot of trouble. Especially me."

"I'm so sorry."

She stood. "Well, I need to start supper. I need to choose the appropriate knife to chop the string beans…"

"Just a moment," I insisted. She sat back down. "Since we're talking candidly—I assume we are, right?—I'm curious. Tell me what you remember of *that* day."

"Oh, no. Please. I'm not going through that again."

"Only what you told the police."

She laughed too long. "They scarcely talked to me. A few words. I was the hysterical sister screaming out of control, the maddened woman by the fireplace woodpile. Other than—if I recall—one remark on the spot. The policeman said, 'You came downstairs to find your sister leaning over the body, right?' To which I nodded, sobbing into a handkerchief, 'Yes, sir, indeed, I did.' And that was it."

"Unforgivable."

"Edna dear, we barbaric Jews are known for our murderous rages."

I tilted my chin. "Well, my desire to slaughter a few folks is certainly there, and well known, I'm afraid, but I resist the temptation. Prison bars do not appeal to me."

She sat back into the cushions. "What happened that day…" She drummed her fingertips against her chin. "A Homeric epic. It was a quiet day, a typical day in the neighborhood. I'd had hot tea and a slice of poppy-seed roll for breakfast…"

"Don't be frivolous with me, please."

She was quiet for a long time, regarding me with narrowed eyes. Then, resolutely, "You are a grim young woman, Edna Ferber. Probably not very likable, although I sense we could become good friends, the two of us sheltered from the storm out there."

Impatient: "Tell me."

"My, my. Another woman destined for spinsterhood."

"Which, frankly, I welcome."

"We all say that."

"I don't say anything I don't mean."

She deliberated a moment. "You know, I actually *believe* that. Most of what I say I don't believe as it's escaping from my tongue."

"Then we could never be friends."

"Just as well." She interlaced her fingers and hid the lower part of her face. I noticed her nails were jagged, with a line of dried blood on one or two. Here was a woman who gnawed at her nails and I wondered why. "Let me see." Now she rubbed an eyeball.

"About fifteen years to the day, Edna. I'm not gonna fool you. No, I know exactly what happened. You have to remember such things clearly. The last day when there was peace in this household. Since then we live suspended in space here. We all held out breaths for years and years…until we disappeared. And since Leah's back home, there is even less air to breathe."

"Tell me."

Her voice got soft, yet matter-of-fact, a mechanical recitation. "In the morning Leah and I went to the market, as we always did. Ivan was home sick—upset stomach, chest pain, and a little bit of a fever. So unlike him, you know. He'd traipse to his shop through blustery winter snow and whooping cough. He didn't trust Morrie. All the men ogled Leah. All the boys, too. Herman and Jacob's school buddies wanting the mother in a room when they visited. Can you imagine? All schoolboys *run* from mothers. Anyway, Ivan lay on the sofa, grumpy and complaining. Here you have a big, growling man, a butcher notorious with a kosher cleaver, reduced to a little boy begging for soup."

"Did anyone visit him?"

That stopped her. "I heard Herman was here briefly early on. Ivan went onto the porch to say goodbye, or so the neighbors told the police. They were loud, but they always yelled at each other. I know Morrie called from the shop. I could hear him yelling on his end of the telephone. He'd had it with Ivan and didn't believe he was sick. That marriage of butchers was coming to an end."

"So Ivan knew that?"

"Ivan was not much fun to be around. In fact, the day before, after supper, he overheard Jacob and Ad on the porch, talking about the...scandal. I know Jacob was bothered by what folks said about his mama, even though he laughed about it, claimed it was funny. Part of the problem was that Ad, his best friend, was then a little too religious for everyday life. Under the sway of old Levi Pinsky, that hand of a malevolent God. Ad defended Leah, though he accused her. I suppose he didn't know what to say. It was...awkward, to say the least. He was intoxicated by her beauty, too. He always got giddy around Leah, which tickled her. All men and boys did. 'It's not *her* fault,' Ad told Jacob. 'Hey, it's not my papa's,' Jacob countered. Back and forth, really stupid. Jacob even shoved Ad. But Ivan, inside, heard the whole thing, and, flying onto the porch, slapped Jacob in the face. Ad skedaddled across the yards, but Jacob was crying, that grown man. You could hear him up and down the street, wailing. So Ivan hit him again."

"What did Leah do?"

She thought a bit. "I don't think she was at

home. Otherwise, she'd have rescued Jacob, her darling boy, the one who shared her beauty. She'd have fought Ivan who never understood Jacob. He really was Herman's advocate, and the porcelain-doll twin girls, Emma more than Ella, of course—but Jacob, the poet, the drifter—no, that boy was a mystery to him. So, no, Leah couldn't have been home."

"But Leah and Ivan fought the very next morning, no?"

"And brutally, I gotta tell you. They *never* fought like that. But Ivan was sick and irritated and fed up, and Leah was feeling guilty about brushing her lips against Morrie's, but Leah can only take so much yelling at her. That—and Jacob complaining that his papa had slapped him—twice. She gave it back, and royally so."

"You heard the whole thing?"

"Most. At first it was stupendous entertainment, I admit, like an over-the-top scene from the Yiddish Theater." For a moment Sarah turned away. She wrapped her arms around her chest and shuddered. Then with a deep sigh she looked into my face. "But it went on too long, you know, a fight that got…dangerous. I don't mean physical—I mean dangerous in a way where people say things they can't take back. Ivan had always been perversely flattered by the ogling of Leah, some badge of victory for the *schlemiel*. Frankly. But Morrie had crossed the line—and Leah foolishly let him. I think Morrie did it on purpose—a slap in Ivan's face. Maybe she was lonely. I don't know. I don't care. Ivan, the older he got, was not *there*."

"But the fight had ended."

She nodded. "It ended. I'd closed my bedroom door upstairs, tired of it, but at one point when I opened my door, I heard her rattling around in the kitchen. Quiet downstairs. Ivan still on the sofa, but breathing hard. Then nothing. I closed my door." She bit her lip. "I know at one point I walked by the window that faces the backyard, and Leah was there, picking tomatoes, putting them in a basket. She had a small garden and liked to putter there. I started reading, and thought the day would drift by as usual."

"Where was Jacob?"

She clicked her tongue. "I was waiting for you to ask that. He's been going crazy since you caught him on that…that contradiction. Edna, Jacob can't remember anything—least of all sequence. Even on *that* day. So now you've made him doubt his memory—and himself. Worse, you've taken a man hopelessly devoted to his mother and planted doubt here. But it's all cockeyed. He was told his mama killed his papa. End of story. Now he wonders. Confused. It's like he wanted to keep believing she killed his papa. Cockeyed, as I say." She pointed finger at me. "Shame on you."

"That wasn't my intention."

"Of course it was. You like to shake the bushes to see what form of life emerges. When you pick up a rock, Edna, I bet you smile at that white worm slithering there."

"I'm not a cruel woman, Sarah."

A heartbeat. "No, I suppose not. Just a pesky one."

"True."

Her eyes danced. "Anyway, the twins were in their lair, but Jacob—in my memory—was not home earlier. I heard him leaving *before* the argument. So he must have missed the battle. But he came back at one point."

"You saw him?"

She paused to organize her thoughts. "I *heard* him. I think I heard his bedroom door shut. I know he said he came downstairs afterwards. He also told you he walked by his papa on the sofa, but—I don't know."

"Leah was still in the backyard?"

"I don't know." She waited. "I heard voices at one point. She was talking to a neighbor over the fence. From the street in back of us. I had stopped paying attention. So I don't know when she came back into the house. I remember she'd told me she'd be running to Maxwell for some groceries. But I heard what I thought was mumbling from the parlor. Ivan, I thought, hacking away. Then a grunt—maybe a shout. Loud. That startled me. Then nothing."

"Then you went downstairs."

"Only later. For a drink. And saw Ivan on the sofa, slumped over, and Leah bending over him, her fingers tinged with blood, this blank look on her face. I started screaming and couldn't stop. I went on and on." A smirk on her face. "I'm not good with murder, Edna. I remember staring at the twins who came flying downstairs. But as I did so, I spotted Jacob. He was already standing in the back corner by the Victrola, leaning on it. I don't know how he got into the room."

"Had he been upstairs?"

"He says he was."

"Maybe he followed Ella and Emma down."

"Maybe."

"Your words indict him, Sarah."

"You asked me what I saw."

"True."

"Don't shoot the messenger." She drummed the table with her fingers. "Everything happened so fast, really. I still can see Leah's face—stark, empty, white."

"It sounds as if you don't believe your sister killed Ivan."

"I don't really know. She could have, I suppose. I could have. The man who delivers eggs on Tuesday. I don't know…"

"I don't understand Jacob's place in all this. I think…"

"Edna." A voice broke in. I jumped, nearly knocking over my glass. Turning, I saw Leah in the doorway. Dressed in a robe tied at the waist, her hair a jumble and her eyes heavy with sleep, she leaned against the doorjamb, her arms wrapped around her chest. She was facing Sarah, and I wondered suddenly if Sarah had seen her standing there, even as she continued talking to me.

"Edna was telling me what really happened the day you didn't kill Ivan." Sarah's voice was chilling.

I gasped, furious.

Leah's face was transfixed on me. Frightened now, those luminous eyes held me, demanding.

"I don't want my children hurt, Edna," she said in a raspy voice. "I told you that."

"Leah, I would never…"

Ferocity in her words, chilling and desperate. "Nothing else matters, Edna. I don't want my Jacob hurt. Do you hear me?"

Chapter Eleven

I worried about Jacob. From the kitchen window as I chatted with Esther or Molly, I'd spot him moping on the sidewalk, or walking in and out of his home as though he'd forgotten something, or, worse, sitting on the front steps with his head dipped into his lap. Once, hearing banging, I hurried to the kitchen window in time to see him slamming a tree limb against a porch railing, over and over, until he flung the branch across the yard. Helping my mother as she made her cherry cobbler one afternoon, I heard Ezra's hearty greeting, followed by Jacob's meek hello, and then the slamming of a car door. The blare of a horn as they sped away.

I worried. Had I fostered this emotional wreck? And Leah's words as I sat with Sarah—those heartfelt, if bitter, words stayed with me. A shattered family had finally assumed some semblance of quiet, and I blazed into their lives, the cocky reporter on a mission. Was I wrong? And yet—

And yet I believed the story hadn't been told. Or, rather, the story had been given the wrong ending, trumped up, convenient. Strings tied around a bloody package. That bothered me.

At breakfast Ad listened absently as I pummeled him with questions about Jacob's state of mind. He didn't want to talk about it, fumbling with the coffee pot, flipping over the pages of the newspaper he held, even eying the doorway into the hallway. Idly, he emptied the drip pan from underneath the icebox, carelessly splashing water on the hard-swept floor.

"Jacob looks so unhappy," I summed up. "I'm bothered, Ad. Aren't you?"

He grunted and turned away.

At that moment my mother was walking in, settling into a chair opposite me. "Is it any wonder?" Her good-morning greeting. "Edna, stay out of it. For Lord's sake. Must we be the guests who arrive with pestilence and doom?"

I ignored her. "Can you talk to him, Ad?"

He shrugged. "You know, Jacob keeps things to himself. Private."

"But Jacob will listen to you."

Esther and Molly walked in, Molly rubbing her lower back. *Tap tap tap.* The cane banged into a cupboard. She'd been muttering to Esther about her lumpy feather mattress but, hearing the end of my words with Ad, she straightened up. "Do you begin every morning at full gallop, Edna?" No kindness in her words, and my mother nodded furiously.

"It's conversation," I said emphatically. "I'm just talking. Ad and I."

Ad eyed his frowning grandmother and grinned. "Jacob's not gonna listen to me."

"I don't want to hurt him."

"A little late for that," my mother grumbled. Ad poured coffee for everyone. My mother slathered a roll with butter, licked her fingers, and watched me over the top of the cup. Her look said, brutally: *Stop this! Stop this insanity now!* I refused to look at her.

"*You* should talk to him, Edna," Ad said finally. "But he's afraid of you."

"Impossible." I was smiling. Then I added, "People *like* me." A pause. "Jacob likes me." Another pause, purposeful. "Everybody likes me."

Said, my words brightened the mood in the kitchen, a ripple of laughter growing.

My mother whooped, spilling her coffee, and Esther giggled. "Your daughter is a hellion, Julia."

"I've heard other words used, I'm afraid."

"I will talk to him," I said to Ad. "He has nothing to fear from me."

Everyone at the table chortled, except for Ad, who shook his head. When I caught his gaze, he saluted me with a wave of his hand. Esther had tears in her eyes but reached over and touched my wrist affectionately. She was still giggling.

Molly wasn't happy and wanted the last word. "Sooner or later everyone you meet will be afraid of you."

• • ● • •

Of course, Jacob didn't cower in fear when I met him on the sidewalk. In fact, he seemed eager to walk to Maxwell Street with me. The handsome face was drawn, true, but he gave me a wispy smile.

"Everyone says you're afraid of me."

That startled him. A long drawn out "Nooo," though there was question in his eyes. "I admit I've been a little…morose. Is that the word I want? You *rattled* me, Edna. Let me just say *that*. I still don't know what to think. I don't like to *think* about things, really, and you…" He went on babbling, a little incoherent. What was really going on? Finally, the sputtered nonsense stopped. "I'm afraid of what you *said*."

"About your mother being innocent?"

"Yes, of course." His lips trembled. "I hate to think of what they did to her." A heartbeat. "What *we* did to her. Me!"

"Because you love your mother."

"Yes."

As we walked, he became jittery. He darted ahead of me as though in a rush, only to stop, lag behind, shuffling from one foot to the other. Peck's Bad Boy, sent home from school.

For a moment he stopped and faced me. "I have to tell you—you got me thinking, Edna, and not good thoughts." His face tightened. "I can't sleep at night. But I'm not *mad* at you. This has to do with me. Maybe I *have* to do this. You opened wounds. In me."

A troubled face, a welter of confused emotions. How handsome, I thought—still, after all the years—but bags under his eyes, ragged lines at the corners of his mouth, wrinkles in his forehead. Puffiness around the jawline. The face of a late-night rouser, some café patron. The man who never slept.

His voice got lazy and confidential. "Your words reminded me of how much I hated my father."

"What are you telling me?"

"These past few days I keep asking myself—why? Why did it happen that way? To my mother. Why? But I mean—how was I a part of it?"

"Were you?"

He winced. "That's just it. I don't *know*. Did I do something? You know, that—that thing with Papa the day before when he overheard me and Ad talking nonsense. The way he slapped me in the face. I saw his face, all bloated and red and...and you know what I saw there? Disgust. He didn't like me. My own father. I always knew it, though he never said anything outright. The way he ignored me. The way he slapped Herman on the back, praised him—'What a mind for finance, my boy! You're a chip off the old block, son'—and I was the Romeo fool writing stupid limericks for the girls who followed me home. I was the one who resembled Mama." A wry smile. "That was my biggest sin. He thought there should be no one else like her."

"He didn't understand…"

He snapped. "I hated him."

"But why *hate* the man, Jacob?"

A perplexed look on his face. "I couldn't help it. I started hating him when he came home from the shop, a bloody apron in a bag for Mama to wash. Blood everywhere. Then the way he slobbered his food. His dirty fingernails. The way he got drowsy and slumped at the table late at night, a bottle of Manischewitz tipped over. The sweet sickly smell on the tablecloth. You know how little things start to drive you crazy? The way he held a glass of water. The way he kicked his shoes under the sofa. Stupid, stupid things like that. And then that day he slapped me. Twice. Me, a grown man. Ad running home like a scared little boy, shocked. His papa never touched him—ever. I used to envy the Newmann family because Sol was the father I could only dream of. Lucky Ad. And I felt a little dirty because the slap had to do with Mama and the way men talked about her. Ad and me talking about it. It made me feel unclean."

"And the next day he died."

"And the next day he was murdered."

"But not by your mother."

A helpless look, pleading. "But that's what they *told* me—us." A sob escaped his throat. "I was in a daze, crying, crying. Edna, I said nothing to defend my mother. I accepted…"

"But now your mother is back home."

"And I still don't know."

"Jacob, you have no idea what happened?"

He stopped walking, planting his body in front of me. His cheeks were streaked with tears. "You know why I can't tell you *exactly* where I was—what I did? Every story I tell is different?"

He waited as I shook my head.

"Because I blacked out. A whole chunk of time is dead to me. How did I get downstairs? They tell me I was upstairs, as I told everyone. Or just coming home. I don't know."

"What are you saying, Jacob?"

"I'm saying that maybe I killed Papa."

I drew in my breath. "Jacob…"

He held up his hand. "I don't know." He

started up the sidewalk, hurrying, aimless, brushing the shoulder of another stroller. Over his shoulder he said, "I can't answer any of your questions." He stopped, ten or so feet ahead of me, waiting.

But at that moment, staring at him, mesmerized by his rocking stance, his arms wrapped around his chest, I felt that he *knew* something. I didn't know why I felt that, only that he was hiding something—possibly something he'd not understood himself, something buried in that roiling, frenzied brain. A secret he would not—maybe could not—face.

It was an awful moment, a close one, but I believed that Jacob's despair stemmed from some kernel of knowledge of who the murderer was. Something had clicked inside him...something bit into his soul...

Part of him believed he'd been the killer. Another part said...no...it was—

But he didn't have the answer yet.

As I came alongside him, he strutted ahead. "Wait, Jacob," I called out. "You can't tell me this stuff and then run away."

He scrunched up his face. "I told Sarah about it back then, fifteen years ago, about my...blackout...and she told me to keep still—that no one would believe me. I should just accept the way things happened."

That bothered me. "Tell me about Sarah."

"What's to say—a woman you can't get at. Like…she put up this shell years ago, and speaks *at* you and never says anything."

I broke in. "I don't know that I believe that blasé front she's created."

He shrugged. "Who cares? When Mama came home, which none of us expected, she put on this act. All lovey dovey. *My sister, my sister! Welcome home!* It didn't even *sound* like her, to tell you the truth. But I'd catch her at odd moments—her lips drawn into a thin line, her eyes just slits. You could tell she was angry." He spat out the words. "She plays the radio so loud—like she wants to make the walls crumble."

"She was used to a household without your mother. You and Ella and Emma."

He gave out a false laugh. "She barely spoke to us those years. Herman was paying the bills, grudgingly. When she *had* to, she talked to us."

"But why? Help me to understand."

"An unhappy woman. She lived her life in the shadow of my mother. 'Oh, you're Leah's sister? Really?' That's gotta wear after a while. You get sick of being the *other* one in any family. The drab sister, though I gotta say a smart one. Trust me, I know."

"Do you ever fight with her?"

"No, we dodge around each other."

"What about the…lover who died in the Spanish War?"

Again, the phony laughter, exaggerated now. "Yes, we heard all about him. She claimed he took her for a ride in a Victoria with two chestnut horses, and the two drank chocolate at a carnival—unchaperoned, no less. Grandfather lost his mind. She made it up. She made it *all* up. He was more a story than a flesh-and-blood man. I never met him. *Nobody* did. The story surfaced years after the war was over. One day she mentions how my grandfather put the kibosh on her romance. I remember Mama saying, 'What are you talking about, Sarah?' Then the story comes out. We stared at her like she was crazy. She *was* crazy. *Abie's Irish Rose. Sarah's Irish Moze.*" He laughed at his own joke. "It was a convenient tool for my aunt to take the light off my beautiful mother."

"You're hard on the woman."

"She hasn't made life in that house easy these years."

I waited a second. "You could have moved out."

"And go where?"

"A life, an apartment, a wife, children. A bungalow on the North Side."

Now he was serious. "I *wanted* all that. A Lake Shore home, eventually. But I didn't know how to make it happen." He scratched his head. "There was always another pretty girl who stared at me when I went to Dreamland or to a basement club. I got"—he closed his eyes a moment—"lost." Then his eyes got wide, brilliant. "I left that life to Herman. Money, a cold fish of a wife, a boy and girl we never see. Ever. We are diseased, we folks on Monroe Street. Herman, I think, believes too much socializing with me, or Sarah, or even the evil twins, will sully the chosen children. We're kept at a distance."

"Unfair."

"Well, you've met Herman." A grin. "By the way, he's on the warpath. Against *you*. Rumor is afoot in the Jewish oral tradition we cultivate here in the quarter. You, Edna Ferber, sort of a female dybbuk with a pad and haystack hair. He sits in temple and prays: *May the Lord protect me from Edna. Her evil eye.*" He laughed out loud. "They sell incense on Maxwell to remove jinxes, you know."

"Yeah, and Dragon's Blood herbs down in the Black Belt."

"Ah, superstitions. Not Herman's cup of tea."

I frowned at that. "I'll deal with Herman."

"A greedy man who treats Ella and Emma like invisible waifs who disappear when you blink your eyes. He watches Ella browbeat Emma, and says nothing. And me, the vagabond non-poet who hasn't written a line in years, the son who still worships his mother."

"What do Ella and Emma think of Herman?"

"They're scared of him, mainly."

"They moved out when your mother returned."

"Herman thought it best. Better for everyone. It would make the household less tense. Emma believes Mama murdered my father because they told her that. She's afraid to change her mind. Ella—well, she's hard to read. Yes no, yes no. Each sees the other as another limb on the same body. So many years now that they can't separate. Herman feeds them money. He feeds everybody money, enough to reinforce his hold. It's a curious form of slavery, wouldn't you say? Buying people. Money takes away the desire for freedom."

"Did it work with you?"

That gave him pause, though he smiled. "Of course. He paid for this summer suit I'm sporting." A boyish smile. "Actually, he manufactured it. His label on the collar. He put a tag on me in case I get lost along the way."

"You don't have to bear it, Jacob."

"Oh, but I do. It's my own medieval hair shirt, Edna. Jacob Brenner howling in the wilderness. I spit three times to protect myself in this unclean place."

I pointed to the entrance of Katz's. "Coffee?"

He checked his watch. As he did so, he grumbled, tapped it emphatically. "Another gift from Herman. Order, precision, time, cleanliness, discipline, morality. Lord, my parents gave birth to a Semite Ben Franklin."

"I believe in hard work, too."

"I don't." He bristled. "But I need to get back. Uncle Ezra is picking me up."

"Ezra. The uncle who lingers on the edge of all your lives."

His face tightened. "What does that mean?" He headed home, and I scurried to walk alongside him. He slowed his pace.

"I gather he's around more these past few years now that your mother is back."

He eyed me suspiciously. "That's being mean, Edna. He *is* my uncle. A blood relative, a…"

"How much was he around those years when your mother was away? Tell me that."

He spat out his response. "Mean, Edna. You're mean."

"I'm only asking."

"Ezra was always around." But I could tell he didn't believe his own words.

"Did he get along with your father?"

He walked for a while, dragging steps. "No, of course not. You've seen him—dapper Dan. Razzle-dazzle man. He sparkles in the sunlight with all those diamonds. Papa was a butcher—down to earth, blunt, happy in his easy chair."

"But Ezra came around after he moved back from Philadelphia?"

"For a while we thought he was interested in Aunt Sarah. A marriage that would be made in hell, frankly."

I touched his sleeve and he stopped moving. I could feel a tense muscle in his forearm. "Uncle Ezra still loved your mother, Jacob."

"Good God, Edna." He stomped his foot on the sidewalk.

"He did. But let me ask you one thing, Jacob. Was he aware of the fight you had with your father? When your father slapped you. Or the fight your mother and father had that morning?"

"Why do you ask?" He started walking faster.

"Humor me."

He stood still then, hands interlaced behind his back, swaying back and forth. A puzzled look on his brow. "There was no reason for him to know all about the fights—mine or Mama's. Yes, he stopped in that morning. But real early. *Before* the fight. I remember seeing his car in front, parked there. I remember thinking—so early he comes to visit? I remember hearing laughter. My mother was in the back garden. Before anybody was awake. God, she'd be out there weeding before the hot sun forced her inside. Laughter. Uncle Ezra's roar. But then, later, as I left, I noticed the car was gone."

"Where was your mother?"

"I could hear her in the kitchen. Singing."

"Did she say anything?"

"I didn't talk to her. I left." He paused. "There was a package on the hall table. Uncle Ezra sometimes dropped off books for me." He was nodding his head, happy. "That had to be it—he dropped off books, said hello to Mama, and left." He reflected, "I know Herman stopped in because I heard him talking to Papa on the porch. Loud—they always boomed at each other, like they were talking at each other from twenty feet away. Ezra was long gone by then."

"So he wasn't around during or after your parents had that fight?" I drew in my cheeks. "Where was he?"

He didn't answer at first. Then, "I don't like what you're saying, Edna."

"I'm not saying anything."

He sneered. "Oh, yes, you are."

As we neared his home, a few houses away, I spotted Uncle Ezra's roadster at the curb, with Ezra in the driver's seat. Seeing us, he gunned the automobile, spinning away from the curb, cruising alongside us and braking so abruptly I smelled burnt rubber. Jacob started, jumped back.

"Uncle Ezra, I was almost home."

But Ezra was focused on me, none too kindly. Staring back, I tried to look winsome, Lillian Gish venturing out onto an ice floe with girlish trepidation. My palms on my cheeks, the helpless ingénue. Menaced virtue, the maiden scanning the horizon for a hero.

"I've been waiting," he snarled.

Jacob faltered, turning from me to him, his face sagging. "We were taking a walk, Edna and me."

"I'm not blind, Jacob. I can see the two of you *walking*." He stressed the word, stretching it out, fierce. He wasn't happy.

His shoulders sinking, Jacob leaned on the fender of the automobile, as though stabilizing himself. The automobile rumbled, idling in place.

"Ezra," I said softly, and waited. "Ezra, we were talking about you."

He ignored me. "Get in, Jacob," he said in a harsh, guttural voice laced with fury. "Now, dammit."

When Jacob didn't move, paralyzed there, his hip against the fender, one hand holding the back of his neck, Ezra leaped out of his seat, slammed the door behind him and glowered. I marveled at the transformation: the sleek, polished man who sat opposite me as I sipped a chocolate egg cream, so purposely charming, the *schmoozer*, was gone now. Instead the distinguished face was flushed and dark, the old man seeming much older now, threatening. The lines around his mouth and under his eyes deepened, got blood red, but what most alarmed me was the look in his eyes: gleaming, frozen agates. I caught my breath.

"What did you tell her?" he yelled at Jacob as he pointed at me.

Jacob stammered, "Nothing. We were just talking…"

His voice broke. He wagged a finger at Jacob. "She wants to pin the murder on *you*!"

"I do not." I threw back my head, indignant.

"She's got you all confused. This was not an innocent walk." Fire in his eyes now, a catch in his voice. "She is not an innocent girl."

Jacob rocked back and forth, his body slipping from the automobile. Ready to sink to the pavement, to curl up, he sputtered like a frightened child.

I touched Jacob on the shoulder. His look scared me—starved, pleading.

"Get your hands off him," Ezra seethed.

Jacob swung around and actually smiled at me, a madman's smile, empty and dangerous.

"What are you afraid of, Ezra?" I was blunt.

"Leave him alone."

I turned to Jacob. "Your uncle is scared. He believes you might be the murderer."

Said, the words punched the air like an exploded firecracker.

Jacob found his voice. "Uncle Ezra is afraid that you think *he* is the killer."

Ezra stalked around the automobile and grabbed at Jacob's sleeve. Jacob fought him, pulling away, but Ezra pushed him against the automobile. "Just shut the hell up, Jacob."

Jacob struggled to break free, but Ezra, though an old man, kept a tight grip on Jacob's shoulder. Jacob shook like a caged animal as Ezra kept barking. "Shut up, just shut up. You always say too much."

"Or not enough."

Ezra glared at me. "You've ruined everything, Edna Ferber. Everything."

At that moment, in a blind frenzy, he smashed his fist into Jacob's shoulder, so sudden an assault that Jacob, groaning, toppled away, bounced off the fender of the automobile. Freed, he let out a squeaky wail, a mouse trapped, and he broke into a run. He moved sloppily, as if he hadn't run in years, this middle-aged man who ran by twisting his ankles and bending his knees, a parody of flight. He headed not to his home behind him but toward Maxwell Street. Wailing, sobbing, distraught. Heads turned, people stepped out of the way.

Ezra stared at me, icy. "Do you see what you've done?"

"You hit him, Ezra, not me."

Chapter Twelve

The heat wave stayed with us. Waking up in the morning, the streets still dark, the windows wide open with night creatures brushing against the screens, I could feel the day's heat. The temperature never seemed to drop with nightfall. Everyone moved with beads of sweat running down their skin, clothing sodden and sticky, irritation swelling in their bellies. Another blistering, appalling day.

Last night Sol grumbled, "The hottest Chicago summer on record. And I've been here sixty years. Too hot to live."

Lying in my bed, I rolled over: too hot to live. Like being in the open flames of the steel mills, the red glow that washed the sky.

Esther was in the kitchen, setting the table for breakfast. As I walked in, she was humming softly to herself, preoccupied, and I startled her. She tittered, "Good Lord, Edna dear, you walk as softly as a kitten."

I gave her a quick hug, "Yet I growl like an old lion."

She chuckled. "Edna, some folks are born to rile the world. You may be one of them." She winked at me. "But that might not be a blessing."

"You're being kind, Esther."

"I *do* love your visit, dear. Remember that." She kissed me on the cheek, then stepped back, eyes twinkling. "It's gonna be another hot day, Edna. Again. Sol will talk of nothing but the weather. He'll quote the newspaper. Only on Shabbas does he stop about the weather. For a few minutes, at least." Laughing, she handed me a cup of coffee. "Fresh and hot. You like it black."

The *tap tap tap* of a cane as Molly, grumpy and sleepy, walked into the room. "I'm gonna die of the heat."

"Some coffee?" Esther handed her a cup. "Fresh rolls from the oven."

"Least downstairs there's a little breeze from the backyard. Though not much." Molly frowned at me. "You're in my old room, Edna. Upstairs. Hottest room in the house, sorry to tell you. The only good thing I got from the stroke I had last year was moving downstairs to the back." She grinned at Esther. "Of course, I had to take over Esther's sewing room." She glanced back at me. "Your room is hell, Edna." Molly was happy with that shared news—the proper place for the errant guest.

"I don't mind. We can't have you falling down the stairs."

"Don't get old, Edna," she told me. "A curse, it is."

Behind her, Esther rolled her eyes.

"It's something I'm looking forward to," I said. "Then I can speak my mind."

Molly smiled but never blinked. "I think you got a head start on that, dear."

Molly sat down while Esther waited on her. She kept the cane at her side, gripped in her right hand, every so often tapping it on the linoleum. Then she'd rub her lower back and groan. I caught Esther's eye, her swift glance telling me Molly would have one of her crotchety days. She'd find fault with her daughter-in-law, the quivering *hausfrau* that Esther was, though Esther had learned something I refused in myself: patience with whiners and malcontents. Molly, at eighty-eight—she insisted she was eighty-six, as though that shifted the axis of the earth dramatically—thought it her privilege to kvetch, to make everyone around her stand at attention. My mother attended the same school.

She turned to me, her chin trembling. "You're up early, Edna. I heard you in the kitchen late last night. Rattling around."

"I couldn't sleep. A glass of water. I was trying to be quiet, Molly. I swear. How'd you know it was me?"

"I heard you clear your throat. Twice, in fact. An old lady is a light sleeper. After all these years, I know the souls of my own home."

Grinning, I teased her. "Molly, you're our Sherlock Holmes."

Cranky: "No, just an old lady who likes a quiet house at night and would prefer for folks not to wander around in the dark."

Lord, I'd tiptoed downstairs, aware of Molly's bedroom behind the kitchen, her door open to catch a breeze, moonlit shadows in the hallway. I'd lingered by the front kitchen window, idly watching the house next door shrouded in blackness except for a light switched on at the back of the house, probably Leah's bedroom. Two in the morning, someone sitting up, a lamp casting a glow out into the backyard. Leah, unable to sleep? Leah, hungry for light? A woman afraid of darkness.

Molly was watching me. "Edna, you enjoying your visit?" Slyness in her tone, an unfriendly sidelong glance at me.

It was an untoward question, and Esther gasped. Hurriedly, Esther began chatting about the warm bread on top of the stove, the black pumpernickel, the failure of the yeast in the dead air. The cold mutton and apple sauce she'd be serving that night. The cherry cobbler, lumpy, dry. Babble, all of it, a little crazy, though I appreciated her attempt to salvage civility.

Molly was oblivious, prattling on. "You prefer the occupants next door." A grimace that showed ivory-blue false teeth, stained.

Esther chatted on. "Well, that Jacob is a handsome…"

Molly interrupted her. "It's bad enough our Adolph insists on keeping that… friendship with that lad. Such a bad influence on Adolph. The mistake we made years back of moving into this house. He could have—I suppose he will"—she deliberated—"flower." She sipped coffee and peered at me over the rim of her cup. "Had Jacob not been next door, Adolph would be a rabbi."

Esther frowned. "Adolph played at that, Molly. The way he plays at being a puller, or a handyman, or a…"

Molly drew her lips into a straight line. "He looks like my father, you know. In the old village. The spitting image, really. So wonderful. I look at him, feel a tug at my heart. His great-grandfather's nose, the jawline, the eyes, even the way he walks—that shuffle, as though he is afraid the earth beneath his feet will cave in. Like my father, he'll marry late and find happiness in old age."

Like you did, I thought horribly, though I was pleased at my own observation.

Sipping coffee, she'd become almost rhapsodic, a beatific smile on her lips, though I noticed Esther, doubtless often the recipient of this blissful song to her shiftless son, fiddled with the loaves of bread and paid no attention. In the middle of this paean to one man's uncharted future, Ad trooped in, his father and my mother close behind him.

My mother was rubbing her eyes.

"Mother, you all right?" I asked.

She put on her aggrieved face, one I'd seen since I stumbled around in pigtails in a Kalamazoo kitchen. "A sleepless night."

"I'm sorry."

"This is an upside down household," Molly said.

Sol grunted at his mother. "The heat is driving everyone crazy. People crack from the heat—go nuts. The papers said…"

His mother, cane tapping the floor, hissed, "We can't change the weather, Sol darling."

"All I'm saying is that…"

"All right, Sol." Esther affectionately drummed her fingers on his shoulder as she moved to the stove.

Molly smiled at her grandson, slumped over the table, head to the side, heavy-lidded eyes, not even trying to stifle a yawn. One leg of his gray cotton trousers was tucked into a high-laced shoe, the other hanging loose. He tugged at it with his fingertips but finally sat back, reaching for a buttered roll Esther slid across the table at him.

"Hmmm." The picture of contentment, the family pet finally fed.

Then, gulping coffee and sitting up, Ad spoke to me, a tickle in his voice. "What happened yesterday, Edna?"

"A lot of things happened yesterday, Ad. Could you be more specific?"

He made a crooked smile, one lip turned up. "With Jacob."

"We went for a walk."

"I was coming home from the hardware store, and I cut through the park on Halsted and Elm. Jacob was there, bent over on a bench, sobbing."

A catch in my throat. "Sobbing?"

"Yeah, and he wasn't happy to see me approaching. 'Go away, Ad,' he yelled. 'Can't a man sit by himself?' But he mumbled your name—or at least I think he did. You…and Uncle Ezra. What in God's name happened?"

Every face on me, waiting, unhappy.

"He had a spat with Uncle Ezra."

"Edna," Molly asked, "what did you tell Jacob?"

I shrugged. "We were talking."

Ad smiled, the rabble rouser. "She made him cry."

My mother sighed. "Sooner or later Edna makes everybody cry."

I ignored her, compelled to say, "Sooner or later everyone tells me that."

Molly grumbled. "That is an unstable family. Look at the lot of them. Jacob—I know you persist in that dead-end friendship, Adolph—is a bomb ticking away, getting worse. I see him from the porch. A *farblondzheter*, that boy. Lost." A lost soul, baffled, confused. "He ambles, he talks to himself, he stumbles, he laughs out loud at a joke only he hears in his head. He slams the front door."

"I don't care," Ad insisted. "A boyhood friend."

Molly rolled on. "The twins are squeamish little mice, though that Ella can be a bully. I've heard her. Lord! Ezra, well, I've known him for decades. He's always one step away from a shady deal. You can't trust a man who wears a diamond stickpin."

"Molly, please…" pleaded Esther.

"That family teeters on the edge of a cliff. Sister Sarah won't give you the time of day. Over the years I tried to be friendly." A deep breath. "And need I mention the unpardonable sinner, Leah, with the knife in the poor slob Ivan's neck?" She stopped, triumphant.

Esther gasped, hid her face over a pot on the stove. Ad stared at his grandmother, dumbfounded, unhappy. Sol *tsk*ed and reached for his pipe.

My mother spoke up. "Really, Molly, your words stun the breakfast table."

Molly harrumphed with a good measure of Victorian bile and venom. "I don't care. A subject long buried when Leah…left us. Over with. Finished. Thank God. Justice in an unjust world. And now, unwanted, back at us. We talk and talk—and our eyes shift over to that horrible house." She aimed her cane at the kitchen window. "And you, Edna, the reporter on holiday, no less. Needling a weak Jacob, having coffee with that murdering woman, throwing our world into chaos. It's unforgivable."

I said nothing because I wanted this conversation to end.

Esther cleared her throat. "You know, that horrible day, that hot, hot day, we sat in this kitchen and listened to Ivan and Leah fighting."

"You could hear it here?" I asked.

Esther nodded. "It was *that* loud. Summer. The windows open. A hot summer. I knew to my soul that life would never be the same. A strange feeling in my gut. It had nothing to do with us—with me—but a chill sweeps through me. Such yelling I never heard. Nasty and cruel and bitter, with crying and…and awful silences in between. Never in my life, I tell you now. Like something ripped open a part of the street, this neighborhood, this quiet block of good Jewish people, law-abiding, God-fearing, and said, Look, look inside, all this simmering evil is here, underneath, waiting, waiting, everywhere…I swear I never thought of people the same after that." She closed her eyes. When she opened them, they were wet.

A long speech, especially for Esther, and so deadened and low that many of the words were lost or slurred, though we all listened closely.

"It was that bad?" I asked. "The fight."

Ad nodded. "Edna, it *scared* us. You can hear noise from over there, people on the porch, the radio, the gramophone." He smirked. "Leah cranking away her Caruso records. Listening to opera on KYW. But that was…ferocious. Mama is right—it went up your spine."

"Adolph wanted to go over there," Molly told us. "We were going to leave, the two of us, shopping downtown, meeting a friend of his, but we just listened. We couldn't move. I told Adolph, no, please no. Stay here. They have to deal with it."

"What was said?"

Molly frowned at Esther, who glanced at Ad.

"It started about Ivan hitting Jacob the day before. Leah had just learned of it—from what she was screaming. Then the—you know—little kiss with Morrie, Leah's apology, her pleading."

"I got real afraid," Ad said. "Ivan was scary."

For the first time Sol spoke. "Such a bitter man, that Ivan. Once so good to everyone. A friend. We smoked cigars together."

"He wouldn't hit Leah?" I asked.

Ad shrugged. "I was afraid of that. We all were. After all, he did hit Jacob twice. A mean man, but he never was...violent. And I knew Jacob wasn't home—I saw him walking up Monroe earlier." He exchanged looks with his grandmother. "You should have let me stop it, Bubbe. Look what happened afterwards."

Molly wasn't happy with the conversation. "You could not have stopped *that*. In the middle of such craziness. Family business." She paused. "Then, suddenly, it stopped. Just like that. Adolph and I left and I saw Leah carrying a water pail from the front porch to her garden out back. Like a normal day. Daily chores. She didn't look up as we walked by. Silence in the house, Ivan somewhere inside. Silence."

"You didn't hear anything later on?"

"We were gone a long time, came back later, tired, Adolph and I upstairs in our rooms. I woke from my nap to hear screaming. At first I thought something happened to Esther because it sounded so close. But then I thought it was Leah's howling and thought, oh no, here they go again. But Adolph comes flying out of his room and yells to me, no, it's Sarah. Sarah is hurt. Something was wrong. You could hear her—like someone was killing her. Adolph ran over, Esther behind him. The neighbors. You know the rest." She frowned. "I've told the story too many times." She bit her lip. "Too many times—and now again."

"The day was hot like today," Sol commented.

"And now," Ad added, "Jacob sits in the park and cries."

"Because," I said quietly, "he has his mother back but he doesn't believe she killed his father."

A collective groan, my mother's falsetto cackle breaking above Molly's squealing protest and Esther's quiet whisper. Ad's look conveyed the notion that I was a pesky disturber of the peace.

Only Sol, portly and fleshy, sitting with his hands resting in his lap, wore an enigmatic smile that alarmed me more than their expected responses.

"What?" I asked him.

At that moment we heard a heavy footfall on the front steps, followed by an insistent *rap-rap-rap* on the front door. Everyone jumped, though no one headed to the door. Finally Sol shuffled to the front door, then followed an irate Herman Brenner into the kitchen. Once there, planted in the doorway, Herman repented his brash invasion, grunting and fussing, half turning toward the front door.

He stammered, "I'm sorry." He addressed Sol, then Esther. "I've come from my mother's. Ezra telephoned her about Edna, telling a horrible tale. Little of it makes sense. Jacob is slobbering and is accusing *me* of God-knows-what. That I *betrayed* our mother. I lay all this at the feet of this questionable young woman who plays with my family's… tragedy for…for sport."

Sol placed his hand on Herman's shoulder. "Sit down, my boy. We haven't seen you in such a long time." He nodded at his wife. "Esther, a cup for Herman. Some rolls with butter. Please."

Rattled, Herman dropped into a seat, his mouth open, suddenly aware of where he was, where we all were. His eyes swept the kitchen and rested on Esther.

A sheepish smile. "Lord, I haven't been in this kitchen for years and years." So simplistic an observation, so naïve that Esther, watching him, teared up. Herman struggled to stand. "I'm intruding. Unforgivable, my temper. I didn't mean…I'm sorry."

Esther placed a cup of coffee before him,

smiling at him, and Sol nodded at him. "Drink some, Herman. Please."

As if by habit, he sipped the coffee, though his hand trembled. He nibbled on the crust of a roll. A smile lit up his face. "Esther, your rolls. Heavenly. As a boy we made sure we wandered in here in the morning. The aroma from the sidewalk…" He stopped.

"Is Jacob all right?" l asked.

Herman's words were bitter. "The happy-go-lucky fool we all got used to now moans and blames and starts at any noise. My mother doesn't know what to do. She walks the hallways, waiting for him to come out of his room. She's crying. He's crying. The only one who isn't crying is Sarah. I stop in and find a topsy-turvy home. Jacob says to me, 'We did a horrible thing to Mama.' What can I say to that? 'We put Mama in hell. Who is the murderer, Herman? I'm afraid it might be me.' Then he looks at me and says, 'Or you.' Can you imagine such words from his mouth?"

Sol nodded toward Herman's coffee cup. "Drink, my boy."

Herman stood up. "No more. I'm sorry. A mistake, my rushing in here. I came here in poor taste—to confront Edna." He nodded at me, not angry now but with a hint of melancholy. "My mother's house is filled with ghosts today. That's what drove me here. I'm sorry. I'll leave you all in peace." He half-bowed to Molly and Esther, even to my mother, but not to me. He was gone.

A minute of stunned silence.

Sol spoke up. "Herman, after all these years— and so crazy a visit."

My mother fumed. "Look what you've done, Edna."

I faced all their stares, but didn't care. "I don't understand why everyone is content to let a wronged woman wear a stigma. What about justice?"

Tap tap tap. Molly exploded. "And you know more than the police, dear Edna?"

"The police never investigated this the way they should have. No investigation at all. Leah was an easy target."

In a small, unexpected voice, timid, Esther began, "I never believed Leah did that horrible thing."

Startled, we all turned to her.

"What?" said Sol, befuddled.

She shrugged. "It just seemed…impossible then. Like the big pieces of a puzzle were missing somehow." She faltered. "A thought, that's all." Then, staring into my face, "It seems to me that someone knows something—if Edna is right."

"But she isn't," Molly screamed.

Ad stood and his glance took us all in. "Nonsense, all of this. Do you hear yourselves? When everyone turned away from that family, left Jacob to flounder, helpless, I was the one who stayed at his side. I got him through it all. I made him laugh again. When people pointed at him on the sidewalk, I …I sheltered him. Me—me. And now, he's slipping back into that black pit. I never thought Leah would be *allowed* back home, but what do I know? All I do know is that it's…it's like somebody took a family photograph way back when, everybody standing in their Shabbas best, but now, years later, someone is shredding the picture, piece by piece, ripping it all apart."

He paused. "And now *we're* in the picture."

Molly sputtered, "Leave us out of it. Your love for Jacob is a curse, Adolph. *A tropn libe brengt amol a yam trern.*" A drop of love may bring an ocean of weeping.

"Stop, Edna," Ad said. "Stop! Can't you see what you're doing to them?" And his outstretched arm pointed at his own family.

• • ● • •

I sat on the front porch, alone, crying softly. What had started as a glance from an old woman on her porch had led me to a conviction that something was wrong. I stumbled through my questions, driven not by meanness but by a heartfelt belief that there was, indeed, rightness to life. If Leah was innocent—as my gut told me, and the smattering of evidence suggested—then there was a murderer among us. One of the folks I'd met, socialized with, talked to, followed, probed, debated. Everyone saw me as hard and insensitive and maybe cruel. But a murderer lurked in the shadows of Monroe Street. When was the world going to be fair to Leah, with her lost life, her dark corners, her fears? "I don't want my children to be hurt," she'd said to me over and over. A prayer. But she also didn't want her children to have a murderer for a mother. What mother did? I believed that. A mission, a—

"Edna!"

I jumped. Sol had slid into a chair next to me.

"Sol, you startled me so."

"You're crying, Edna."

I turned my head away. "I'm all right."

Sol shuffled his seat, edging it closer to mine. He reached out and grabbed my hand, squeezing it tightly. "Dear Edna," he said with affection, "a problem for you, this whole story." He waited. "Look at me."

I faced him. Strangely, he was smiling. "Sol…"

"No, no." He put his hand in front of my face. "You're young, a modern woman. Maybe one of those girls I don't understand. It's a different world nowadays. I'm old. But you want to do the right thing, always. You want to make the world *better*.

Most people don't. Yes, they *say* they do. Everybody is on the side of right. Everybody jumps back from evil. From doing the wrong thing." He waved back toward the kitchen. "Everybody believes they are good people. And they are. But you're—what?—a different girl. You *do* things, Edna."

"And everyone hates me." Self-pity, a trait I disliked in others, especially myself.

"No one hates you." He chuckled. "Maybe a little irritated with you, I tells you, yes. They don't understand what's inside you. You push and push." He laughed. "They should make you a puller up on Maxwell. Imagine the sales!" Then his voice deepened, serious. "Edna, don't worry. Follow your heart. You gotta be...Edna. Yourself. Like the Talmud says, 'A man's name is his soul.' You understand? That's you...inside. They"—again he pointed inside—"can never understand a girl like you. The passion."

"I believe in Leah."

A long pause. "So do I."

Startled. "What?"

"I'll tell you a secret. Like my Esther, I never believed she killed poor Ivan. She *loved* that man, and he was a hard man to love sometimes. Not good with his children. Mean to Jacob, so bad. I used to ache for what he did to that boy. One time I says to him, 'Leave the boy be. Jacob is a good boy.' And he says for me to mind my business. Okay, so they fought. But we all fight. I seen her that day when the police come here—frozen, dead eyes. The face of a grieving woman, not a murderer."

"Then who?"

He shrugged. "I don't know."

"That's why I…"

"I know, I know. And let me tell you something, Edna. I'm proud of you. You need to do this. You are a girl with a heart so big it makes others tremble. You know the saying, yes? *Dos hart iz a halber novi.*" I shook my head: no. He watched me carefully. "'The heart is half of a prophet.' You walk on a road that looks into the future. The others…you can't help the way they thinks. You will always be a mystery to your own mother. In the end they will still love you." He winked. "As much as they can."

"But this isn't going to have a happy ending."

"It don't matter. It will finally have a…ending. That is enough."

Chapter Thirteen

Minna Pittman telephoned me to check if we were still on for the theater on Sunday. "I hope you don't cancel," she said nervously.

Of course not, I told her, annoyed. I'd been wishing to see Sigmund Romberg's *Blossom Time* at the Auditorium on Michigan Avenue.

"But," Minna went on, as though I'd vacillated, "I am really excited about it. We are, Ad and I. But this whole thing with Jacob and…" Her voice trailed off, a squeak at the end. She waited. Then quietly, "I hate when people don't talk."

"Minna." I raised my voice, confused. "What are you saying?"

"Ad told me about Herman barging in and how Ad told you to…he told you to leave things alone. To *stop* it. Hurting his family."

"Minna, is that why you're calling? I am *not* mad at Ad. Is that why he's been sulking around?"

She didn't know what to say. Finally she blathered, "He thought he hurt your feelings."

I shook my head "Good Lord, Minna. Tell him—oh, never mind, I will tell him."

She hung up.

So that explained the silence in the hallway, Ad's sheepish avoidance, the hesitant hellos and goodbyes. Our minor kerfuffle over breakfast was forgotten, though my mother had reminded me, once again, that I was a guest in the house. Good Lord—how thin-skinned did Ad think I was? Though, considering it, I smiled to myself: ah, the unnecessary gentleman that he was.

So on Sunday as I walked with Ad and Minna up Monroe to Maxwell Street to catch a streetcar, Minna did most of the talking, Ad silent beside her, grim-faced.

"Ad," I told him, "I'm a big girl."

He made a face. "The women in my family— and the woman in *your* family—told me I wasn't… polite to you."

I laughed out loud. "Ad, didn't you ever learn to fight back?"

"I only win battles with Minna." He flicked his head toward her. "She lets me."

The remark seemed dismissive. The girlfriend with lukewarm water in her veins, the faint-hearted child who lacked the iron blood the women in his household possessed. Minna—destined to be the *alte moyd*. The spinster much pitied yet coddled.

At that moment, listening to him, Minna heard that condescension, and I watched her squirm, bite her lips.

Curious, that scene, because Ad immediately sensed his error, stammering, "Minna never finds fault with me." But that cavalier line was dreadful, a deeper cut, utter disregard. Finally, groping for an apology, he simply walked ahead and muttered over his shoulder, "I should keep quiet."

"Advice most men fail to learn," I commented.

Ad showed me his crooked smile, which failed to charm.

Minna was blinking her eyes rapidly, an idiosyncratic behavior I'd noted once before in her—a girl who would never be comfortable in the matriarchal world of Molly Newmann, Monroe Street martinet.

"Jacob won't answer the door." Ad spoke suddenly, a line not directed at Minna or me.

"I told you, Ad—he's sad. Leave him alone." Minna touched his elbow, reassuringly.

Ad banged one fist into the other. "I knock on his door. Yesterday. Today. He won't answer. I'm getting worried. It's always been him and me. Blood brothers. He *knows* that. Through the bad times. I held him up when he fell apart." His eyes got wide, round. "Now, I'm afraid."

"He'll come around," Minna said softly.

Ad's eyes rested on me. "His mother told me *she's* worried. Edna, you should've seen her face—like…like a ghost."

I glanced back down the block. "I need to stop in to see Leah. She hides away, too."

"Everybody hides in that house." Ad breathed in. "It's a locked-up fortress. Sarah, the guard dog at the gate. Jacob's mad at the world. His knuckles bruised—a fist against his bedroom wall." Then, a helpless look. "But he cannot be mad at me, can he?" He shook his head back and forth. "It's crazy."

Minna touched his elbow again. "Call him later."

He scowled at her, impatient. "Why would he be mad at me? He always *comes* to me."

"C'mon, Ad. Please."

He had no interest in the play, though I did. The American version of the Viennese musical, *Das Dreimäderhaus*, Sigmund Romberg's adaptation of Franz Schubert's melodic tunes, was a jolt of old-fashioned melodrama, depicting the sad (and final) days of the celebrated composer. Lovely, I thought, a soothing balm after the open wounds on Monroe Street. "Serenade," an enticing ballad, made Minna cry. It made me miss my father.

Ad fidgeted throughout the musical, though the spirited song of "Three Little Maids" did elicit a snicker from him. Minna was overly solicitous, tugging at him, the mother hen with her awkward runt offspring, though Ad shrugged her off. At intermission when he was away in the lobby, Minna whispered to me that Jacob's new disaffection was Ad's only story.

"Ad doesn't like people being mad at him." She leaned in. "You know that Jacob had a real bad breakdown after his mama was taken away. Ad cried for days."

When Ad returned, Minna's jerky laughter confused him, and he shot a penetrating look—not a kind one—at me. Edna, the spreader of gloom and doom throughout the Western hemisphere. The wicked stepsister rubbing her foul hands together with glee over the cauldron of steaming poisons.

Ad offered to treat us to coffee and dessert at Henrici's Fancy Bakery and Café on Randolph Street, though I said no—since he'd provided the tickets, that snack would be my pleasure. Minna squealed as if I'd paid for catastrophic surgery. But we were all in a genial mood now, the afterglow of splendid theater, always so bolstering for me, covering us, making us giddy and foolish. Ad played the clown as we strolled along—he warbled "Bei Mir Bist du Schein" too loudly, and purposely off-key, but Minna frowned him into silence.

Over walnut rolls and robust cherry phosphates,

I faced the two of them in a booth. Ad had whispered something in Minna's ear, and she'd blushed to her ringlet roots. Watching Ad's curiously distant yet still solicitous gestures, I understood, yet again, the calculus of their love. Ad would be the perennial bachelor under his aged grandmother's doting care, Peter Pan in a Friday night yarmulke. The boy who never wanted to leave his bar mitzvah party.

I wasn't paying attention to their bantering, engrossed as I was in my own splendid summation of the overgrown yeshiva boy before me. I was startled back into the conversation by Minna's uncharacteristically brusque, clipped tone. The surprising mention of Herman Brenner. Minna had been talking of Herman's abrupt visit to the Newmann kitchen, followed by his tepid and embarrassed apology, but her mention of Herman's name seemed particularly bitter. Amazing, I thought, how someone can say a name—in the case, *Herman*—and the word dripped with bile. What was Sol's quotation from the Talmud? *A man's name is his soul.*

I sat up, alert. "Herman?"

Minna narrowed her eyes. "I mean it."

I had no idea what that meant. Unfortunately, now as a habit, I never listened to Minna.

Ad was shaking his head. "Edna, Minna has a history with Herman."

I turned to her, this pencil-thin, frail woman, as brittle-boned as a skeletal bird, forgettable. Or not. "Tell me."

"Nothing to tell," she stated, her eyes dipped down at her plate.

Now those words always infuriated me. They were any inquiring reporter's least desired response, an indication of so much left unsaid, the rich ore under the sandstone earth. *Nothing to tell.*

"Tell me." I spoke so sharply Ad spit soda pop onto his sleeve.

"My first beau." Said quietly, an epitaph etched in the soul.

"Herman?"

She giggled. "Impossible, no? That…that stiff collar, that over-starched man."

"When was this?"

"We were young, well, eighteen, nineteen. For a real short time. A foolish time, let me tell you. Our parents arranged it, of course, as they did back then. They planned for us to *love* each other, very Old Country, no? And we were determined to be real Americans, red, white, and blue to the core. We enjoyed being together, me and Herman, though always under the eye of one parent or someone. Ice skating at the Midway Plaisance, box suppers in Humboldt Park, volunteering at the Davis Square Settlement House because they had an ice cream parlor downstairs. As proper as can be, our relationship. And Herman used to laugh a lot back then, before he was told he wasn't supposed to."

"What happened?"

Minna wrinkled up her face, which made her look like a disgruntled ferret. "His father took a dislike to me."

"Can you imagine that?" said Ad, tapping her wrist.

"Ivan? But why?" So innocuous a girl, so invisible in a room.

"He never gave a reason...I always felt he wanted someone else. Like he was *thinking* already of someone else. But Leah *liked* me. We spent a lot of time in the kitchen. She once told me that maybe Ivan favored a rabbi's daughter from North Chicago, Rabbi Goldman's distant relative. Some money there. Living up on Calumet Avenue. But my parents and Leah arranged..."

The more Minna talked, the more shrill her voice got, edged with a fury I'd not thought her capable of showing. She, this diffident woman, twittering around the Newmann family for years, had mettle. And spirit, though that spirit was tinged with smoldering resentment. A spitfire woman here, and I marveled at this delicious new revelation. Ad, the un-handyman of the neighborhood, would be no match for the redoubtable Minna Pittman, once aroused and passionate.

"Ivan the Terrible," I said.

She rapped her knuckles on the table. "Herman was a coward, despite his bluster and yelling. 'I don't care what my father says'—that's what he told me. But he kowtowed to his father, though Leah fought him—quietly. Ivan always talked to me like I was a dumb farm animal. I'll never forget it."

I widened my eyes. "So Herman left *you*?"

Ad was nodding furiously. "But lucky for me."

I didn't know about that, frankly, a dull buffoon like Herman giving way to a layabout gadfly like Ad, two members of the male species who'd fallen out of the monkey tree.

"He left me," Minna thundered. Her eyes blazed. "He said he still loved me. He would always love me—the love of his life, said with the passion of a scared boy. Imagine that?" Her eyes got moist. "We *did* love each other. Then. I mean—then."

"Yeah, sure," Ad said. "Herman was always a bump on a log." He winked at Minna. "I remember when you and Herman courted."

Minna pursed her lips, unhappy with the depiction. "My parents were nervous about Ad marrying me." She grinned. "I told them that he'd once thought of being a rabbi."

Ad laughed, too. "No one believes that. Jacob could never understand that dream of mine."

"I don't see you as a Talmudic scholar, Ad," I grinned.

"I had a moment—way back then." His eyes got sad, dark. "Long, long ago. Before Ivan's murder. Jacob *fought* me. A baseball player, a hot dog vender, a ditch digger. But not a rabbi. 'Don't get crazy on me,' he said. That was my holier-than-thou year, preaching and spouting Scripture like some Jewish Cotton Mather, thunder and lightning. God, you should have heard me at Nathan's Meat Market."

"Why there?"

"Because of old Levi Pinsky," Ad told me. "You know, the ragpicker that still squats in the empty shop. A religious Jew, that one, fanatical, he wouldn't even sneak a pretzel on fast days." He chuckled. "He watched everyone, quiet mostly, except when he came in with some Biblical truth. He started talking to me about old Judaic lore, myth, superstitions, and I guess that's what got my attention—for a while. But I couldn't stay with it. He's not happy with me to this day."

"What kind of teaching?"

"Stories of how in Rome Jewish girls lined the Appian Way and sold dream charms and notions to those walking by. How demons carry on in the shade of trees—in the shadows cast by the moon.

How demons are all around us, invisible, because, if seen, we'd go crazy. Demons everywhere, waiting, waiting. The night before a boy's circumcision is the most dangerous one in his life." Ad stopped, embarrassed by his enthusiasm. He dropped his eyes. "Stuff like that, designed to make a young man curious. I got…caught up. Most don't know stuff like that. So I talked to our rabbi, but he wasn't happy. He said Levi had some confused view of our religion—true stuff, but not what I should be focusing on.

"The rabbi set me studying seriously, on the path that petered out. Once I got past the late-night spookiness of medieval Judaism—hocus pocus and razzmatazz—once I stopped boring my friends with bits and pieces of history, I lost interest. Hebrew floored me, made me black out. Not the memorized routines of the bar mitzvah but the sheer power of the language, the sheer weight of its history. Suddenly my religion was so…important. Magnificent. It was all so…beautiful, that history, so awesome. I couldn't…" He shrugged his shoulders. "I couldn't do it. I walked away."

"Hmm," I said. "I suppose Levi thought he was doing the right thing. Levi the Teacher."

Ad's voice a low rumble. "Yeah, the ragpicker prophet, sorting clothes on the butcher block tables where carcasses once lay. No one cares anymore.

Morrie Wolfsy, a couple nights a month he's there, alone, collecting rents, away from his wife and her French Provincial furniture and the gold-gilt bathroom fixtures, behind the locked doors of the upstairs apartment. Or he's downstairs, sitting with old Levi, the two lost in the past over cigars and knishes bought from a cart on Maxwell." He laughed. "Go in sometimes. The front door's unlocked. A big bare room now."

"Obviously Levi's still disappointed you abandoned your studies."

He thought about that. "He didn't seem to notice at the time. After Ivan's death, Morrie discouraged the men from haunting that back room, a place we loved. I loved—a place to hide away. Morrie lost interest. Even old Levi disappeared for a while. He was unhappy with the whole nightmare. 'Jews killing Jews,' he screamed one afternoon. 'Is that what we do now? Ain't it bad enough the Russians got a head start?' Then, one day, I heard he was back. But Morrie told everyone to stay away. He wanted to close up shop. So I never returned there. Jacob, of course, stayed away. How could he go back there? Ivan was gone. Morrie liked the back room—the talk, talk, talk. Then he didn't." A dark smile. "Another thing Levi taught me. When bad luck touches you, you and your family can't shake it off. It stays, grows."

"No one ever suspected Morrie of the murder?" I wondered out loud.

"Yeah, of course. The partner? The man who wooed Ivan's wife? We thought the cops would question him—but they didn't. Nothing came of it."

I grumbled, "The police already named the murderer."

He nodded. "Yeah, on the spot."

"Tell me about the back room."

He raised his eyebrows, suspicious. "A place where we could smoke cigars and talk about things."

"Talk about women."

Ad squirmed. "Sometimes." He sighed. "A refuge that wasn't shul. I felt at home there. So did Jacob."

"The women never came in?" I asked.

"Leah would step into the doorway, but Selma never did. Morrie's wife. But the men would, you know, watch Leah…"

"Barnyard antics," Minna piped in.

"She'd smile at us." Ad reminisced.

"I'll never understand Leah's…indiscretion— if that's what it was—with Morrie, Ad."

Minna spoke up. "Edna, Morrie never *liked* Leah either. He thought her foolish, a distraction. He didn't like it when she walked in. Everything in the shop went off kilter."

Ad went on. "He used to push the boys—

me, others—to joke with her—to make her uncomfortable."

That news flabbergasted me. "Why then the... indiscretion?"

Ad sat back, smug and confident. "You wanna know why? Simple. Because he *could*. Because he could take something away from Ivan. Ivan was talking of breaking up the shop, going out on his own. Morrie found a way to hurt him."

"My God!" I exclaimed.

Minna concluded, "Little boys playing rough in the schoolyard. Nasty." A wide grin on her face. "The land of the cavemen."

"C'mon, Minna," Ad admonished her. "It wasn't like that."

"Well, Ad, when you bar women from your door, you risk chaos in the land. You men won't be content until you make yourselves extinct."

"That makes no sense, Minna."

Minna's expression was blissful. "Edna understands what I'm saying."

• • ● • •

The land of the cavemen. The infernal back room. The dark recesses of the male species.

Ad and Minna decided to look at the shop windows up and down Michigan Avenue, but the afternoon sun exhausted me. I headed home.

Turning onto Monroe, I stopped at the corner by the entrance to the old meat market, caught by the dusty plate-glass window, the faded signs over the door, the yellowing cardboard notices in the window advertising chicken and beef for so much a pound. On sale this week. Today. A kosher market, unintelligible Hebrew (to me, at least) in black lettering, chipped now.

On the hot afternoon the front door was wide open, a block of wood under the bottom of the door, securing it. Staring in, I expected to see old Levi sifting through piles of old, smelly clothing, hunched over, a Uriah Heep with the bony scalp and hawk nose.

"Hello." My voice echoed against the back wall—all those empty cabinets, those glass-topped display cases, the racks, the shelves, everything empty of the deadly paraphernalia of butchery. A shell of a store. No one answered.

Too seductive, of course, an invitation to probe. That sacrosanct back room, the lair of the clubby men. "Hello," though now I expected no response, and happily so. I stepped through the doorway and moved quickly into the back room, a cluttered hovel: mismatched chairs with torn fabric, a Franklin cast-iron stove with a broken hinge, tables with overflowing ashtrays, not emptied in years, stacks of newspapers and magazines, even a scurrilous *Police Gazette* propping up the uneven leg of a table. Empty bottles, dirty glasses, a turned-over box of hoar-frosted peanuts. The stench of unventilated mayhem. Along all the walls were the counters and cabinets where, doubtless, poultry and beef carcasses made their inglorious entrance from a back door, preamble to dissection and trussing with cleaver and twine. Three of the walls held cubbyholes and ramshackle drawers, some half-open with papers and receipts and yellowing pulp spilling out. One wall once held knifes, the slots empty now but menacing, a knife-thrower's vaudeville act or, rather, the basement of the Spanish Inquisition. Torquemada's private pleasure. Chills ran up my spine seeing that vacant wall of deadly weapons, stripped now, but haunting. Had the knife that pierced Ivan's neck come from here?

Standing there, overwhelmed by the packed and worthless accumulation, I thought: There are secrets here, a story unexplained, a room that no one wanted to touch. I doubted the police, in their hurry-up investigation, considered pulling out even one of the drawers—or peeking into one of those jam-packed cubbyholes.

What notorious talk in this back room led to the murder? What questionable comment? Or did it?

I sensed an answer buried among the mountains of decay and dread.

My fingers gingerly touched the pull of an oak drawer, slightly ajar.

A voice bellowed from behind me. A gargled grunt.

I swirled around, my hand sweeping up thick gray dust, to face Morrie Wolfsy and Levi Pinsky, both furious.

"What means this?" Levi bellowed, quaking. "*Vos iz das?*" The veins in his temples bulged dangerously, blue-black, purple. Nostrils flared. Shoulders shook. A bony finger accused. "Trespasser."

Morrie, arms folded over his chest, simply said, "Edna Ferber." As though he were a jury foreman rehearsing a death sentence.

"The door was open and I…"

"Trespasser!" Levi screamed again. He sputtered, "You…you…*noodsh*." A pest.

Morrie approached me. "The stories come back to me, Miss Ferber. You befriend the murdering woman and they tell me you get ready to point the finger at me, the surviving partner. They tell me you suspect me." He pointed to the rack that once held all those knives. "Morrie Wolfsy, he took a knife." Almost a child's chant, the words rhythmic. He said it again. "Morrie Wolfsy, he took a knife." Singsong, Lizzie Borden—that awful refrain.

And took from Ivan his precious life…
Morrie Wolsy took a knife…
"But I never…"
"Word on the street, Miss Ferber."
"I give you my word."
"*Ikh zed azoy lang lebn.*" I should live so long.

Levi rocked back and forth, this ninety-year-old hunched man, a bell-ringer of doom. "The good Jewish girl belongs in the home. Her mama's kitchen. Not here." His arthritic arm took in the cave. He shuddered. Disgust covered his features.

In a flash, I realized that Levi, the old crusty celibate, despised women. An unhappy man. I thought: Ad studied at his feet and learned the persistent alienation of affection. Another thought: poor Minna found the back room amusing but didn't realize it was most likely the wellspring of her perpetual engagement. She'd never walk down any aisle that was not stocked with gefilte fish and macaroons.

I was through defending myself. I marched between the two men, striding boldly, Scylla and Charybdis parting seamlessly.

"Goodbye."

Behind my back I could hear Levi cursing Leah. "Such beauty in so horrible a woman. Lilith, that demon woman with the long, long hair. Lilith who fled the Garden of Eden. A curse on all of us."

Chapter Fourteen

Detective Tom O'Reilly's name had been mentioned in the newspaper accounts of the murder, but fifteen years later, he was reluctant to talk to me. Ready to retire, he told me—"The old ticker needs Florida, Miss"—he sat behind a desk with two pieces of paper on it, one of which, doubtless, was his retirement application. The other paper a brochure of a clapboard beach home in Porto Gordo, Florida. He was a pot-bellied officer of the law with out-of-focus eyes surely in need of spectacles, and a few strands of vagrant white hair teased and encouraged over a bald head—a hopeless journey from one grotesque floppy ear to the other. A button red nose, speckled with polka-dot red blood vessels, and a tobacco's chewer's gamey breath. Detective O'Reilly eyed me with a look that suggested I'd interrupted a day of calculated idleness.

"Miss Ferber," he chortled, "they tell me you're famous."

"Hardly. A novel of mine…"

"I don't read."

"I could have guessed that."

His eyes narrowed. "Captain Mooney ushered you in, all buzzing and waving his arms. He claims he knew you when."

"Yes, when my family first moved here after my father died in Appleton, Wisconsin, we lived with my mother's family for a few years over to Calumet. Jimmy Mooney was a young patrolman on the block then, someone the neighborhood liked and respected."

"Yeah, yeah," he broke in. "A real sweetheart, that Mooney. Blarneyed his way up to captain."

"He remembers the Brenner murder."

He sucked in his breath. "Not much to remember about it."

"You were the chief investigative lawman."

"Open-and-shut case, my dear."

"Are you sure of that?"

That gave him pause, and considerable digestive surprise, given the rumbling and rasping and clucking that erupted from his throat and bursting belly. "Sort of dim in my memory—after all, this is Chicago where folks kill for sport. You have heard of our beloved mobsters, no?—a husband catches a wife *in flagrante delicto*, a spat breaks out, real messy, and the good wife kills cuckolded husband."

"In twenty words or less."

"You're the reporter, lady."

"I am that. But if you'll indulge me, sir, I'd like to review the evidence."

His eyes got wide. They flickered a moment as if I'd shined a light into them. "A young woman like you playing detective? My, my, my." He chuckled. "How times change!"

I didn't chuckle. "As I say, sir, indulge me."

He'd been leaning back in his swivel chair, his tremendous girth suggesting imminent catastrophe, but now, quick as a slap to the brow, he shot up, spine rigid, and banged a fleshy fist on the desk. "I sent the killer away, Miss Ferber."

I smiled winsomely. "And now, would you believe, Detective O'Reilly, Leah Brenner is back home, cooking in her kitchen. Grinding poppy seed in a mortar and pestle."

"What?" He tapped the desk impatiently. "They let her out?" He stared over his shoulder as if he expected Leah Brenner, white-haired now and demonic, to smash through the wall, cleaver at the ready.

"The asylum, I suppose, deemed her suitable for the safe streets of Chicago."

"Very funny."

"Thank you. Most of my humor is met with derision—or bafflement."

His face tightened. "Look, Miss Ferber, I heard all about you because of that novel you wrote about Chicago. So I suppose now this…this conversation we're having is the stuff of a new book, though why you want to dredge up some domestic squabble is beyond me. You can read all about it in the papers"—I nodded—"but police business is police business."

"The news accounts in the *Chicago Tribune* suggest a rush to judgment."

"She was caught red-handed."

"Without a knife," I broke in. "Without *evidence*. How is that *red-handed?*"

He struggled to stand. "I don't think I can help you, my dear."

"Sir…"

He scratched his neck. "Oh, I don't think so."

Unceremoniously, I was pointed out without any goodbye and certainly with no thanks from me, only to find myself downstairs facing a grinning Captain Mooney. Still with that red, boyish face and round blue eyes that I remembered from years ago, Captain Mooney was scratching his head. He watched my face, admittedly set in a stony grimace, and held out his arm. In it a green-backed folder, thin, bound with cords.

"He's a bastard," Captain Mooney whispered.

"And lazy." He pushed the folder at me. "Here is what you want."

On my way in I'd told him my mission, though he'd not spoken a word. Clever boy, this old beat cop, and kind.

"Sit in there"—he pointed to a small alcove, windowless but with a door—"and leave it on the table when you leave."

"You'll be in trouble?"

"This will be the least criminal act committed in this building today." Laughing, he motioned me toward the open door. As I went to thank him, he simply bowed, threw out his arms like a stage performer at the end of a revue, and disappeared.

A quick hour, but an intense one, focused, my pencil scribbling furiously in the notebook I'd carried in my purse. A skinny file, granted, but its chaotic notes—was that Detective O'Reilly's illiterate penmanship?—intrigued me. Notations later ignored or forgotten—and ones that never made it to court or to the skimpy Fourth Estate accounts. What particularly intrigued me were the desultory—and largely trivial—interviews with relatives and neighbors. O'Reilly misspelled names, and in one case began a paragraph describing Sarah, quoting her, and then at the end of the same paragraph decided the quotation was by Ella (which was crossed out and "Emma" inserted).

Folderol, most of it, a man in a hurry to head to Bath-House John's Groggery or to his browbeaten mistress in a fourth-floor walk-up.

But what I gleaned made the visit worthwhile. After all, I was at the point of asking the central question: Who was where that fateful day? How did the hapless players in this sordid drama move, interact, or absent themselves from the fatal scene? Yes, I knew what I'd been told by the players, some reinforced by the skimpy reportage in the *Chicago Tribune*, but here, in the detective's rambling and bumbling narrative, was a beggar's opera of tidbit and anecdote.

First, Jacob, the wandering Jew, the sensitive artist whose perfected art was avoidance—and now absence. The report said he was upstairs the whole time, all morning, emerging only with Sarah's screaming. So his current story of walking in and seeing his father on the sofa was perhaps fanciful, failed memory. Or perhaps he'd lied to the detective. I'd lie too, confronting that supercilious buffoon who'd convict out of convenience.

But there was an appended follow-up to Jacob's scattered behavior that day. Leah, dazed and silent, had been taken to Cook County Hospital, which surprised and pleased me, though, according to Detective O'Reilly, her moaning essentially admitted guilt. I gathered he somehow deciphered the words "fight" and "Ivan" and "sorry" from the sounds she spilled out. All of which the perfunctory detective interpreted as an outright confession. That same night, released from the hospital, she'd been summarily arrested for murder. Jacob, sitting in the hospital hallway with Uncle Ezra, wailed and smashed his fist into the wall. His intended target was supposedly some cop who was holding onto Leah, but Jacob, maddened with a welter of confused emotions, missed, bloodying his knuckles on a doorjamb, an inept assault on a police officer that luckily spared him handcuffs and arrest.

That same night Jacob disappeared. Sarah called the police the next morning, saying her nephew hadn't returned home, nor had he taken a suitcase or a change of clothing. The notation on the typed sheet stated, crassly, "Out on a drunk? Drowning his sorrow? Or at Hattie Beeber's brothel?" I imagined the smirk that accompanied such scribbling.

When Jacob was gone for a week, even the cops sat up and paid attention. Another murder perhaps? All in that misguided and hot-tempered family? A call from an old cousin in Bloomington Hills, Michigan, however, let the family know that Jacob had arrived there, distraught and exhausted, the night before. He wouldn't say where he'd been the day before, though his grubby clothing and unshaven, haggard face suggested tenderloin flop-houses and waiting rooms in train stations.

He refused to return. "Dead. Everything's dead there." Jacob's words on the telephone, as recorded.

Uncle Ezra asked Adolph to ride with him to Detroit because Jacob said he'd only speak to Ad. Nothing followed the summary, save a remark that Jacob was finally coaxed to get into the automobile. He returned home.

There was nothing written about the nervous collapse Jacob shortly would experience.

Sarah's comments were routine, cursory, though she seemed to contradict her own statements on her second (and apparently final) interview, the first that afternoon, the second the next morning after being informed of the arrest. I recalled that she'd told me emphatically that she'd *not* been interviewed at all. She'd lied to me. At first she told the police she'd spotted a knife on the hardwood floor, feet from the dead Ivan. But, questioned further, she'd balked—she was so hysterical she *looked* for a knife. After all, Ivan had been stabbed. You could tell from the blood on his neck. On his chest. She swung around. The afternoon light through the curtains, the tilt of sunlight, the shadows. But she was wrong. Of course, she was wrong. As she was quoted, "There was no knife.

We all know that now." She'd also said she'd rushed down the stairs to find her sister standing back from Ivan, just by the kitchen entrance, immobile, facing *her*. That detail was transmogrified within the same interview to Leah's bending over the body, inches away, as though she'd topple onto him. But one fact was consistent both days: Leah said nothing. She stared blankly at a questioning and screaming Sarah—and couldn't speak. Now and then a low moan. The awful silence, the stillness that underscored the horror of the tableau.

Sarah did provide information not in the news accounts nor, obviously, in her brief talk with me. And I wondered how true—or forgotten—that information. She told Detective O'Reilly that she'd been reading upstairs and vaguely heard the front door open. She was asked why not the back door—the door that led to the garden where Leah had been earlier. Or the side kitchen door. Had Leah left for errands? No, Sarah insisted, it was definitely the front door, massive and oak and a little warped, so that it made a dragging sound, a creaking wail. No other door did that, but only on opening it. When you closed it, there was only a quick *pop*. So, she said, she thought maybe someone had entered through the front door. But in her second interview Sarah said she wasn't sure now—it might not have been that afternoon. After all, folks walked in and out all the time. She thought it was that afternoon—but—

I scratched a note on my pad. What was that all about? If true, something very different was evident: someone walked in from outside when Ivan was in the parlor. Through the front door. No knocking or bell ringing. Jacob, returning? Which door had he used earlier? If, indeed, he'd been out earlier. Ivan on the sofa, watching. If true, that person was free to approach Ivan. But who? Leah returning from errands? Wouldn't she have used the kitchen door? Unless she was sitting on the front porch. That was possible. But would the door be shut behind her? Herman? Ella and Emma? Morrie, sneaking away from the butcher shop.

The butcher the baker the candlestick maker…

Sarah, upstairs, waited for the *pop* as the door closed. It never did. The door left open?

The police had found Morrie at his store, surprised at the visit, greeting them in a bloodied apron and gripping the cleaver he'd been using moments before they arrived. No, he told them, he never left the shop. A cup of coffee upstairs, running up, few minutes maybe with his wife there, his counter helper, Manny, still downstairs with customers. Even upstairs he could hear the front door jingle. No, no, Ivan was home sick, yes, no, no, such a busy morning it was, yes. Such a story you tell me now! Oh my God! Let me sit down, collect myself, let me.

Morrie's story, recorded by a transcriber, complete with vaudeville dialect.

Buried deep in the paragraph was a brief mention of Levi Pinsky, described as "Morrie Wolfsy's helper," a man who came out of the back room having eavesdropped on the conversation, and said one thing to the cops, which totally baffled them: "Evil everywhere, you men. Demons. Everywhere the night falls during the daytime." With that, he turned and retreated into the back room.

That made no sense to me.

Morrie had confided to the detective, "Everything that happens can be found in some line from the Torah."

Which made no sense to Detective O'Reilly who noted, "Crazy kike."

Nice touch, I thought, his sorry attempt at alliteration.

I skimmed through the comments by random neighbors who'd gathered on the sidewalk. A half dozen names that meant nothing to me—and offered nothing concrete. But what did startle me were the words offered by Esther and Molly Newmann—not Ad, I noticed—who stepped onto the Brenner lawn that afternoon. Molly, I gleaned from the notes, had considerable nonsense to offer, none of it of value, so labeled by O'Reilly—"An old biddy next door thinks I'm there for coffee and a cruller"—while Esther, described as "the old lady's niece or daughter," kept tugging on Molly's arm, directing her back home. As Leah was led away, Molly muttered, "You reap what you sow," to which Esther, suddenly sobbing, reached out to Leah, trying to lay a comforting hand on her, though she never did. A bad scene, Molly playing Greek chorus to that awful tragedy. And decent Esther, always forgiving, an ineffective antidote to her mother-in-law's nasty and unnecessary homily.

• • ● • •

Back on Monroe Street, fevered, my notepad bursting with jottings, I knocked on Leah's front door. She seemed surprised to see me, wariness in her eyes. Dressed in a shapeless Mother Hubbard, coarse gray, with a white lace shawl thrown casually over her shoulders, she held a book in her hand, clutching it to her chest. Despite the broiling heat of the afternoon, she appeared chilled, her skin pasty, clammy. She'd pulled back her white hair into a careless bun, bound with a red ribbon, but vagrant strands broke free, giving her the look of a wagon-train gypsy.

"Edna," she whimpered, but offered only a cool, distant smile.

"Are you all right?"

She winced, her voice thick. "Has something happened?"

"No, no," I said hurriedly. "Ad told me Jacob is troubled—won't talk to him. Hiding away…"

She motioned me inside, watching the street as I moved by her. A woman expecting to be shadowed, watched, questioned.

"I don't know what to do."

"Is this my fault?" I asked quietly.

She sighed. "I suppose it's all my fault, if you think about it. I did come back home."

"It *is* your home."

Resignedly, "I suppose so. But what that means I no longer know—a roof over our heads, sure, but too many ghosts in the woodwork."

"I'm sorry, Leah, if I hurt you or your family."

"I know you are, Edna." A sigh. "Nothing to be done about it now."

She pointed to a chair, but I didn't sit. "I'm not staying. I'm expected home. I wanted to see about Jacob."

Her eyes brightened. "Thank you."

She was turning away, glancing toward the stairwell. Jacob, upstairs perhaps, listening. Or Sarah, eavesdropping. Ghosts in the woodwork. I longed to question Sarah about her remark to the police about the front door opening, but this wasn't the time. The atmosphere had shifted in the home since my first visit. Then, there'd been warmth, a soft glow to the light, bodies eased into overstuffed armchairs, the tinkle of ice in glasses, conviviality. That was my visit with Leah, of course. My scattered talk with Sarah on the sun porch was a different matter. Now, however, late afternoon shadows swept the parlor, darkening corners, exaggerating the stark light from a solitary lamp switched on in the hallway. A mausoleum, that room—that house. Sarah's gaudy figurines an eerie circus panorama. A crypt in a Gothic romance. Leah sat at the edge of the shadows, most of her face in darkness.

I seemed an intruder now, a violator of a hard-won serenity that was dangerously close to being lost. My fault. Mea culpa. My blame. Edna, who never allowed herself the luxury of guilt—now consumed by it.

My voice choked, I turned to go. "I only wanted to help."

Suddenly Leah grasped my shoulder, made me face her. The move seemed to surprise her as much as it did me, but she spoke tenderly, a catch in the back of her throat. "You've done nothing wrong, Edna."

My head turned toward the stairwell. Jacob

and Sarah, up there, listening. The hum of a radio. "But…"

She was rocking me gently, a mother's soothing grip. "Nothing. You don't think I wondered all those years? You don't think I felt blessed when you stepped onto my porch that day?"

Tears escaped the corners of my eyes. "This can't have an happy ending."

"Nothing in my life will ever have a happy ending, Edna. It can't be, not now. Not after all these years." She let go of me. "All I ask is that it have…an ending."

● ● ● ● ●

The Newmann kitchen was alive with preparations for supper as I walked in. My mother was peering into a huge pot of boiling water, preparing to drop in handmade rolled egg noodles. Esther sat at the table, dicing burgundy-red beets into thick fleshy slices, her fingertips tinged red. Molly, leaning against a counter, her cane resting at her hip, was breading chicken legs, dipping the pieces into egg and then rolling them in the flour. A deep-dish apple pie, heavy with the smell of grated cinnamon and nutmeg, sat on a wire pie rack, cooling, tantalizing. They'd been chatting amiably, but they stopped, almost on stage cue, as I banged through the back screen door.

"Edna," my mother said, "we expected you hours ago."

"Research downtown." I told the truth.

"Truck farms in High Prairie? The Dutch farmers?"

I nodded, dumbly, but I said to Molly who held up flour-coated hands, "I didn't know you and Esther spoke to the police the day Ivan died."

My mother groaned, ready to explode, but Molly squinted at Esther, puzzled. "So? All the neighbors did. We stood on the front lawn, watching." A pause. "And how did you know that?"

"You were quoted in the police report. Lots of people were."

Molly stared, unfriendly. "And what did I say?"

"In Leah's yard. 'Reap what you sow.'"

Suddenly the three women exchanged looks, a gurgle rising from Esther's throat, and then they burst out laughing. Though I had no idea why, I joined in, that infectious community of women sharing some laughter in the steamy kitchen. "*What?*" I manage to say. "What?"

Esther had tears in her eyes. "Molly *always* says that. To Sol, even now. To Adolph and Harriet when they were little babies. To me." The corners of her mouth twitched. "Especially to me."

"Wisdom for the ages," Molly added, nodding.

"Perhaps you should heed it, Edna." She glanced at my mother, nodding back at her.

I got serious. "But why hurl it at Leah that afternoon? She was a stricken woman."

Molly was perplexed. "If I remember correct, I was saying it to Sarah. Leah was already gone. Not to Leah."

Now that made no sense. Leah, the rumored adulteress. Leah, the murderer. Leah, the neighborhood leper. Sarah, the skittish spinster sister.

"But why Sarah?"

Molly waited a heartbeat. "Well, I suppose it *was* for Leah, a shameless harlot. But they were already carrying her off. Sarah was standing there, a snippy look on her face that said to me: Get off my lawn. This is not your affair. I don't *like* you."

Esther faced me. "Molly and Sarah have had long clashes over the backyard fence."

Molly pouted. "She once accused me of being a yenta. A busybody. That Sarah was always a brat. Leah was the pretty flower, vacant as an abandoned house, so far as I was concerned. But Sarah, she was like sandpaper against my skin. 'Mind your own business,' she says to me. She complained about me to Herman who talked to me. Said he'd send the rabbi to talk to me. Imagine that! Him and his wife, Naomi, that dreadful cold fish. Both of them

are like Sarah, a form of life best left under rocks."
She smiled maliciously. "So *there!*"

"I didn't know this," I said. "The feud between
the Newmanns and the Brenners. The Hatfields
and the McCoys."

"No feud," Esther insisted. "Leah had coffee
with me at this table. She was my friend—one of
the few I had."

"Against my wishes," Molly said. She banged
the cane against the cupboard door. *Tap tap tap.*

"Sarah also suffered that day—what she had
to see, no?" asked Esther.

Molly would have none of it. "She put her
two cents in. That's why I tried to catch her eye
on the porch."

"What are you talking about?"

Molly covered the platter of floured chicken
and then rinsed her hands in the sink. The cane
rattled to the floor as Esther rushed to pick it up.

"Edna, that bruising fight that morning.
Above Ivan's yelling and Leah's wailing there'd be
Sarah's voice yelling, 'Stop!' or 'Just stop!' It was
almost comical—like a child trying to stop a speed-
ing train."

"You never mentioned Sarah as part of that
fight."

Molly shrugged. "I told the police."

"It isn't in the report."

Molly's voice cracked. "That ain't my fault." She paused. "I must have told them."

Now Esther spoke up, befuddled. "Molly dear, you *never* heard Sarah then. This is the first time I'm hearing about it."

The old woman teetered a second, squinted. Now she deliberated. "Or was it another time?" She tossed her head back. "What does it matter now?"

"It does confuse the story," I said.

"Edna, you're being ridiculous. I can't remember *everything*."

Ad opened the screen door and walked into the kitchen, Molly wagged a finger at him. "You're late."

"I didn't know I was expected." He kissed Molly on the cheek.

His mother poured him a glass of lemonade, which he gulped down. "Adolph," she asked him, "tell Edna about the fight Leah and Ivan had that morning."

He rolled his eyeballs. "Didn't we have this talk before? A thousand times? Is this the only story left in the world?"

"Your grandmother now says Sarah kept telling them to stop." She waited.

"What are you talking about?"

Molly jumped in. "It's no big deal, dear. I recall

Sarah stepping in and trying to end it. We all heard her, no? She yelled 'Stop!'"

Ad started to walk across the room. "I didn't." He smiled at Molly. "Are you sure? We talked about it, you and me, as we went shopping. That was *all* we talked about. That I remember. I know their house was quiet when we walked by—the fight over with, but…no, Sarah was not part of it. This is the first I'm hearing about it." A heartbeat. "What is this all about?"

"I must be losing my memory." She lifted a dishcloth off the platter of chicken to inspect her work. "It was a brutal fight, those *two*."

"Do we gotta relive it all over again?" Ad complained. "Didn't it color too much of our life? Days afterwards, horrible. The world turned upside down. Maybe if I'd gone over there, that day… wouldn't have happened."

Molly cried out, "Oh, Lord no. I didn't want you anywhere near that craziness. Ivan would have turned on you. Leah waving that knife… You could have been…" She stopped, her voice shaky. "You could have been *hurt*." Her voice shook. "Exhausting it was, listening. Then, later on, Sarah crying out like that. To wake the dead, that woman's screams. I can still hear it. I woke from my nap and thought the screaming was here—in this house. I thought somebody—my Esther—fell, maybe—hurt. I rushed across the hall and pounded on Adolph's door."

"And scared me half to death. You yelled, 'Something happened to your mama.'" He shook his head. "But I knew it was Sarah, I could hear her myself."

Molly's lips quivered. "Everything changed then. Everything. Leah, that harlot…"

Esther *tsk*ed, glanced at Adolph as though he were five and not forty. "Now, now."

"That woman." Molly smiled. "I was right what I said then. You do reap what you sow. So many times I was convinced that Ivan would kill Leah. He had such a temper, that man. A husband made a fool of. Sooner or later he'd kill her. She drove him to it. That woman was too…alluring. You gotta know—that beautiful woman was a curse on both our houses."

Chapter Fifteen

Another Saturday afternoon on Monroe Street, the pavement breathing its silence. Shops closed, doors shut, no distant sounds of two-wheel pushcart vendors drifting over from Maxwell Street. A family in black moved down the center of the street, headed to shul. Mostly the street was silent, deserted under a white hot July sun, heat waves rippling above the pavement. A toddler squealed in its mother's arms. A street that watched and sighed under a day meant for God.

By myself, I strolled the empty streets after lunch, listening to the bark of a chained dog or the sudden blare of an unreligious horn or the profane violation of a husband and wife spat or the hint of the passing Illinois Central.

Back home at mid-afternoon, I found Sol Newmann sitting on the front porch with Ezra Brenner. That gave me pause. But of course they knew each other, friends from years back. But not exactly the friendliness of two old men leisurely smoking cigars on a hot afternoon—Ezra sat upright, one hand holding the arm of the chair as though ready to flee. Although his posture might have been the result of spotting me strolling up the sidewalk.

I cringed. How I disliked the man, especially after that unnerving altercation the other day as he tried to drag an unwilling Jacob into his automobile.

Sol waved to me, cheerful. "Edna, you disappeared after lunch."

"A walk through the quiet streets."

Sol continued, "My favorite day on Monroe. You can almost hear the prayers in folks' houses."

Ezra frowned at him. "Sol, you're not a religious man."

"No, Ezra," Sol answered, a smile on his face. "And you're not a religious man. No decent Jew wears such a tie on Shabbas."

For, indeed, Ezra, dressed in a sharp-pressed gray linen suit, sported the most ostentatious turquoise tie and accompanying handkerchief. With his black-and-white shoes and snappy spats, his white hair under a summer straw sailor hat, he resembled a barker from a rag-tag Punch-and-Judy revue.

Ezra laughed. "Jealousy is an awful thing."

"Are you visiting next door?" I asked him. I waited a second. "And found no one at home?"

"Edna, with such a tart tongue you'll not find a husband."

"Then I need to employ my tongue even more than I do now."

Ezra leaned into Sol. "Ah, the modern woman, Sol. Bicycles and lawn tennis and Camel cigarettes and dance slippers and…and miscast votes."

But Ezra was through with the banter, bored, his eye watching the street. "I wondered if Ad has had any luck?" A question to Sol. Again, the sweep of the sleepy street.

Sol followed his eyes. "Poor Jacob."

I moved closer, panicked. "What happened?"

Sol made a dismissive wave of his hand. "The lad wanders. You know that."

Ezra fretted, tapping his cigar against the rail of the chair. "As you know, poor Jacob, distressed over the latest turn of events"—with this, he narrowed his baleful eye at me, registering blame where he supposed it to be—"has pretty much hidden in his room, even cold-shouldering Ad. I thought I'd drive over to take him for a spin." He sucked in his breath. "I seem to be the only one he'll talk to. Even poor Leah finds herself excluded. But he'd—fled."

"Ad went searching for him?"

Sol spoke softly. "I sent him. We think maybe

Jacob went to visit with an old school friend, Sy Bloom, over to Roosevelt Boulevard. Ad, too, old friends from school, but years ago. Sy calls now and then. A wild goose chance, we figures, but why not?"

"We got to do something," Ezra said.

"I never knew what was wrong with that boy." Sol shook his head.

Ezra was nodding. "A lad who never had roots, that one. An adventurer."

Yes, I thought: an adventurer who never stepped away from his father's home, the middle-aged man who wrote one poem in a magazine and then drifted through five or six streets, this adventurer who now hid in his mother's house. Hardly the circumnavigating hero headed around the world. A man committed to nothing, though he wrestled with demons inside that no one took seriously or, at worst, ever even noticed. Poor Jacob, indeed.

"So you're worried?" I asked Ezra who was doing his best to act friendly toward me, a plastered-on smile covering his features, though his eyes were wary, distrustful,

"Of course. It's as though the murder of Ivan happened yesterday. It's an open wound with him, that emotional, that..." He hesitated.

"That unanswered," I finished for him.

A flash of anger in his eyes. "So you say. Poor

Jacob talks like a crazy man, colorful nonsense. He acts like a…" His voice trailed off.

A shock to the system, that sputtered sentence, because at that moment, like a wallop, I experienced an epiphany: Ezra feared that Jacob in his confused, rambling state would *say* something. But what? A confession? Or something else? Maybe something about Ezra? Or someone else? Staring at Ezra, the polished mannequin so shallow and decadent and *fin de siècle*, I realized that he might believe Jacob was, in fact, the murderer. He wanted to shield him—or shut him up—or…or what? To silence him.

All along I'd felt Jacob had something to say but perhaps didn't realize what it was. Now, more than ever, I was convinced of it. Something crucial, deadly.

"…a murderer?" I finished for him.

"No," he stumbled. "God, no!" His voice broke as he hurriedly went on. "Edna, no one seriously considered Morrie Wolfsy, the disgruntled partner, the smarmy…seducer. Did you know that the day before—the day *before*, let me repeat—Morrie waved a cleaver at Ivan? They were at each other's throats, and Ivan got so scared he hid in the small bathroom in the back room. He locked himself in. All the time he's yelling, 'Help! Help! Call the police!' While in front Morrie is waiting on customers lined up, weighing out a pound of lean beef, some rib-eye steaks. A customer told me this later, of course. Customers were lined up, and Ivan in back hollering 'Help! Help!' It was almost comical, really, some zany skit out of a Yiddisher nickel show."

"What happened?" asked Sol, fascinated.

"Nothing, it turns out. They always fought, even before the…the thing with Leah. A half hour later, calmed down, Ivan opened the locked door, stumbled out, and got behind the poultry counter. 'May I help you, Mrs. Rabinowitz?' he says to the next in line. 'A good-looking bird, plump, this one, the best, look at this wonder.'"

"Then why do you say they should consider Morrie as a murderer? If, in fact, they entertained each other with these little spats."

Ezra drew in his cheeks. "Because Morrie never took them seriously, but Ivan *started* to. He *did*. Near the end. A game to Morrie, the customers even laughing, but after Leah and the nonsense there was a look in Ivan's eyes—and at the end Morrie saw it. The violence under the chitchat. Hair-trigger moments. Sooner or later…"

I wasn't happy. "Based on what? All the police information puts Morrie solidly in the shop that morning."

Ezra scoffed. "Yeah, that reliable witness, Levi Pinsky."

"Do you know anything?"

Ezra stood. "I told you everything I know."

And with that, positioning his hat on his head, adjusting it carefully, and putting out the cigar in an ashtray, he nodded at Sol but not at me, and stepped off the porch.

• • ● • •

That night, long after sundown, the heat of the day making the air sticky and close, I left by the kitchen door, skirted by the Brenner yard—there was only one light switched on, at the back of the house—and strolled up the block toward Maxwell. People sat on front stoops, fanning themselves. A few children ran after balls in the street, though such activity was listless. The whole street seemed to sweat, to wilt. Ad had never returned home, so I didn't know if he'd located Jacob. An automobile squealed by, Ezra with the top down, elbow resting on the open window ledge, a cigarette drooping from the corner of his mouth. Coming from Leah's? Searching for Jacob? I doubted that—the preening peacock. I disliked the fact that such a dissembling, devious weasel could so infuriate me.

A light flickered in the front room of Nathan's Meat Market, the door propped open, and I expected to see a doddering Levi Pinsky issuing a proclamation rescinding woman suffrage, scribing his diatribe on a piece of ragged linen cut from a five-cent tattered trouser leg.

Sitting quietly in the center of the room, leafing through a stack of papers under an overhead naked light bulb, was an old woman, eyeglasses slipping off her snub nose. I was staring, true, surprised, but she stared back, then raised a welcoming hand in the air.

"Edna Ferber." Harsh, bold, her voice dropping.

I started. "Why, yes."

"My husband described you perfectly."

"I can imagine…"

"Late thirties, sallow skin, short, reedy, a nose from one of the lost tribes, and a hayfield bonnet of wiry hair."

"How attractive."

She grinned. "Morrie is not a nice man. And never to women, unless they're beautiful and in need of money."

"You're his wife, I take it."

"A badge of dishonor I refuse to relinquish, don't ask me why."

"Why?" I asked, stupefied.

Her eyes got wide, not amused.

She was a smallish woman with a little girl's bony frame, four-feet-five if she exaggerated, thin papery arms and neck, so scant they resembled twigs, breakable; a face lined with deep wrinkles that nearly eclipsed the small nickel-sized round eyes, as metallic as dull silver. A homely woman, one who'd never been pretty, but a woman who, with advancing age and teeth-clenching grit, had become doggedly handsome, like a piece of ancient statuary rusted and weathered in a forgotten park. The patina of forgotten silverware. As I watched, she simply dropped the stack of papers to the floor where they scattered, some sliding under the chair she sat on. She shrugged and ignored them.

"I'm Selma Wolfsy. You gathered that already. You're smart. At least you're smart enough to realize that Leah Brenner never killed Ivan."

That shocked me.

"You know that, too?"

"Of course." She smiled at me.

"But you never told the police."

She roared in a thick, whiskey voice, ending by coughing into the back of her wrist. "What do I know? Do you think I have evidence? I'm talking common sense here."

"Then who…?"

She groaned. "Oh, please don't ask me that. You've probably bored everyone on Monroe Street with that tired, unanswerable question. Do you really expect an answer from one of the crowd around these parts? Everyone naming Leah but secretly pointing to their least favorite person. A wink—look at *him*. Look, look. It's bad enough my husband thinks you're planning to pin the murder on him—the fool—an idea whispered by our own resident misanthrope, Levi Pinsky, who fears he might actually touch my hand by accident some-day—so Morrie spends his waking hours hiding upstairs and running from you."

"Does he have anything to hide?"

She laughed and wagged a finger at me. "Dear, we all have things to hide. By the time you're my age—I'm seventy next month—you'll probably be annoyingly famous and hated by most folks you've skewered in your writing, and living alone, hiding your loneliness with wisecracks."

A beat. "I do that now."

"So you found your destiny early, young lady. Good for you."

"Why are you sitting here alone?"

She waved a hand around the room. "I want to sell this firetrap. I've been begging Morrie for years since he closed up shop. I rarely come here. But I had to sort through some delinquent leases. Apartments we own. The Russians we rent to make believe they can't read English. They're all hiding in shul today, of course. Morrie is visiting someone over on Canal. He'll be back in a bit." She grinned.

"You better not be here, Edna Ferber. You'd hate to see an old sickly man topple over in fear, right?"

"Will Morrie sell?"

"Morrie is a sentimental fool. He remembers with affection the old days, the rough-and-tumble off-the-boat days, the romance of being poor in squalid houses. He holds onto the old ball of string that tied his first rump roast together. Lord! I'm a practical woman. I like my new kitchen with the electric refrigerator and the electric stove and…and my green lawn and sycamore trees. Even if Morrie comes with the package."

"A loving marriage."

She watched me closely. "Sarcasm is unattractive in a young woman. In an old woman it's sometimes all we have left."

I leaned against the doorjamb. "You don't care for him?"

"Of course I do. I love him. It's just that I've never *forgiven* him."

"For Leah Brenner?"

She grunted. "You don't know the half of it."

"Tell me."

A harsh, unfriendly grin. "You *are* a public nuisance, my dear. The rumors about you don't do your peskiness justice. In other centuries they'd have burned you at the stake. To thunderous applause, I'd say." She laughed at her own joke.

"Leah Brenner. Ah, where do I begin? A woman born to woo ships into the rocky harbors. Not her fault, you'll say. Let me ask and answer all the questions here. Well, that's true, but it's no great consolation for a plain Jane like me. Or, sad to say, you, my dear. We're the scraggly ragweed growing on the side of the road, wild-blown, dusty, as the speeding roadsters sail past with Lorelei with her red lipstick cooing in the driver's ear."

"You can't just blame a woman. A man—your man—is part of the equation."

She shook her head back and forth. "And don't I know it, but I can still condemn Leah. Look, dear Edna Ferber, Leah was only one, maybe the last, of a series of women over the years. Some I closed my eyes to, others I confronted. Leah was one frivolous afternoon, a second in time. Nothing happened. There were so many others—a week, a month, so long as Morrie had nickels and dimes for the nickelodeon—or an evening at Haverley's Minstrels followed by supper at Gold's. Cheap girls, all spangled up and shiny under a streetlight. He destroyed our marriage years ago, but Leah was off-limits. She was the partner's wife. Ivan's wife. Lord, there have to be some boundaries, no? You can't be friends with a woman who looks—*looked*—I mean, she's an old woman now—like *that*."

"She suffered a horrible fate—for a murder I

don't believe she did. But to accuse her because she was beautiful…"

Sharp, angry. "Who cares? C'mon. Who cares?" A sliver of a smile. "I actually met her a few days after Ivan unearthed—is that the word?—the tawdry moment, the kiss heard round the shul? She was shopping with sour Sarah of the salt mines. That unhappy woman. Leah approached me, brazen, and apologized. Can you believe that? Her arms filled with packages, the dutiful *hausfrau*, shopping for Shabbas supper, and she gets teary-eyed and begs forgiveness. I turned away."

I swallowed. "But it must have pained her. It took courage to do that."

"Sarah stood there with a smirk on her face. A big joke to her. Laughing at me."

"But Leah wasn't laughing."

For a second she closed her eyes. "Everyone in the neighborhood was. A disgraced woman—*me*. Not her. I kept away from shul for a month. 'Here's the prune-faced wife. How sad! How horrible! Married to a squat, spindly Lothario with loose coins jangling in his pockets.'"

"You stayed married to Morrie to make him pay?"

A slow, lazy grin made the old wrinkled face contort. "Now, at last, you understand the whole story."

I shuddered. "I wouldn't be you for a million dollars."

"I agree. I wouldn't be me for a million dollars."

I glanced toward the back room, jerked my head in that direction. "All the fantasies and foolishness that came to life in that room. Men with their games. What happened in there, I believe, was the hotbed that ended with the murder of Ivan. Something those men never expected."

She followed my gaze. "A no man's land. A dump. But you're right. The men schmoozed and planned lives they never got 'round to leading… fantasies that couldn't be realized or—or…"

"Or had dreams that had no hope. Women breathe hope into men's souls. We temper men's folly."

She chortled. "Ah, a feminist. I should have suspected it. The New Woman. Susan B. Anthony casting off her ritual wig."

"You sound bitter."

"Actually, I'm not. I'm enjoying this conversation. You're tremendously innocent of things."

I bristled. "You make innocence sound childish."

"And it isn't?"

She stood, tired of the talk, and glanced at the wall clock. "Morrie is late." She was peering into the back room, dark now, the door half-shut. "What a pigsty. If we sell the place—if I twist his arm enough—it'll take a month to clear out those shelves and cubbyholes. Can you imagine if it caught fire? A fire you could see from the rim of hell."

I stood beside her. "Lucky you."

She faced me. "It always surprises me that someone *wanted* to break in there."

I started. "In the back room? What?"

She laughed pleasantly. "For a nosy detective, you sure miss a lot, Edna Ferber. No one told you? On the same day Ivan was stabbed to death, maybe around eight that night, dark out, someone pried open the back door. Morrie and I were away, maybe at the police station, I don't know. But when we got back the door was smashed. The latch…"

"What was taken?" I broke in, eagerly.

"A small tin box with some change was emptied. The box was knocked onto the floor. Maybe five dollars in quarters, nickels, dimes. Nothing. Pocket change."

"Nothing else? Was anything moved around?"

"Hard to tell. Back then, especially, it was the same disgusting pile."

"Did the police investigate?"

She narrowed her eyes. "Well, somebody came out. But keep in mind Ivan's murder got more attention than some petty burglary. There were other break-ins in the neighborhood that summer.

The police thought it was just one more. Some youngsters, bored, daring."

I rushed my words. "But didn't the police make any connection with Ivan's murder? The same day, a break-in at his store? It seems to me…"

Her hand in my face. "For Lord's sake, Edna, you do take wonderful leaps of imagination. By that time they'd already condemned Leah to perdition. Based on what—I'll never understand." She smiled. "A body and someone standing over it. Case closed."

"But…" I stammered. I wanted to yell: madness, this investigation. Something happened that night, yet no one decided to add one and one to get two.

"Pittance, Edna. Change. I don't see how you are connecting those dots. It would be one thing if we stepped on a bloody knife, conspiratorially dropped onto the floor. Or lifted a bloody shirt. Follow a line of bloody footprints out the front door. Or upstairs. Evidence pointing to Morrie. It was nickels and dimes. Hardly a pirate's booty."

"Somebody wanted to get inside that back room, and it had to do with the murder."

"Preposterous." She stepped away. "Enough. Really." She headed to the front door but shot a glance back at me. "So, my dear, what have we concluded?" The gravelly, irreverent laugh. "Have I given you the answer you need?"

"I'm thinking about that break-in."

Her eyes flickered. "You think it had to do with the murder?"

I didn't answer her.

"Now you're trying to scare me." Her voice was hollow.

I shook my head back and forth. "I don't think that's possible."

Chapter Sixteen

Late the following morning Esther walked in from watering the flowers on the front porch, a puzzled look on her face. She held up a long white envelope, sealed. "*Vos iz dos*? For you, Edna dear. And no stamp on it. Dropped onto the porch. How odd." The envelope simply said "Edna Ferber" in thick black ink that had smudged at the edges. "A mash note?" A twinkle in her eye.

I took it from her. "More likely a death threat."

But those were poorly chosen words because Esther drew in her breath and scrunched up her face.

"I'm joking, Esther."

"I hope you are, Edna. I don't understand today's humor. You young folks."

Sitting across the table, spreading boysenberry jam on some toast, my mother quipped, "This new generation of young women refuses to be humorous."

"No, Mother," I answered back, "we just refuse to be humored."

Perversely, I declined to open the envelope, though both women insisted I do so. Molly, hobbling in, wondered what the fuss was about. Told of the note, she gave me an in-my-day-no-respectable-girl look that left nothing unsaid about decorum and civility and suspect missives dropped casually onto a fair maiden's doorstep.

Back in my room, hurriedly, I ripped opened the envelope. What I found intrigued me: a yellowing piece of paper, typescript on one side, and neat penmanship on the back. It was, bizarrely, from Jacob, though I was baffled why he chose to drop it onto the front porch.

"Edna," it began. "It came to me—at last—about years ago. I finally remember you. I was cruel." Below that:

> *Edna, Edna, sugar and spice,*
> *An orchid locked in frozen ice.*
> *Edna, Edna,*
> *Not nice—*

Dramatically he'd drawn a huge "X" through that bit of old childish doggerel, and below it wrote:

> *Edna, Edna*
> *Let's hope I'm wrong.*

When I sing you a comrade song
That goes on too long.
Edna Edna
Here's some advice
An orchid in ice
Please be nice.

And below it, separate from the silly verse, were two words in bold block letters:

TO ME!
Please be nice to me!

At the bottom he also scrawled: "This is the first poem I've written in seven years."

Hardly poetry, I thought. Not exactly a love-smitten Robert Browning writing to (and wooing?) the frail and welcoming Elizabeth Barrett. The scribbling was, frankly, unsettling.

None of this made sense, except as indications of Jacob's disturbed state of mind. Jacob, playing a game. Jacob, groping along in some darkness he'd fallen into.

Jacob's mind taking him back to the past—and remembering me. Finally. But also, I wondered, what other bits and pieces of the past were at last surfacing in his mind these days.

The paper crackled in my hand like opening an old letter, long stowed away in a drawer, brittle. On the back I found what was obviously an old poem from the days when he listened to some poetic muse. Poorly typed, under the title "Poem," with cross-outs, hatched lines, a fading typescript read:

> *The movement of my mother*
> *Suddenly turning in her beautiful flesh*
> *Makes us watch*
> *Stars move through untouched heavens*
> *And the boys gather from the street:*
> *She lifts pots from the stove*
> *And licorice from the cabinets.*
> *In summer she sees them to their end.*
> *I shouldn't be here, this moment—*
> *Lapping tongues that mock.*
> *Not my fault.*
> *Even the dead know more than I do.*

I reread the old words—a rough draft? Rambling, confused, and, for some reason, I thought of Stephen Crane's stark, enigmatic verse, which always intrigued me, though I never liked it. Was it an accident, Jacob's choosing this old sheet of paper with that particular poem in order to pen the doggerel intended for me? Who knew?

What was he telling me?

Jacob worried me. I watched for him to leave his house. I drifted to the side windows overlooking the Brenner yard, or read on the front porch, or glanced out my bedroom window late at night, unable to sleep. I waited, holding my breath.

Which, surprisingly, was how I finally spotted him: at midnight, the houses and street silent as dust.

Just after midnight, as I sat reading by a small table lamp, unable to sleep, I noticed a light switched on at the back of the Brenner house—on for a minute or so and then extinguished. I switched off my own light and peered outside, where I noticed a faint shadow moving out from the back steps, someone leisurely walking around the side of the house toward the street. A man, I could tell from the build. Jacob Brenner, obviously. The erstwhile poet wandering under a hazy moonlit sky.

Hurriedly, foolishly, I threw on my robe over my dressing gown, tied a sash at the waist, and quietly, cat-like, opened my bedroom door, closed it carefully, and moved down the stairs. The old house creaked and moaned with night noises, the labored breathing of old boards, so my careful footfall on the oak stairs produced a few groans and sighs as I walked. I wasn't certain of my behavior. Certainly I could never follow the nomadic man through Chicago streets at this unseemly hour, especially dressed for bed and unchaperoned by my dowager mother. Yet curiosity overwhelmed me. The front door squeaked as I opened it, so I paused, waiting. No one in the house stirred. Molly probably popped awake—but so be it. The rest of the household sound sleepers, I trusted—as I usually was.

Though the night remained unrelentingly hot, a slight chill made me shiver. Nights in Chicago usually shuddered under the wind that came off Lake Michigan. Even in the dog days of summer, boiling, no one could forget the awful power of any Chicago winter. So now I shivered, drew in my robe tighter, and huddled in a corner of the porch. Silence: no one visible. Jacob Brenner, disappeared.

Gingerly, in violation of all I considered proper, I walked down the steps, surreptitiously secreting myself behind an overgrown bank of hedges, and peered up the block. Not an automobile, not a soul in sight. The darkness was relieved at regular intervals by fuzzy streetlamps. Dim lights in some apartments, here and there. A tomcat disappeared under a car fender. But mostly blackness on this quiet, respectable street of hard-working lives. The streetlamp in front of the Brenner house cast blocks of yellow onto the pavement.

Moving in the middle of the street, slowly, dully, was Jacob's shadow. From my hidden spot, I could discern his lanky figure moving, moving, moving, and steady, with purpose. At the corner where Monroe met Maxwell, he stopped, conveniently under a streetlamp. A tiny figure now, almost difficult to see, except for the movement of arms that waved at nothing in particular. He stopped directly in front of Nathan's Meat Market—that lodestar at the heart of his papa's murder. He stood there for a long time, though perhaps it was but minutes, and soon I saw the ghostly silhouette headed back.

Quietly, I slipped into the house, tiptoed into the parlor where I stood by the front window, concealed in darkness, my hand pulling back the curtains. Within seconds, Jacob reappeared, still in the middle of the street, as though savoring the exquisite freedom of a city street with no automobiles, no bustling strollers, no noontime yelling and rattling.

Yet he danced around, loose-limbed, a marionette freed from the confining strings, because he swirled, stepped left, stepped right, a tap dance on the pavement. I heard—or imagined I heard—a humming, or was it a plaintive keening coming from his throat?

He stopped, stooped down, hunched over, and rocked on his heels. He stared at his dark home. Silent now, arms folded on his chest. He was waiting for something. But what?

Then he moved quickly. I jerked back in the parlor, gasped as I bumped a table, a box falling to the floor with an loud thud. Energized, he walked toward the Newmann home. Had he spotted me on the porch earlier? Had he caught my reflection in the window, a shadow caught by moonlight and flickering street lamp?

He stopped in front of the house—directly in front of the window where I stood, paralyzed now, helpless to move. As I held my breath, he crouched down again, the same frog-like stance he'd assumed before his own home. Now, rocking like a children's play toy, he stared at the Newmann home and I feared he'd be there all night, with me—the nosy investigator—afraid to shift my body lest he catch sight of me. Dawn would find Jacob still on watch, and my mother would discover her wayward daughter wrapped in a parlor curtain like a pesky servant spying on the household.

I waited.

But of course Jacob finally moved, standing, nodding as though waking from a dream, and walking home. No jerky movement now, no flailing of arms, no *danse macabre*. Simply a man strolling home without a care in the world.

I slipped into an armchair and realized I was breathing heavily, my heart pounding. Good Lord, I thought, what was that midnight romp all about? What demons drew poor Jacob from his hot bed and compelled that midnight trek?

My mind sailed to the scrap of doggerel he'd

sent me—a message? Trivial, a lingering vestige of the old, flirtatious Jacob? The ladies' man, Romeo, the foolish gigolo. But then I thought of the poem on the back, that dark poem to his mother, the neighborhood cynosure of the hungry boys, and that haunting last line:

Even the dead know more than I do.

The dead? His father? For, indeed, his father knew his assailant. Yes, I thought: Ivan let the killer come near. No stranger, of course, that killer. Someone free to approach him, to bend over and stab the man to death. A knife to the neck. A curious place to strike—as if by chance, anger, confusion. Unpremeditated?

Ivan knew his killer. And well.

At that moment, I guessed that Jacob knew the name of the killer.

• • ● • •

A police car pulled in front of the Brenner household, and the street held its breath. Late afternoon, a lazy and sweltering day, I sat on the front porch with my mother, Esther, and Molly, scarcely moving, nursing tart lemon phosphates and saying little. Too hot for conversation. Earlier Molly had asked me what I was doing roaming around the house late last night. "I recognized your steps in the parlor. Something dropped on the floor—knocked me wide awake."

"Sleepless," I'd told her. "The heat."

Still eying me suspiciously, she dozed off, a whisper of a snore coming from the back of her throat. Every so often a passing car—a horn tooting or an explosive backfire—would startle her and she'd open her eyes, surprised to see the rest of us staring at her. Esther was talking in a weary drawl about the wilting of her petunias alongside the front steps.

My mother pointed. "Look."

The policemen stepped from the squad car, adjusted their trousers, and one shifted his body and nodded to the other.

Roused, excited, Molly wanted to walk to the Brenner home, but Esther, alarmed, held up her hand: No, please, no. Not our business. No.

Within minutes the front door opened and the two lawmen escorted Leah and Sarah out.

Molly made a rasping sound and shook her head. "What new black spot is that woman bringing to our street?"

Esther stared her down. "Really, now, Molly."

I walked to the edge of the porch, quietly watching. What I saw told me that this was no arrest. The police walked alongside the two women, one of them leaning into Leah's neck, saying something. But the way he held his body—the tilt of his neck, the way he held onto Leah's elbow—suggested comfort, solace.

And Leah looked shattered, drawn, stooped over, an old dragging woman. None of the vibrancy or spunk I'd seen in her before. Even Sarah, stone-faced with her head thrown back, her fingers gripping a handkerchief, seemed unusually solicitous, her hand touching Leah's lower back. That rare display of intimacy scared me more than the policeman's reassuring touch. Sarah, the woman with sass and vinegar, her sister's harsh critic, now lending comfort.

It had to do with Jacob. I felt it to my core. Standing there, I trembled.

Then, like that, they were gone.

Molly's craggy, lined face was ghostly, white. The life of the street had shifted again, and she knew it to her marrow. The new twist on old news. When I turned to Esther, she was sobbing.

• • ● • •

We knew nothing until later that evening when Ad, ashen and shaky, walked into the house. Sol, home from the cigar store, was the first to approach him, his hand grazing his son's shoulder.

"My boy," Sol said, his voice a rumble. We stood, all of us, to greet him, panicked.

Ad pulled out a kitchen chair and toppled into it.

"Ad…" his mother said anxiously.

He was shaking.

"Jacob?" More my statement than a question.

He nodded, his eyes moist.

"He's dead?" From Esther.

"Thank God, no." Ad smiled thinly at his mother. "But he's hospitalized. He's unconscious. In a coma."

"Tell us," I demanded.

Across from me my mother sat with her eyes closed.

Ad sighed. He didn't know where to begin, a run of incoherent speech, a voice so soft that his mother nudged him quietly. "Please, Adolph. I don't understand."

His voice cracked. "I heard it on the street so I stopped back at their house. Leah was at the hospital but Sarah had come home." He sucked in his breath, his words broken. "Sarah told me the horrible news."

"Is he going to be all right?" Real concern in Molly's voice. "That poor boy."

Ad deliberated. "I don't know."

"But what happened?" I begged. "Jacob doesn't leave the house. He hides away." Except nights, midnight ghosts in the deserted street. The dancing shadow silhouetted against a white-hot sky.

"Uncle Ezra got real worried. He stopped in but Jacob refused to see him." A sad smile. "The same with me, his oldest friend. Shutting us out. Going a little crazy, maybe. But Ezra kept at him, even banging on Jacob's bedroom door. He talked to Jacob, whispering through the door, demanding, according to what Leah told Sarah. Leah told Ezra to leave him alone. But he convinced Jacob to go with him. Leah, rushing in from the kitchen, saw them speeding off in Ezra's car."

"How did Jacob look?" I asked.

He shrugged. "She only saw them leaving. She was surprised—and bothered. She doesn't trust Uncle Ezra."

"No one does," I commented. "Too oily a confection."

"Edna, for Lord's sake." My mother cast a baleful eye on me.

I wasn't happy and drummed my fingers on the table. Ad's eyes watched my nervous hand, mesmerized. "Jacob had something to say," I told him. "I'm convinced of it. Ezra wanted him to keep still."

"How do you know that?" Ad asked.

"I don't."

My mother *tsk*ed. "Edna, please stay out of this."

Impatient, I cut in. "Tell us what happened."

"Well, Ezra's version."

"He was there?"

Ad bit his lip. "Right there. He was trying to shake Jacob out of his blue spell, afraid there'd be another period of…of depression, so he breezed around the streets with Jacob, out to the lake, stopping at a chop suey place on Thirty-first Street, stopping for ice cream at Nathan's Ice Cream Parlor, even going to a movie at the Vista up on Forty-third Street. Weird, he said, the way Jacob acted there. They saw *Within the Law*, you know, the Norma Talmadge movie. I saw it last week with Minna. Halfway through the movie, Jacob got agitated, jumping up. He left the theater and Ezra followed him. Outside Jacob said the movie put salt in the wound he'd already opened."

"I don't know that movie," I said. "Tell me."

Ad volunteered. "It's about this girl, Mary Turner, a shop girl at this emporium, falsely charged with stealing, a trumped-up charge. She's sent to jail for three years—even though she's innocent. She didn't *do* it. Maybe the scene where she gets out of prison got Jacob all riled up. She wants revenge, but within the law, the people that did her dirt paying for it—but make them pay in a way she couldn't be touched. Anyway, Jacob ran away from Ezra, up the street, pushing through the crowd, bumping into folks, rude, staggering, loud. Ezra says he caught up with him, grabbed hold of Jacob's shoulder, trying to hold him back, maybe calm him down, but Jacob shrugged him off. 'Stay away from me. All of you.' That's what Ezra said he kept yelling. Embarrassed, folks staring at them, Ezra stepped back." Ad paused, hesitant to go on. His mother reached across the table and touched his wrist.

"And?" I prompted.

"And Jacob was standing on the corner as the streetcar approached. Ezra said Jacob was quiet, even turning toward him with a slight smile on his face. So Ezra relaxed, as they stood shoulder-to-shoulder with crowds of folks ready to cross the street. But someone jostled the crowd, some woman slipped, someone reached out to grab her, to pull her back to the curb. Everything shifted suddenly and Jacob stumbled, just feet from him, toppling in front of the streetcar. He was knocked to the ground and smashed his head."

"Oh, my Lord." Molly was trembling.

My mother's face tightened. A mixture of sadness and accusation. Lightning flashes in my head, a roar in my eardrums, panic. I turned away from her look.

"Or a suicide," I said into the silence.

Esther gasped, covered her mouth with her

hand. "Oh no, it had to be an accident. Street-cars hit people all the time. I've seen…people stumble…"

Molly was staring at Ad, her jaw set, rigid. "What do you think, Adolph?"

"I don't know. I wasn't there."

"What do you think happened?" I asked Ad.

A long, unhappy silence, Ad fidgeting with the buttons on his shirt until he snapped one off. It rolled onto the floor, and Esther stooped for it. Ad's mouth went slack, his eyes half-closed. Finally, breathing in and out, almost melodramatically, he faced me. Me—not his mother. His eyes were dull pieces of stone.

"You wanna know what I think? I think Uncle Ezra pushed Jacob in front of the streetcar."

"Adolph, no!" From his mother.

Molly gasped, clutched at her throat.

But Adolph gathered steam now, his voice booming across the kitchen. "C'mon. Face it. Uncle Ezra murdered Jacob."

"But why?" his mother pleaded.

"Because Jacob had learned that Ezra was the one who killed Ivan."

Chapter Seventeen

Jacob Brenner lay in a coma.

Two days passed, suspended time, all of us holding our breaths, frantic yet calm. Waiting. A deathwatch. Conversation muted, if at all.

Renovation completed, the five-room apartment we'd booked at the Windermere Hotel in Hyde Park was ready for us, lovely spacious rooms, morning walks to Lake Michigan one block away, to Jackson Park. My routine for summers: writing nine to four, a walk, back home for a bath. Quiet rooms, except for the rumble and toot of the Illinois Central suburban trains as they passed.

But now I was hesitant to leave the Newmann home. Not yet, a few days more, graciously invited by Esther and Sol, and the reason was Jacob Brenner. Though my mother said nothing, I sensed she also wanted to be nearby. A harsh woman, my mother, but one easily made sad by the agony of others.

Esther busied herself in the kitchen, baking a Black Forest cake that we'd all ceremoniously carry to Leah's home that afternoon. I'd called, asked whether such a visit might be acceptable, and Leah hadn't spoken for a moment. An awkward moment, but she finally said yes, though I could hear the hesitation in her voice.

Hearing of our planned visit, Molly balked. She was snide. "Have a good time."

"Please," Esther begged her.

"You bring cake after a funeral," Molly insisted. "Not before."

"We've known Jacob all our lives."

Molly said nothing. The old woman was sitting on a kitchen chair, her lethal cane resting on her lap. At Esther's "Please" she gripped her cane, tapping firmly on the floor, her fiery punctuation.

Molly turned to my mother. "You going, Julia?"

Tap tap tap.

My mother was startled, unhappy being singled out. She glanced at Molly, and in a croaking voice said quietly, "This visit is for Jacob, Molly."

Molly snorted, struggled to stand, waved the cane menacingly in the air, barely clipping Esther, who ducked, and slowly tottered out of the room, exaggerating her movement, her slight limp.

Esther whispered, "I'll pay a price for this long after you two leave."

I spoke up. "Leah will wonder where she is, no?"

Esther shook her head. "She'll *know*. Molly harbors a lifetime of resentment. You don't give up such dislike easily." A thin, mischievous smile. "Her first words about Leah, I recall: 'A beautiful woman ain't no gift from God.' Then she said, 'No good will come of this. You mark my words.' So, I suppose, Ivan's murder and Leah's arrest proved her…her dire prophecy. Molly has never been one to forgive—or forget. Ask her about the time Sol was fifteen and forgot to come home from a park for her birthday." She shuddered. "Still talked of."

"She has one weakness, though," I noted.

"What?" Esther stared into my face.

"Ad. She indulges your son as though he's the golden child,"

Esther bit her lip. "I know. Poor Adolph, the heir to the throne. But what throne? My Harriet, two years younger than Adolph, a quiet and pretty girl, smart as a whip, was ignored."

"How sad!"

"That's why she married young and moved to Cleveland. She got tired of sitting in darkness, though Sol and I fawned and flattered. Adolph got all the smiles. So…so Old Country, no? The man is the…chosen of God."

My mother, surprisingly, muttered the old ritualistic prayer. "'Thank God I was not born a woman.'"

"How sad!" I repeated.

Of course, I'd spent a lifetime in the shadow of my sister, Fannie, now married and happily away from my life. True, my mother grudgingly accepted the generous alms I offered from my increasingly large bounty. A short story sold to *Cosmopolitan* garnered her that new fur coat she coveted or some glittery bauble, shrilly demanded but then denigrated. So I understood Harriet's flight from family…but I was bound, the indentured servant in the Ferber household…

Esther was talking softly. "Molly has spent all of my married life waiting for me to blunder. After over forty years of a good marriage, Sol and I, I still got to prove myself." She sighed as she glanced toward the doorway. "It gets a little…exhausting."

As she said that last word—an "exhausting" that was world-weary but strangely comical, elongated and in a purposely Old Country inflection—my mother and I burst out laughing. Then Esther, surprised at herself, joined us, and we sat there, giggling like small girls in a schoolyard.

● ● ● ● ●

Leah's house was an oven. The windows were shut

against the afternoon heat, the quiet rooms deadly. As Sarah let us in, deftly taking the cake from Esther's hands and disappearing into the kitchen with it, we noticed Leah standing back against the fireplace mantel. She was staring over our shoulders, probably for Molly, but I was watching my mother, whose exclamation of "The nerve!" had begun my treacherous journey into the facts of the murder. A flicker of disapproval in her face, though she was long practiced in the art of deception, the actress who'd learned to deal with the annoying patrons of the family notions store she once ran back in Appleton. So her smiled "Hello" was acceptable, though I noticed she didn't extend her hand. Leah pointed to chairs in the dining room, and we sat down around the table.

Sarah served iced tea and the cake, but she said nothing, watching us warily. Once, accidentally, I caught her eye, but her stare was difficult to read—peculiarly, a trace of anger that baffled me, though in seconds her eyes assumed the blank look she always wore. That also troubled me.

Surprisingly, Leah was dressed in a current style, not the dowdy, matronly dress she'd worn before, but, rather, a modish lavender blouse with filigreed lace around the neck, and a straight-lined black skirt, snug at the hips, knee-length, modern. She looked younger than her sixty or so years, nervously jumpy—someone wide-awake because something unexpected might happen. Her snow-white hair, luminous, was pulled into a schoolmarm bun, secured with a black velvet bow.

"Any news on Jacob?" Esther asked.

Leah shook her head and suddenly, gulping, began to sob. She turned her head away, closed her eyes, and breathed in. "No, he's dying."

Said, the awful words stung the room, sucked the air out of us.

"Oh, my Lord," Esther whispered. "We're sorry."

"He never woke up."

"A horrible accident," Esther said.

Sarah made a growling sound, deep and loud, that made us start.

"Yes?" I asked.

"There are all kinds of accidents," she told us.

"But Ezra said…"

Sarah broke in. "Ah, yes, beloved Uncle Ezra, tour guide through the dangerous Chicago streets, the guardian angel."

Leah snapped at her. "Stop this, Sarah. For heaven's sake."

"I'm only saying what you are thinking."

The two sisters eyed each other, a penetrating look I couldn't read.

"You've never been able to read my mind, Sarah," Leah countered.

Sarah smirked. "Just as well. Dark, unchartered territory there."

Leah made a clicking sound, her dark eyes flashing.

Esther was following the nasty exchange, confused, ready to cry. Exasperated, my mother bridled, shifted in her seat, half-rising. She adjusted the sleeve of her dress, pulling at it, a nervous gesture I recognized—a signal to me that she was ready to leave.

"*Nu*," she said, "we must go."

No one had touched the iced tea or the cake.

But I wasn't ready to leave. "Sarah, certainly you don't think someone pushed Jacob in front of that streetcar? On purpose?"

My mother screamed. "Edna, have you no decency?" She glanced at Leah, who was watching me carefully. At that moment our eyes locked, and I realized she'd also wondered. She was nodding her head.

I didn't apologize but addressed Sarah. "Now what are you saying, Sarah?"

"You've met Uncle Ezra."

Leah reached out and touched her arm. "Maybe not now, Sarah."

Sarah jerked back her arm. "Then when?"

"Not now."

Sarah flicked her head to the side and rolled

her tongue over her lips. Flushed, jittery, she was readying some remark when the doorbell chimed. Leah turned to her sister. "Who?"

Reluctantly, Sarah ushered Ella and Emma into the dining room. They stood behind the chairs, not happy to discover the neighbors sitting at the table. Speaking in a low, trembling voice, one of them said to Sarah, "We've come from Mount Sinai."

Leah tensed up, her hand raised against her cheek. "And?"

"Nothing. No change." She stared blankly at her mother.

"Sit down, Ella. Please." Then she spoke to the other sister. "Emma, I'm happy you've come."

Emma glanced at Ella, as if to say: Are you satisfied? I came, after all. Emma, the twin who believed in her mother's guilt. The prodigal daughter, grudgingly visiting the home she'd left three years ago. She sat down and avoided the staring faces, the stranger at the wrong party.

Ella had an edge to her voice, "Emma wanted to come."

Emma scowled as her head bowed into her folded hands in her lap. But when she caught her mother's watchful eye, her face softened. "I'm sorry," she said simply. Then, a catch in her throat, she echoed her own words, but louder now. "I'm sorry."

So she'd moved past the belief in her mother's guilt, at least for now, perhaps because of Jacob. Or, more likely, Ella's emphatic order. No matter, because her words "I'm sorry"—heartfelt, spontaneous—cracked something within her, and her body slumped in the chair. She'd wanted to come home, I realized. She'd wanted this overdue reconciliation. Silent now, but content as an old cat by the hearth, she half-closed her eyes as though ready for sleep. A curious transformation—the reluctant daughter back at home. Strangely, though, Ella, the sister who visited her mother, the one who professed her mother's innocence, now was on edge, anxious, her eyes blinking rapidly, as if she'd been accused of some transgression and didn't know how to respond. She was the one ready to flee the room.

Leah asked Emma about Hull House. "I understand you're working for Jane Addams with the young Russian immigrant girls."

Emma seemed surprised that her mother had heard that news. "Volunteering. Three afternoons a week. I'm teaching sewing to young girls. And English at the same time."

Ella grumbled. "There's no money coming in." She shot a look at Emma. "This won't last."

"I like it." Emma's voice rose. She smiled at

me. "I was working two days a week as a seamstress. For a cruel woman. We both did, me and Ella."

Ella's tone got bitter. "But we need money for the rent, Emma."

Emma frowned. "No, we don't. Herman pays…"

"For everything," Sarah finished. "The rich brother."

"I don't like it," Ella said. "Emma is making a mistake."

Leah put her hand to her head as though squelching a headache. "You can move back here, Ella."

Ella jumped. "Oh, I don't think so."

"We may have to," Emma said, surprisingly. Then she whispered, "Although I think I'd like to live on my own."

Emma, the dormouse under Ella's severe control, had found some spunk. Feisty, I thought, this girl who'd had a taste of independence, and now, so late in her life, was daring to counter her sister.

"A single woman can't live…" Ella began, but stopped.

Sarah snickered, "Just like when you were little girls. If one said left, the other said right."

Ella bristled. "I always knew what was best for Emma. Because…"

Emma glared at her.

Leah finished for Ella with a nervous laugh, "But they both ended up headed in the same direction."

"Because of Ella." Emma's voice had no kindness in it.

Ella glowered at Emma, the muscles prominent in her neck. "Not anymore."

Silence in the room, my mother again mumbling about leaving. This time, nudging me, she stood, adjusted the seams of her dress.

The doorbell chimed again, but before Sarah or Leah could move, the front door opened. Uncle Ezra walked in. Nothing sheepish about his entry, unannounced, because he planted himself in the entryway, his face flushed. Leah started to speak but Ezra spoke over her words. "No one answers the telephone in this house. Why pay for that infernal contraption if it's not used? It seems to me…"

"Because we knew it was you," Sarah said snidely.

He narrowed his eyes. "I told you I'd call at nine, Sarah."

"I know," Sarah said again, cheerfully. "As I said, we knew it was you."

"I was at the hospital," Leah said, placating. "I didn't…"

Ezra addressed Sarah, "At times like this, a family must come together, support…" He paused. "You know…*mish pokhe*…the family."

Sarah rolled her eyes. "Oh, please, Ezra, don't you get tired of being an ass?"

"Enough," said Leah. "Ezra, please sit down. Join us. We have guests."

But he didn't. He surveyed us all, his steely gaze condemning. Finally he rested his stern glance on me, and waited.

"What?" I asked.

"I'm surprised you are here, Edna."

"I'm concerned about Jacob—and Leah."

He grunted but said nothing at first. Rather, he tapped his foot on the floor, the pouting child. Then, purposely, he spat out the words: "I suppose you came to apologize."

My mother spoke up. "My Edna doesn't need to apologize for anything."

I held up my hand. "I can fight my own battles, Mother."

Ezra, eyes bright, mimicked a look of innocence. "This is a battle?"

I glowered at him. "A skirmish, really. My opponent woefully at a disadvantage."

"And why is that?"

"You don't understand that you've already lost."

That confused him, but he stopped talking. Sarah was grinning, actually pointing a derisive finger at him.

"Outnumbered, dear Ezra," she told him flatly.

"Look around you. Women in the kitchen, in the dining room…they *overwhelm*." She counted. "Seven against one. Lucky seven. You make us unlucky, Ezra—eight is doom."

Leah was tired of the squabble. "What's wrong with you two? Do you hear yourselves? We should be thinking of one thing now." Once she started, she went on and on, a sad ramble, until all of us—not me, really—tried to look penitent and sorrowful. Ezra, too—he never altered his look of disgust and condescension.

The doorbell chimed. "Good God," Sarah said, "is this a hub of the Illinois Central?"

A sheepish Ad walked in, trailed by a jittery Minna. Ad said nothing and seemed surprised and bothered by the number of folks gathered there, but Minna entered talking, thrusting out a white box tied with twine. "Cookies from Bremmer Cookies." She was holding out the box toward Sarah but recognized her error, swung around and bumped into Ad's side as she searched for Leah. Ad watched her, annoyed, but Leah approached her, accepted the box and embraced the woman. Minna stepped back, colliding with the edge of a table, and kept muttering, "Sorry, sorry, sorry." She viewed the room in a panic and said, "I haven't been here in ages."

Leah followed Minna's gaze. Perhaps some in the room flashed back to a time when Minna had been the sweetheart of Herman until Ivan, finding fault with the bumbling girl, had nixed that union. Minna once sat at that very table…dinners, plans, dreams. Leah, of course, had given them her blessing, so she'd liked Minna—something apparent now as she held her, Minna's face buried in her shoulder.

"Ad told me. I didn't know. How is…?"

Leah shook her head slowly, comforting. "It's all right, Minna. Sit, sit. Please."

Ad sat at her side, though all the attention centered on Minna, frail and trembling. I watched Ad. Drawn, weary, shattered. He'd shaved but missed a spot near his left ear, a faint patch of beard stubble that seemed endearing to me. The Arrow collar he'd clipped to the pale blue shirt was coming undone, poorly fastened. Despite his sharp-pressed pants and the polished button shoes, he looked disheveled. A man who hadn't cared that morning as he bathed and dressed for the day.

"Were you at the hospital?" I asked him.

He nodded. "Yeah, I stopped in before I got to Minna's. Nothing doing. They wouldn't let me into his room."

Ezra spoke up. "Family only, young man."

Ad's face got hot. "Jacob is my best friend. Always has been."

"It's all right, Ad," Leah reassured him. "He

knows you're his best friend. No matter what. Some things don't got to be said."

Ad's expression got dreamy. "I keep thinking about my last talk with him. A few days ago. Just before he started to avoid me—to avoid everyone. He shuffled along like an old man, shoulders down, droopy eyes. You couldn't shake him out of it, and I kept asking what was wrong. 'Tell me, tell me. C'mon, Jacob. Tell me.' But he'd get this funny look in his eyes, that lazy sleepwalker's look he sometimes had, and stare at me. Like he was already far away from the world. Lord, it scared me. It was so—crazy…deep. But at the same time I felt he wanted me to *help* him. So close to me, the way he stood."

"What happened?" I asked.

Ad stopped a second, catching his breath. "What he said chilled me." Another pause, his eyes half shut.

"What?" I prompted.

Ad peered into my eyes, but he glanced for a second at Leah. "He said he'd failed his mother."

Leah tensed up. She wrapped her arms around her chest, and swayed. "But he never failed me. He knew that. He had nothing to do with…"

Ad couldn't look at her now. "He believed he *did*. Then, like that, his eyes got hard as glass, real scary like, and he said to me, a finger jabbing in my chest, 'Don't you know it's time?' 'What?' I asked. 'Time, time, time. It's time.'" Ad swallowed. "It was like some chant."

Sarah spoke too loudly. "What does that mean? Are you saying he planned to kill himself?"

Ad gasped. "God, no." Then, fiery, "No, dammit." He shot a look at Ezra, then at me. Ad had announced Ezra as Jacob's attempted murderer last night. Now, as Ad's eyes focused on him, Ezra squirmed. He'd been lighting a cigarette and dropped the wooden match. He swore under his breath.

"Ad," I said, "Jacob was sinking into his troubles. It's hard to know what he meant by that."

"I dunno." Helpless, a whimper. But he went on. "Then he said, 'Should I let the past stay dead?' He mentioned those days when we all sat around the back room at Nathan's. 'Disgusting, all of it,' he said. Then, like that, he closed up."

Sarah said, "If Jacob comes out of his coma, maybe he'll tell us what really happened."

Ezra glared. "Be realistic, Sarah. He's not going to make it."

Ad shot him a look. "How convenient."

"What does that mean?"

Ad didn't answer.

By chance, I'd been watching the twins as Ad told the story of his last conversation with Jacob.

Ad had a drifting, rolling voice. His narrative was intoxicating. I watched his handsome face, the deep lines under the eyes and at the corners of his mouth that, in a man like Ad, added to his charm. Though not to everyone, especially Ezra, ready to pounce. But to Ella and Emma, rapt and attentive, mouths slightly open, heads tilted back, Ad's tale was powerful, the stuff of heroes. It struck me then that both women, bound by sisterhood and spinsterhood and the awful poverty of women on their own, shared an abiding infatuation with Ad, one that probably dated back to childhood years. The plain, forgettable sisters watching the handsome, debonair playboys, Ad and Jacob, cavorting on the porch, in the yard, squiring the popular girls to basement clubs and sandlot baseball games. Quietly, they held onto their hunger, unspoken maybe even to each other, but clearly still alive. Ad must have known—how could he not? Such unabashed devotion in their eyes. Because even now, sensing their riveted looks, he faltered, smiling, and then, embarrassed, he reached for Minna's hand.

"We have to leave." He nodded toward Leah.

Ezra made a dismissive sound, then seemed to regret it.

With a mystical power I'd not anticipated, Leah slowly began to shoo us toward the door, the loving mother hen, tending, pecking, a flicker of an eyelid, the curve of her chin. It was magnificent to watch, so effective, so seamless. There she was, the woman sprung from isolation in the leper colony, the disgraced woman, the alleged murderer of the man who once lived in that house with her—there she was, benignly leading everyone to the door, the schoolteacher herding stubborn or dim-witted children. *Thank you, thank you, so kind…*

As Emma and Ella moved, they whispered to each other, saying something we couldn't hear but nevertheless communicating some bitterness. Bickering that would probably end with a sisterly feud that would last for years—the deadly silence, the nasty gossip, the noxious bile. I knew that cruel story because my sister Fannie and I didn't speak for years at a time. So, too, Ella and Emma, Siamese twins joined at their loneliness, had now found a way to leave each other. Ezra seemed loathe to leave, smiling at Leah who ignored him—that sleek, expensive man, gussied up with pomade and moustache wax and a flashy garnet pinky ring—a man no one ever trusted, could never trust again. And Sarah, watching her exiled sister take control of a house she'd ruled for years, the prison matron with the cruel jibe—she herself stood back, watching, her jaw set in disapproval, her eyes wary.

And, of course, Jacob's spirit hovered over us,

the lost lamb, shattered, now dying…or already dead…

I was the last one to leave, trailing after my mother and Esther. Ad and Minna were the first, in a hurry. Ella and Emma and Ezra moved, then stopped, debated, then left together.

Leah shook her head as she leaned into my neck.

"Edna."

I turned back. "You all right, Leah?"

"Of course, I am." A pause. "I have no choice now." Then her voice trembled. "You know, Edna, I didn't kill Ivan, but somehow I destroyed my family."

She walked away.

Chapter Eighteen

The trouble began as daylight waned. All afternoon the heat built, miserable, the air clammy, and we waited for the thunderstorm that would do nothing to end the long hot spell. The sky darkened and we waited. A few drops fell, a sprinkle, teasing us, wisps of steam rising from the hot asphalt. Then the light began to fade, the heat getting worse, a furnace. Everyone wilted. I sat on the porch and waited for the storm to come.

Herman Brenner and his wife, Naomi, pulled up in his town car, idling in front of Leah's home. They debated stepping out—I could see Naomi's head swiveling back and forth as though she were arguing with her husband—but finally Herman stepped out and slammed the door. He wasn't happy.

A shadow moved in the rear seat, leaned forward to say something to Naomi, and in seconds Emma opened the door and walked out. Naomi stayed in the car.

Emma yelled to her brother, "She won't get out."

"Then leave her, for Christ's sake."

Emma without her sister? Sitting in the backseat of brother Herman's automobile? So here was the recalibrated twin, long convinced of her mother's guilt and hammered into obedience by Ella, now visiting—without her sister.

She spotted me on the porch, said something to her brother, who waved indifferently. He walked to the passenger door, leaned in to say something to Naomi, and she finally got out, though not without grunting her unhappiness. The three stood on the sidewalk, waiting, watching one another. Naomi glanced up into the twilight sky, and pointed. Again, Herman waved, but this time the gesture seemed a salute, very Prussian military. I waved back. Then, in a body, they moved toward me.

"Edna," Herman yelled, "no one answers my telephone calls to the house." He jerked his head toward his mother's home. "Have you seen signs of life there?"

"I have no idea, Herman. I don't keep track of the neighbors."

He scoffed. "Edna, Edna. You expect me to believe that?"

"Believe what you will, Herman." I turned to Emma. "Emma, a return visit? Where is Ella?"

Emma waited for her brother to answer for her. When he didn't, she said, "My sister is not happy with me."

"And why is that?"

Naomi bent into her, her fingers brushing Emma's sleeve. As she whispered something I couldn't hear, Emma shrugged her off. "She resents my...I was the bad sister, the unforgiving one. She trumpeted my mother—I refused. Now I want to return home and she...she's unhappy."

"I don't understand."

Herman was glaring at Emma, but he spoke to me. "You don't have to, Edna. This has nothing to do with you."

Naomi was tugging at her sleeve. "Could we go and get your mother?"

Herman explained to me, "The doctor called earlier. We need to be there now."

"Jacob."

"We're losing him today."

My heart raced. I stepped off the porch. "I'm so sorry to hear that."

Herman stepped closer to me, ready to say something, but simply stared at me.

The door behind me opened, and Minna strolled out onto the porch, though she was speaking to someone behind her. When she spotted us, she stopped, alarm in her face, took a step

backward, and then forced a smile. "Herman."
Again, her voice lower, "Herman."

Probably Herman was a man who rarely
got flustered, had long practiced his stoicism,
but staring up at the woman he'd once planned
on marrying, the woman he swore undying love
to and then abandoned, he stiffened, his mouth
twitching, and insanely one of his hands gripped a
thigh. His shoulders hunched up. He stole a look
at his frowning wife, someone doubtless aware of
her husband's first love affair, but Naomi wore a
cruel smile, nervously pleased with her husband's
unexpected discomfort.

"It's been a long time, Minna," Herman got
out.

"Yes, it has." Cold, distant, so unlike the
bubbly, scattered Minna who giggled into Ad's ear.

"How've you been?"

"Fine." Minna managed to make the throwaway remark biting. She was wearing a pink bow
in her hair, a Mary Pickford affectation, and she
checked to see whether her little-girl look was
intact, running her fingers through her ringlets.
A failed move, however, because she made it lopsided so that she seemed the madcap ingénue in a
vaudeville farce.

"It's been a long time." Herman repeated the
words, then regretted them, flicking his head away.

Emma tried to maneuver him away, but he was rooted to the sidewalk.

It dawned on me then that Herman still loved Minna. Settled now, middle-aged, moneyed, the father of two children, ages fifteen and thirteen, and a loyal if plodding husband, pragmatic Herman still held a lingering romanticism about the girl he had loved when he was a young man. A carefree bachelor then, his father's awful edict—exiling unacceptable Minna—had driven him into a marriage that probably satisfied his father but no one else, least of all Herman. Minna represented a moment of freedom he'd walked away from. And a real love had blossomed in the mechanical man. Now, on the hot sidewalk as we waited for the thunderstorm, Herman froze. This was what his dead father Ivan had wrought. This…this awful paralysis.

"Fine." Minna repeated the same word. A curse now, wrought with steel.

Herman shrugged. "You visiting Esther?"

Perhaps he didn't know about Minna's long courtship with Ad, though that surprised me. Yet it was possible. Since Ivan's murder fifteen years back, Herman was an infrequent visitor to the neighborhood, and the Newmanns kept their distance from the cursed house next door.

"I'm marrying Ad."

Herman seemed puzzled. "Adolph?"

"Of course."

He squinted. "But I'd heard you were seeing him *years* ago."

She faltered. "Yes, we were—I mean, are. Have been…" The troublesome conjugations threw her off, and she finished with: "We'll be…still."

"Minna." My voice was sharp. "Minna, go back into the house."

She didn't move. There they were, the two of them, back twenty years ago, ignoring the intervening years of other marriages and other engagements and other disappointments. And the horrific murder next door—something not to be imagined.

Minna dropped into a chair, her face crumpled. Oh my God, I thought: Don't let her cry. Not now. Not on the porch.

At that moment Molly came outside and, smart woman, understood what was happening. "Minna," she said firmly, "Ad is waiting for you." Then, cane tapping, she addressed Herman. "Herman, if you are intending a visit to your mother, you'd best be on." She lifted the cane and pointed dramatically to Leah's home.

But Herman still didn't move.

A sudden *wooza wooza wooza* jolted us, as Ezra pulled up in his roadster. He leaned on the insulting horn again, pulling alongside the three people standing on the sidewalk. Emma let out a mouse-like squeal, was embarrassed by it, and then giggled. Naomi, eying the interloper with steely eyes, took a step toward the idling car and cleared her throat. Herman, however, produced the most bizarre response—he cursed Ezra roundly, a string of *goddamn yous* while raising his fist into the air. I could never imagine Herman so out of control, so maddened, nor could he, because almost at once he froze in place, blinking furiously, affronted by the behavior of a street lout.

Meanwhile, Ezra put the automobile in gear and slid to a halt in front of Leah's home. He threw back his head as though he'd just heard the most hilarious story. By the time he stepped out of the car, Herman was right there, face crimson and hands flapping at his side.

"My heart went into my mouth," Herman roared. "That infernal horn. Do you have a brain in that head of yours?"

Ezra ignored that. "Is Leah home?"

"She's not answering the telephone," Naomi told him.

"Maybe she's not home."

The two men stood there, facing each other, their dislike palpable. Ezra was spiffy in a charcoal gray summer seersucker suit, a creamy white shirt open at the neck, and a rose-colored silk handkerchief peeking out of his breast pocket. On his head he wore a bleached straw bowler. Next to him, Herman, the younger man, came off as the drab poor cousin in his wrinkled black suit, buttoned up to the neck, an old-fashioned businessman's black cravat, and a brimmed cap with attached goggles that he always donned for motoring. A tad ridiculous, his look, especially the ludicrous goggles, and made more so next to the dapper uncle. Herman's blurted out curses made no secret of his dislike of Ezra, and Ezra—long used to being the despised blood relative who visited—couldn't have cared less.

"I thought I'd take her to the hospital," Ezra said. "To see Jacob."

Herman glanced back at me—and his eyes lingered on Minna, watching from a seat on the porch. He sneered, "I *still* don't know what happened that day with Jacob."

That surprised Ezra, who fumbled. "He slipped..."

"And you couldn't stop him?" Tense, snide.

Ezra squirmed. "I couldn't reach him."

Herman persisted. "I can't get a picture of it, Jacob falling, toppling." A sneer. "With you at his side."

Ezra spoke through clenched teeth. "You have more of an interest in your brother *now* than in all the years he walked these streets." He glanced up and down Monroe Street.

"What does that mean?"

"C'mon, Herman. You never *liked* Jacob."

"He's my brother."

"You saw him as a lazy, foolish poet, some silly boy who looked like your mother and flirted with the girls."

"He's my brother!" Yelling now.

Ezra insisted, "I'm the one who was his friend. Me, Herman, my boy. And Ad next door. His own family laughed at him."

Herman stepped closer. "For three years now you slink around here since our mother is back home. You don't think I hear about that? Uncle Ezra, knocking on the door. Uncle Ezra, bringing baskets of food. Uncle Ezra, taking little Jacob for a ride in his tin lizzie. Uncle Ezra taking Jacob for a boat ride on the river. Ezra, Ezra, Ezra."

Ezra snarled, "So what?"

"The truth is that I don't think you ever cared for Jacob. It's my mother you were visiting."

Uncle Ezra glanced at the Newmann porch. Minna had stood up, moving closer to the front steps, though Molly reached out to touch her elbow. "Meaning?"

"You know damn well what it means. You've crawled around here for years now, even when Papa was alive. *He* knew it. He warned you. I *heard* him tell you to get lost. Mama tossed you over for Papa but that didn't stop you. Flattering, smiling, laughing, a silly little boy. My father warned you to stay away." He faltered. "A…a *shedim*…you demon."

Ezra said nothing, checking out the quiet street. He glanced up into the sky, watching for the thundershowers. The sky was darkening. Finally, he grumbled, "A street brawl, Herman? Is that what you're reduced to?"

Red-faced, Herman poked him in the chest. "The way you ogled my mother."

Ezra stepped back, unsure of his footing. "*Everyone* watched your mother, dear Herman. A beautiful woman. Ivan *liked* that. He had his precious little doll. He got meaner and meaner as he got older and older, jealous, cruel."

Herman's voice was a low rumble. Another poke in the chest. Ezra flinched. "You want to jump back into her life now. You want to go back to when you were young and…and you thought *you'd* be marrying her." Unwittingly, he spun around and stared at Minna on the porch. It was a knee-jerk reaction, its meaning not lost on himself, or me, or doubtless the listening Minna. She tensed up, a trickle of tears streaming down her cheeks.

"C'mon," Herman's wife pleaded, tugging his

sleeve. "Do you realize how foolish the two of you look in the street? Street urchins, pushcart boys."

Herman ignored her.

Ezra put his face close to Herman's—and suddenly, bending his neck, spat onto the pavement. Herman sucked in his breath.

The door behind me swung open and Ad, hearing the brouhaha in the street, stormed out, slamming the screen door behind him. "Jesus Christ," he yelled, "what's going on out here? I'm in the kitchen…" He hesitated. "Minna?" She stood there, crumpled up, tears on her cheeks. "What the hell happened?"

"Ad," I began, "it's nothing. Don't…"

"Minna, what's the matter?" He glanced toward the skirmish in the street. At that moment, regrettably, Herman heard Ad's bluster and turned, though his eyes rested on Minna. Ad fumed. "What did he say to you?"

"Nothing," she muttered.

"Ad," I went on. "Nothing."

Molly said to him, "Go back into the house, Adolph."

Ignoring her, Ad touched Minna's shoulder, a quick, comforting gesture that made her sob harder, which in turn enflamed him. Always the neighborhood knight, the tilter of imaginary windmills, Ad repeated, "Minna, did he say something to hurt you?"

She shook her head vigorously and tried to smile. "I don't know why I'm crying, Ad. It's all this...yelling...Herman and Ezra...in the street. Jacob is dying and..."

Her words ignited Ad's temper, and he pounded one fist into the other. Madness—the next act in this silly street revue, men acting like loutish boys.

"Herman," Ad yelled.

But Herman ignored Ad's fury. Instead, he'd turned back to Ezra who was sneering something about the roly-poly burgher in the rumpled suit. Herman said something unintelligible and stepped back. He nodded at Naomi, though she regarded him coolly, then sought Emma who'd stepped off the sidewalk and was standing in a clump of bushes.

He took a step away.

But Ezra, still raging, lunged forward and, thrusting out his arm, slapped his nephew full in the face.

So resounding and unexpected a blow, so marrow-deep ugly, so...so *wrong*. I breathed in, and Minna, behind me, cried out, "No!" She started to hiccough.

Stunned, Herman blubbered, rubbed his face with his palm, and sputtered, "You..."

Emboldened. Ezra pushed his palm against

Herman's chest, and Herman stepped to the side. His foot turned and he nearly toppled, but he grabbed onto Ezra's sleeve. His uncle shrugged him off, but slapped his face again. Herman bellowed but then, grunting, hunched over and plowed his head into Ezra's chest. Ezra let out an *oomph* sound, the air out of a balloon, and staggered back against the fender of his car.

Out of breath, heaving, the two men stared at each other, eyes hooded. An ugly space between then, wrestlers ready to grapple.

Suddenly Herman's eyes found Minna, locked eyes with her.

Ad, incensed, flew off the porch, nearly falling over, and stood between both men. He spun around, furious, pointing first at Herman, then at Ezra.

From the bushes, bent over as though in pain, Emma whimpered, "Jacob. Think of Jacob."

Ezra stormed at her. "Yeah, you love your brother, little sister."

She cried out, hurt.

Ad yelled at Ezra, though his frantic glance took in Herman. "Yeah—Jacob. How he hated the way you…you followed his mother. He stopped. "Evil Ezra."

Brutal, frightening words, belligerent. Ezra scrunched up his face. "You—you hypocrite. Ivan warned all the boys…even you."

Ad made a fist, but it was Herman, rubbing his cheek and breathing hard, who gripped Ad's arm. "No, no. He's not worth it."

But Ad would have none of it. Hotheaded, spinning around like a wobbly top, he wasn't sure what to do. Back on the porch, Minna was rocking, mewing loudly, her tiny hands fluttering around her face like jittery birds. "Ad, no, no. Please." Her voice hollow, words so mumbled that only I could hear her.

"Damn you, Ezra." Ad was panting. "Jacob dying—my buddy." His voice a ragged blend of yelling and sobbing now, sailing over the street. "He wanted you away from the house—because of his mother. He went with you to keep you from coming *into* the house."

"Nonsense," Ezra hissed. "Funny, though. These last days the *only* person he'd see was…me. Not you, Ad—he kicked everybody away from him. Only me. *Me*."

A long, dead space. Ad spat out, "You thought that he killed his father…" He stopped. "He told me *you* kept *asking* him—'What do you remember? That day. Tell me. Tell me.' Why did you ask?"

"Because he *knew* something."

The words made Ad see red. Blindly, he thrust out his arm at Ezra, an ineffective jab that grazed his cheek. Surprised, Ezra punched the air, grunting, but immediately grabbed onto Ad's sleeve, tearing it.

"Goddamn you," Ad swore, and spinning around, yanked Ezra's necktie, bunching it in his fingers.

Ezra made a gurgling sound, stumbled, but, sidestepping around Ad, lunged at Herman who'd taken a step toward him. Ezra barreled into him and Herman staggered back. Getting his footing, Herman assumed a cartoonish pugilist's stance, one foot in front of the other, fists thrust out in front of him, elbows bent.

A dark laugh escaped Ezra's throat as he pointed at Herman, mocking his ridiculous stance. Dancing around Herman, Ezra didn't expect his nephew's sudden punch to the mouth. Ad laughed out loud.

Ezra, mumbling that Ad should get out of the way—"Mind your own goddamn business"— ran the back of his hand across his mouth. A smear of blood from a cut lip. He whimpered, blubbered "Blood, blood," as Herman, still in that outlandish pose of a gentleman boxer, rocked on his heels.

Ad shot a look back at the porch. Minna was sobbing. He hesitated—waiting. But I realized—and he realized—that Minna was staring at Herman, her body trembling.

Huffing, head bobbing like a circus clown,

Ad crashed into Herman, who toppled back and bounced off a car fender. He slapped at Herman's face, but Herman kept striking out, loose-limbed swings that missed his target. Circling the other two men, Ezra poked and jabbed, the pesky gnat. Herman kicked Ezra's shin, and he howled. The three men slammed against one another. A tangle of awkward bodies—tripping, bumping, arms and legs that aimed but mostly missed. Roustabout vaudeville slapstick. Helter-skelter sad sack comics executing exaggerated kicks that knocked them off balance.

Then, out of the tangle of flailing arms, a vagrant kick—Ad's foot into Ezra's groin. The old man bellowed, fell to his knees, and cried out.

Exhausted, the men fell apart, bodies sprawled on the hot pavement, Ezra moaning, Ad wheezing, Herman's breath a scratchy rasp.

Over—the slapdash scuffle of men who never thought they'd ever raise a fist at another. A trickle of blood across Ezra's cheek. Herman picked street gravel from a bruise on his forehead. Ad's head buried in his shoulder, a patch of bare flesh exposed where his shirt had ripped.

It was over—we waited. A stunned Greek chorus, we held our breath. Emma whimpered in the bushes. Minna had fallen into a chair, her face buried in her lands. Naomi had disappeared—I spotted her inside the car, the door open.

An eerie silence—only the labored breathing of the men.

Herman rolled onto his knees. Ad struggled to sit up. He grasped Ezra's forearm, pulled him into a sitting position.

A crackle of thunder, the sky suddenly dark and awful, the air heavy, the setting sun masked. In the distant sky a flash of lightning, brilliant. Big droplets began to fall, *splat splat splat* on the hot pavement. Hobbling, bent at the waist, Ezra hurried to put up the top of his convertible, clumsily falling into the automobile. He rested his head on the steering wheel. Herman groaned as he lumbered to his car to crank up his windows, then sat still inside, his head inclined against the seat rest. Only Ad didn't move. Standing now, he wrapped his arms around his chest, swaying. Raindrops covered him. He was sobbing.

Dark now, the storm gathering steam.

One drop, another, *plop plop. Splat.* A hot breeze blew rain onto the porch. The thick-leafed maples rustled. No one moved now, Ezra and Herman still in their cars. Naomi in the passenger seat, facing out, the door still open.

The front door of the Brenner home opened, and Leah walked out onto the porch. She'd been home all along, though she was dressed in a nightgown and robe, as though she'd spent the afternoon napping under the covers. She walked to the edge of the porch, looked up at the looming heavens, and then at her family. Her confused glance swept from Emma to the Newmann porch. Her eyes rested on Ad, still standing in the street, shoulders heaving, sobbing. Seeing her, Herman stepped out of the car.

The rains broke, ferocious, hard.

She spoke to Herman, her voice flat. "They just called me, the doctors. My Jacob is dead."

Dripping wet, Herman sucked in his breath, but then pointed at Emma who was running toward the porch. "No one cries. Do you hear me? No one cries. I don't want tears."

A strange line that made little sense.

But Leah, watching him, began to cry.

Chapter Nineteen

After the funeral, Sarah invited everyone back to the house where Leah sat quietly on a low chair, stunned, lovely in her dark sadness. No one spoke to her, though a few approached, began words of consolation, but then, startled by the stark upturned face, retreated, apologetic. Hers was, I told myself, the frozen face she wore fifteen years ago—the haunted look that greeted the police when they first arrived at her doorstep. That unfathomable mask that led them, in their glib dismissal, to assume her guilt. Now, tucked into a chair in a corner of the room, her arms wrapped around her body, her feet planted solidly on the floor as though she feared she'd lose her balance, Leah occasionally surveyed the small group of mourners gathered in her home. Surprise there, and wonder. What was wrong with this day?

She was dressed in a dull black silk dress with a frilly lace collar, ankle-length and a little worn at the seams. A small black ribbon pinned to her chest. A dress from an earlier century, found in an unused closet, with a musty mothball scent, though she looked seductive, the alluring grief-stricken woman, the alabaster skin and the snow-white hair and the black-shadowed, inky eyes. A Renaissance portrait, this woman, painted by Raphael. She reminded me of another Jewish mother, grieving over a crucified son.

An exaggeration, of course, my words, on the impact of her sitting there. Such beauty that was paradoxically so unapproachable.

Sarah buzzed around, officious, greeting the scattered few who came into the home. The presence of Leah, returned from her confinement, must have kept many away, though others visited out of perverse curiosity. A gaggle of loose-limbed middle-aged men in a pack came out of love for the hapless Jacob, a man who'd made so many women smile or wilt or fantasize. Most of the women stayed away.

Sarah urged the few of us to try the whitefish. She kept whispering, "It's from Lyon's Delicatessen," as if that imprimatur would create appetite in us. "Eat, eat," she hummed. "B'rith Abraham delivered it. An offering."

My mother nibbled on a bit of fish on a piece of bread. Earlier that morning, before we'd dressed for Jacob's funeral at Congregation Sinai, with

Rabbi Glickman officiating, she'd packed her hide-bound travel trunk and pushed it into the hallway outside her bedroom door. Her brocade valise was open on a stand in the room, pieces of clothing placed inside. When she saw me watching her, she nodded toward my room.

"Best be ready, Edna."

For, in fact, early the next morning we'd be leaving the Newmann household, headed for Hyde Park and the Windermere Hotel, where my luxurious rooms were ready. Quiet days, long walks, outdoor concerts at Ravinia. During the rest of the long hot summer, away from the Newmann home, I planned on finishing my novel. Serial publication as "Selina" in *Women's Home Companion* that fall, a book from Doubleday next spring, probably as *So Big*, then painful oblivion for me as a writer—my feeble tale of a battered farm wife and her contemporary, shallow son. A book in which nothing happened, the climax a wagon ride to market in the deep of night. I feared a scolding letter from Nelson Doubleday himself.

"No, Mother, that can wait," I'd told her. "A little unseemly to pack now. We have a funeral…"

She'd interrupted. "Unseemly? Edna, I'd suggest you rethink your vocabulary. After all, your horrible behavior set into motion this…this catastrophe."

"That's cruel."

"But true."

"All I wanted was justice for an innocent woman."

She'd smacked her head, dramatically. "After all *this*"—she pointed through walks toward the Brenner household—"you still persist…"

"I know now who killed Ivan."

She'd gasped and peered down the staircase from the landing. "Quiet, Edna. For God's sake. You know *nothing* of the sort."

I'd whispered to her. "Things have happened and it seems to me…"

She'd interrupted, pulling her face close to mine. "It seems to *me* that you're going to accuse an innocent person—and the nightmare you've created will continue, worse than ever. Leah Brenner killed her husband, Edna. Can't you get that through your thick skull?"

I'd held her eye. "Oh, I don't think so. I *know* so. Because the pieces fit together, maybe sketchily, though I regret them." A long, deep sigh. "But I don't know how to prove it—after fifteen years."

"Then leave it alone. We have a funeral to go to, Edna."

"For Jacob's sake, and for his mother's, the murderer must be named. There has to be a rightness to things."

For a second she'd closed her eyes. "It's going to be a long day."

"I'm afraid you're right, Mother." I'd whispered to myself, "For once."

• • ● • •

Someone was saying something to me, so I focused. Emma Brenner was talking about her mother. "Jacob was always her favorite. I suppose because when you saw his face, you saw her. The rest of us—Ella, Herman, me—took after our father—the unlovely children. There were too many mirrors in this house to look into. Jacob was the only one who liked them."

Mirrors on the walls, though thankfully covered today.

"You're hard on yourself, Emma."

She tossed her head back. "I'm a realist, Edna." Then, a crooked grin, she added, "How the world loved poor Jacob. The girls giggled and fussed. Once, in shul, sitting quietly on Yom Kippur no less, humble, the rabbi found a note on the floor, Jacob's name on it, dropped by an anonymous girl. Girls followed him off the streetcars, boys wanted to be his friend. Everyone wanted to walk with him. He had it all." A melancholy tone entered her voice. "Except ambition. A dreamer, my brother. But sad all these years since…that day…"

"Yes, he took his father's death hard. The breakdown." I watched her face closely.

She shook her head back and forth. "Not because of Papa, Edna. Because of what happened to Mama. Too sensitive, Jacob always was. Even as a boy he'd hide away, lips trembling, acting out parts from the dime novels we all read. The murder"— she glanced across the room at her mother—"the murder leveled him. You know, I think he was waiting to die from that day on, spiraling downward, waiting, waiting. You could see it in his eyes. He was never happy again. Something…drained out of him. I believe some people wait for death—they *decide* that. It's like the book is done with. I'd catch him crying, alone, slumped over in the bushes outside. We thought we'd lose him that first time, that awful breakdown." She clicked her tongue. "And now we have."

"He was never close to your father? Even as a little boy?"

She spoke too loudly for the quiet room. "Lord, no. He *hated* Papa. Well, Papa never understood Jacob—mocked him, spanked him. Worse—looked *through* him. Too mean to him. Jacob was a little boy who kept bringing him gifts that were ignored. Worse—ridiculed. 'Papa, Papa, look at me.' Papa was a hard man to love, Edna. Very Old Country. When he got old, the worst stuff inside of him surfaced. He wouldn't even go to shul. 'Obey me, do you hear?' We couldn't talk at the supper table. Silence. No warmth, no weakness."

"Jacob had Ad, thank God."

Emma nodded. "Thank God. The defender of the fortress."

"What?"

She laughed. "That makes no sense, I know. But one time, a couple years back, we all went to see the movie *The Golem* at the Apollo Theater. You know, the Jewish hero created from mud, the defender of Prague in the middle ages. A stupid melodrama but Jacob and Ad joked that they were *our* heroes—me, Ella, even Minna. One made from clay, the other from mud. But Jacob, for days, walked around saying, 'I wish I was a real hero.' There was something so sad about it."

"Everything about Jacob turned out sad," I said.

Emma's lips trembled. "Poor Jacob."

I changed the subject. "Are you reconciled with Ella?"

She started, resented the question. "I'm moving back here, I decided. We both are. But I want my own room now. We're not little girls anymore. I have a job at Hull House, which I love, something vital, important, and maybe it'll lead to something else, maybe a salary—but Ella fights me. She still works as a seamstress. I quit that. What she's afraid of…she wanted to remain little girls, scared, the two of us together, feeding into each other's loneliness. I won't have it any longer. It used to be easier not to fight her."

"That can only last so long."

"Edna, she always told me I wasn't too bright and I believed her." She threw back her head. "That proves she was a little bit right, then. No? If I learned anything from what happened to Mama, it's that silence covers a multitude of sinning. Strangely, what happened to Jacob lately…it sort of liberated me. I watched him sinking…lost, and I woke up and thought about my world. I may be an inconvenience to Ella—to others, though Herman grudgingly accepts me—but I don't care. An inconvenient woman is just what a family sometimes needs to straighten itself out. Do you understand me, Edna?"

I tapped her on the back of her wrist. "Of course, I do. Inconvenience may not be the word I would choose, but it'll work. I like to put myself in the way of folks' expectations. Women need to do that more. Sometimes they'll notice you. Sometimes they'll listen."

She giggled like a little girl. "Tell that to my sister. Look at her."

Ella was sitting across the room, watching us

talking, unhappy. Uncle Ezra was chatting into her neck, but she was focused on us, not him. Absorbed, he didn't seem to notice.

Herman and Uncle Ezra kept their distance, except for exchanged hard and angry stares, the two weary soldiers separated after carnival fisticuffs no one won. At the services Ezra sat at the back, refusing to join the family. When the twins sobbed, he bowed his head, and from where I sat I could see his pale face. Surprisingly, he was dressed in a conservative suit, sans flashy and colorful handkerchief, though the *kippah* he withdrew from a pocket and placed on his head was a brilliant sky blue, inappropriate. He spoke to no one, though I noticed him nodding at Leah. I was surprised he'd come back to the house, but he remained at Ella's side, protectively, assuming his new role as her confidante. At moments, she did her best to slide away from him, not even subtly, once rudely turning her back on him. He didn't seem to care. No one else in the family acknowledged him.

When I'd first arrived, he was one step ahead of me. He'd turned on the top step and watched me. My mother, at my side, squinted at him, disapproving, but he held his unyielding stare. A mixture, I'd concluded, of disdain, wonder, and, fantastically, humor.

"What?" I'd said, perturbed.

"Oh, nothing at all, Edna dear. It's just that you are always one step behind someone, the barnacle on the underbelly of a hurting family."

"A refreshing image," I'd quipped.

He'd hurried inside, disappearing into the kitchen.

Lagging behind me had been a resistant Molly. The old woman mourned Jacob—that dismissive epithet "poor Jacob" would be the way he'd be remembered forever, sadly—and said yes, indeed, she'd go to the services. She'd even give condolences to Leah, the woman she believed began the decline of the Brenner dynasty. It was only fitting and right, she lectured, the dictates of a loving God.

"I'm an old lady," she announced to us at supper. "I don't need someone telling me how to behave."

Leah watched Molly and her family walk toward her. If she was surprised by Molly's extended hand and murmured sorrow, she didn't react. A simple wispy smile, a quiet thank you, and Leah added, "Jacob always loved living next door to your family. He was always at your home as a boy. You were his family, too."

The words touched Esther, already weak with grief, and she burst into sloppy sobbing. Immediately Sol draped one arm around her shoulder and used the other to touch her face. She smiled at him, a soft and loving look, and it was, I thought, a beautiful tableau of a long, cherished marriage. The man who spoke so little but always so aptly, Sol bent over Leah and took her hand, squeezed it. Again, the perfect gesture because Leah's face relaxed, softened.

Minna dragged Ad to Leah, though he resisted. He'd sobbed loudly through the service, the loudest keener, his shoulders shaking as he swayed back and forth, a mournful metronome. Disconsolate, he'd walked out, stood on the sidewalk smoking cigarette after cigarette. Minna tried to talk to him, but eventually gave up, herself crying softly. Nearby, his father watched him but didn't approach. Sol kept nodding at Minna: Help him. Help him. Help the lad. Molly kept an eye on him as well, though she seemed embarrassed by his public histrionics.

Jacob and Ad, a boyhood spent together. Grown men, the friendship now ended.

Inside Leah's home Herman sidled up to Ad and tapped him on the shoulder, muttered a soft "I'm sorry for…outside." He flicked his head toward the street. Ad didn't answer. Herman said something I missed, but Ad slowly nodded, his handkerchief dabbing his eyes. Finally he slumped into a chair, staring at the carpet, with Minna hovering over him, a twittering hummingbird, solicitous, anxious. "Ad," she kept whispering at him. "Ad."

A dreamlike world, that gathering, a lazy stream of Jacob's friends coming in, awkward, not knowing whom to talk to, and then, relieved, turning to leave. A heartfelt *mitzvah*. The rest of us sat or stood, mutely watching them, until finally the few of us lingered there. Molly kept nodding to Esther and Sol, an obvious nod accompanied by her redundant cane tapping, signaling a need to leave. But Esther and Sol were reluctant to leave Ad who was nestled into an armchair, his body heavy and immovable, as though he'd lost the will to stand.

"Esther," Sol said to his wife finally, "we gotta leave the family now. They gotta grieve by themselves."

Sitting shiva for a dead son. A hard-backed chair, low to the floor.

Mirrors covered.

Seven days.

Seven nights.

The door opened and Sarah cried out. Morrie Wolfsy and his wife, Selma, walked in, accompanied by a bent-over Levi Pinsky. No one expected Ivan's old partner to visit the home, though all three had been at the services that morning. As expected. Morrie paused in the entrance, doubtful of his welcome, this old partner who'd battled the dead Ivan—and whose illicit moment with Leah had begun the sweep of trouble that ended in Ivan's murder. Herman bristled at seeing him. The twins actually glanced at each other. Uncle Ezra, though, was smiling thinly, reveling in the happenstance juxtaposition of old acquaintances who never should be in the same room together.

No one moved.

"Hello." Old Levi yelled out in the silence.

It was an unintentionally comical moment, the old man's crackling voice breaking at the end. Uncle Ezra smirked.

My mother nudged me. "Edna. Leave."

I had no intention of doing so.

Levi waited for Leah to address him first, so he watched her closely.

Leah struggled to her feet, disoriented, but she stepped forward, extending her hand to Morrie's wife. The poor woman, obviously uncomfortable, was relieved and muttered condolences. And like that, as if Leah had sprinkled some midsummer night's magic elixir on the room, everyone settled, eased into chairs, sipped cold water, gabbed, and smiled. Leah herself fell back into her seat, assumed her silence, though her eyes watched the room. It was a marvelous transformation, her magic trick, however she achieved it, and even Molly gave the grieving mother a look that had equal parts wonder and admiration in it.

For some reason Levi began to share stories, recalling a young Jacob hanging out in the back room of the old meat market late at night, sitting by a small green-glass secretary's lamp, fashioning his poetry. "Alone. By hissef. Everybody gone home. He said he liked the quiet, the feel of the old room."

"That back room." Herman spoke up. "I never understood its attraction." He nodded at Ad. "You, too. You and Jacob sitting there with the older men."

"A home for us," Ad said.

Levi glowered at him. "You was gonna be a rabbi."

Ad raised his eyebrows. "Ancient history." But for the first time that day he smiled. "We felt so grownup there. Well, Papa and…Morrie." He pointed a finger at Morrie, then stared at Levi.

"I never liked it," Herman said, "A couple times there and I stopped going."

"I never felt welcome there," Ezra added. "But it didn't stop me from going."

Ad watched both of them. "It was like a private club."

"No Jews allowed," Ezra said, snidely.

Ad faced him. "Maybe you weren't Jewish enough."

"Being Jewish is not a…gradation," Ezra said.

"No," Ad said, "but it can be a special beat of your heart. The bond that…"

Ezra scoffed. "Yeah, that special haven. A filthy room packed with junk." He purposely eyed Levi. "A ragpicker's paradise."

"And yet someone broke in to steal," I added, loudly.

Old Levi furrowed his brow, squinted at me. "Yes, so strange, that. The long darkness of that day. On the very night that poor Ivan died. Like God telling us something."

Silence in the room: images of Ivan with a knife slicing into his neck. In this very house. On that sofa. A knife. Blood. All over. The paralyzed widow. The screaming Sarah…the murder… murder…

Emma started weeping loudly, her face buried in her sleeve.

"I'm sorry," Levi blathered. "I talk too much."

"Or enough," I said.

"Edna, please." My mother nudged me in the side.

Everyone turned to look at me. "I always thought it strange—the coincidence—both events on the same day."

"No connection," Morrie said hurriedly. "A

few coins stolen. Those days a few robberies in the
street, I remember."

"But the police never investigated."

"What's to investigate?" Morrie shrugged.
"They come out for a minute. A petty burglary. It's
nothing. A broken door. Pennies."

I stood up, raised my voice, the moment I'd
wanted.

"Edna." My mother, warning.

"What are you saying?" From Herman.

A hissing sound from deep in Uncle Ezra.

I heard gurgling from Leah, behind me. I
ignored it.

"I've wondered about that break-in. I'm sorry,
but I want to say something here. Tasteless but
necessary. Now."

"Edna." My mother, thunderstruck.

Esther tittered, reached for Sol's arm. Molly
gripped her cane. *Tap tap tap* on the floor.

"This is not the time for…" Sarah's voice
broke.

"Am I the only one to wonder about that? A
knife never recovered. Perhaps bloodied clothing.
After all, a stab to the neck. All evidence disappeared. When I saw that cluttered back room, walls
of…of *stuff*, and then learned about the break-in, I
thought, what a wonderful place to *hide* evidence."

"Stop!" Ella, furious.

"The knife."

Two words, explosive in the room.

Ad spoke up. "That makes no sense. Why there?"

"The police would naturally search Ivan's workplace. The back room. Such evidence would then cast suspicion on Morrie. A logical suspect. If the cops found it *there*—well…" I glanced at Morrie. "Or a place to hide it permanently…or to be removed later, at a safer time."

"Oh my God," Ella cried out. "Have you no boundaries?"

My voice trembled. "Why not there? Not in *this* house. Away from here. Maybe a place that lots of folks always gravitated to, comfortable, reassuring…"

Ezra scoffed. "You're saying one of us hid the evidence there? In the…rubble?"

"Maybe."

"Maybe not."

"Could be still there."

"Preposterous."

"Crazy," said Sarah.

Then the room exploded. Some yelled out, others cried, others damned me. Molly, bewildered at the cacophony of noise, banged her cane on the floor but no one listened to her. Ad was shaking his head, a quizzical grin on his face.

362   Ed Ifkovic

In the din I said, loudly and purposely, though I didn't believe a word I was saying, "If it's still there—and I believe there's a chance it is, all these years later, a knife and maybe incriminating clothing. Hidden in a convenient cubbyhole. If so, then there could be a way of identifying the true killer."

I didn't believe a word of it.

More pandemonium. My mother banged on a table, maddened, grabbing at her errant and improper daughter, whose disgrace had no limits. Thank God her bags were packed. After my inappropriate and unforgivable outburst in front of a grieving mother and her family, we'd have to make a hasty retreat out of Dodge.

"The police need to be called," I went on, gathering steam.

Leah had folded her body into a ball, curled into the chair like a scared child, but her eyes locked with mine. Slowly, trembling, her lips formed a curious smile. A nod of her head. One hand lifted from her curled body, and it was, triumphantly, a benediction. We nodded at each other. Her blessing to me. Mine—to her. A *mitzvah*.

Suddenly Ella was at my side, too close. Her hot breath covered me.

"What?" I said into her wide-eyed face.

"Edna Ferber, you're a dangerous woman. You should not be in this house."

Chapter Twenty

My mother had pushed her travel trunk into the middle of the hallway, purposely in my path, a bulky monument to the failure of her daughter to behave. It sat there as a reminder that we'd be moving to our apartment in Hyde Park early the following morning after a robust breakfast Esther insisted on making for us. I stared at the trunk with its plastered-on shipping and city labels my mother generously applied: Berlin, Budapest, Vienna, Paris, Rome, Florence—the grand tour of cities we'd visited just before the Great War, returning on a German boat as the 1914 war erupted. Now, after more than two weeks at Esther and Sol's there'd be no labels stuck on, of course, unless there was one mimicking Hester Prynne's inglorious "A"—in this case, perhaps a "D." For Disgrace, Dismay, or Disdain. Disaster? Or, simply, Dunce.

Because, emphatically, as we left Leah's house earlier, no one spoke to me, except the occasional *tut tut* or *tsk tsk* that slipped from Molly's cranky mouth. Tight-lipped and stony-faced, my mother said she'd skip supper, though I didn't. Esther had a savory roast in the oven, paprika-speckled potatoes, and a beef-barley soup simmering on the stove. Esther picked at the meal, Molly ate one potato and fussed about it, but Sol had an appetite and devoured two helpings. A man after my own heart. He who does not value good food, especially in moments of abject shame and humiliation, is a weak-kneed sap. As far as I was concerned.

Finally, the women gone from the table, I sat alone with Sol as he drained the last of a frothy glass of root beer, homemade and kept in an oak barrel in the basement. A twinkle in his eye: "You done a good thing, Edna dear."

"You think so?"

He shook his head vigorously. "You beat the bushes with a big stick, my dear, hoping a jack rabbit will scurry out."

I smiled at that. "A dangerous game."

"It had to be done."

"So you believe me, Sol?"

"I always have."

"I figured that…" I stopped because, in fact, I knew exactly what I'd been doing.

He was still shaking his head. "But the old back room. You think somebody stuffed a knife and bloody clothing in there? Broke into that place? Fifteen years ago? And still there?"

"Not at all."

"But clever, what you said." He raised his eyes to the ceiling and pointed upstairs. "You drive people crazy, Edna."

"So I've heard. I don't do it on purpose."

"Yes, you do."

A sigh. "I guess I do."

"So everybody goes into hiding." He chuckled, but sadly. "Maybe nobody believes you about the back room, but maybe somebody wonders…what? What's there? Maybe this Edna knows something. Maybe not the back room but somewhere else. Something hidden—in plain sight? Maybe…Who knows? Someone running around now. Nervous like a chicken with its head cut off. Give themselves away, stupid. I bet Morrie Wolfsy is pulling out the drawers in that room, piling up the papers and junk dating back to the last century." He chuckled softly.

"I doubt it. Not now. Did you hear Selma after my…performance? She grabbed him and said, 'I need to get home. Now. Away from here. These people.'"

"The air was filled with poison."

"Yes, from Edna, the anarchist's bomb, hurled into a grieving room. A good way to begin shiva."

Sol shook his head. "Ad took Minna off to

the movies tonight. Up at Central Park Theater. A comedy, he tells me. A night like this—a comedy? Can you figure that? Chinese food at Joy Yen Lew's, to top it off. He tells me as they're leaving, 'What in the world was that Edna thinking?' Minna whispered, 'A troublemaker, Edna is.' And I tell both of them, 'Maybe we need to have more such trouble in our lives.' So Ad punches me on the shoulder like I'm an old school chum and they go off to laugh at some antics on the screen. Movies—I never seen one, you know. Don't want to. Young folks, not caring. A movie today. A box of popcorn. A quarter for nothing. A walk home after dark. Young folks. *You* young folks. Such a generation." He waved a hand at me.

Though I said nothing, I thought Sol's definition of "young folks" somewhat skewered. Ad, at forty. Minna, fortyish. Me, careening unhappily toward forty. I was young when McKinley was president. I was young when it was hardly a golden age. Now *these* were days I reveled in—me, the short story writer in the pages of *Ladies' Home Journal* or *Everybody's*. Six months in New York, six in Chicago. A novelist. A move from short story land to novel country. Furnished apartments with oriental carpets, Victrolas, and supercilious doormen.

…with my mother…

…whose trunk was a punctuation mark on a failed day.

I stood up. "I'm going to hide in my room."

Sol winked, grandfatherly. "Under the covers where the goblins can't get you."

● ● ● ● ●

I turned the doorknob slowly. At first the old door refused to give. No one locked that door, I knew, probably hadn't for years. After all, Levi walked in and out all day, left the door wide open. There was nothing left to steal except his piles of used clothing, unsorted, smelly, worn, sifted through. A vacant room now, though the stink of raw meat and gamey bird lingered, odors that warred with the stink of mouse droppings and old paper pulp. After he shut down his butcher shop, Morrie never locked up. No need to. Everybody knew that. And, maybe, others. At least one other soul who might surprise me.

…with any luck…

Eight o'clock at night, dark now. At the Newmann household all was quiet. My mother was in her room, probably writing letters before she turned in. Esther and Sol in their room. Molly, when I walked into the kitchen for water earlier, was in her bedroom at the back, the hum of a radio on low, some staticky song. I heard her coughing, some phlegmatic jag that alarmed. But then silence. The radio suddenly switched to another station, and then switched off. A house that went to bed early, and happily. That middle-aged youngster, Ad, was at the movies with Minna. Or treating her to chop suey on Clark Street. The house creaked under the summer heat, the steamy attic, and the groaning eaves. Another hot night.

I'd slipped out by the back door, pushing open the screen door, edging my way up the sidewalk until, away from any possible sighting, I hurried toward Maxwell. At the corner I paused to check out Morrie Wolfsy's second-story apartment over the meat market, but saw only darkness. Home with his wife, probably reviewing my shameful performance. "I told you she was a crazy person, that daughter of Julia's. Imagine the nonsense that comes out of her mouth." No one around now. A streetlamp cast flickering shadows on the façade, black-sooted like so many Chicago buildings, the awful dirt and grime of distant I. C. trains carried by wind and rain until so much of Chicago resembled a darkswept Hogarth print.

The door gave, though it squealed and yawned, loud enough to make me hesitate. But not for long. Inside, sweating but calm, determined, I switched on the light, and the miserable room lit up: counters of unsorted clothing, empty butcher-block surfaces, sagging shelves, and on the floor a nasty crumble of old, dried sawdust. Quietly, I moved across the room, reached the back room, found the light switch, and turned it on. I rushed back to the front entrance, switched off that light. The same procedure in the back room, as I located the small bathroom at the back, turned on that light, went back to switch off the back room light. On off, on off, a frantic rhythm. I pulled a hard-backed chair into the bathroom, shut the door but not completely, an inch opening perhaps, and then plunged the small space into darkness.

A little foolish, I sat in complete blackness, hands folded in my lap. And waited. Waited. Waited—though I thought—not only is this most likely a waste of time—but *foolhardy*. Proving what? A suspicion I'd had the day before—a mishmash of bits and pieces that led me to suspect someone of murder? Impossible to prove—except…maybe *this* plot…this…this sitting in the dark. Would someone show up? So there I sat, waiting.

A knife had been thrust into a man's neck, probably a sudden, unplanned moment, quick, quick, the spurt of sudden blood. The horror of it all. Not pretty, any of it. Ivan's murder had been impulse, chance. I believed that. Someone not used to murder. Someone surprised at the act itself. One of *us*.

A murderer who now felt safe, untouchable.

Except for something—maybe *someone*— unable to be controlled.

But…what possibility fifteen years later? So much to lose.

Getting away with murder. The perfect crime, the murderer untouchable. Maybe forever.

I waited.

An hour passed, uneventful. Bored, hot, I nearly dozed off in the tight, close room, windowless, when I heard the creak of the front door. I shot awake, spine stiff, eyes wide. My heart raced. I sucked in my breath.

Now.

My God. Now.

The answer.

At first nothing. Then a tentative step, almost inaudible, the front door closed, a dragging sound as though something were being shuffled across the floor. Through a crack in the bathroom door, I saw the light come on in the back room, though I sat back, in darkness, hidden, scared now, heart pounding. For a moment I closed my eyes: lightning flashes of red yellow blue, blending, colliding, sparks flying. I nearly gasped out loud.

Then I heard it: a wall cubbyhole opened, a drawer pulled out. One drawer, followed by a crash of papers and something metal. Something clanging onto the floor. A pause, deafening. Then a second drawer, opened, rifled through. A rhythm, though sloppy and rushed. I waited.

A tapping. Something moved. *Tap tap tap.*

I had no choice. I snapped on the bathroom light, swung open the door, and heard a woman's piercing shriek, breaking at the end.

Molly Newmann faced me, her face ivory with fright, one hand grasping a sheaf of bound papers, the other gripping her cane. *Tap tap tap.*

I stared, frozen, my mind blank, my throat parched.

A low hissing sound from the back of her throat. "Edna, what…?"

"Molly." I barely got the name out.

She dropped the papers, spun around, banging into a table with that cane and hobbled toward the door. She hesitated a moment, faced me with sad and stark eyes, ready to blather some excuse—*I lost my way, I wandered—I—I don't know how I got here*—

Shoulders dropping, resigned, she ignored me, leaving the back room but, nervously, switching off the light behind her. Plunged into darkness, I reached for the bathroom door, got my bearings, but my body refused to move. When I touched my cheeks, I felt hot flesh, my skin tingling. I burned with shame. It was like opening a door to find someone naked sitting in front of you. You, the intruder, stammer, apologetic, babbling. The naked soul, aware of her own nakedness, simply watches you. In the case of Molly, she simply walked out the door, though slowly, an old woman's fragile step. My whole body shook.

• • ● • •

Molly sat in her kitchen and ignored me when I walked in. I'd stayed in the back room, righting the drawers, obsessed with returning the room to its original look. But it was more than that, really. I couldn't bear the sight of the aged Molly, crippled now, moving down the sidewalk. *Tap tap tap. Tap tap* tap. She was headed to the house where I was a guest. So I lingered, sad and dizzy, until I had no choice but to follow her dead man's path.

She was preparing a cup of hot tea. As I watched, she carefully removed the tea leaves, added a bit of cream, two teaspoons of sugar, and took a sip. She watched me over the rim of the teacup. A civilized woman, but the cup rattled when she replaced it on the saucer.

"I need to understand." I sat opposite her.

She watched me for a while, her face horrible, wrinkled, old, old. "It wasn't supposed to come to this."

"Tell me."

"I knew you'd come to suspect"—she faltered, the word catching—"him."

Her clipped words, so blunt and hurting, were

like a jolt to the system. Of course, she'd sensed that I knew. The little slip-ups. The little nagging suspicion and inconsistencies that suddenly came together, flashed before me, emblazoned.

"Ad." One word, awful in its fearsome weight.

She closed her eyes.

She mouthed one word: Adolph.

Her hand knocked the tea cup, the tea sloshing out.

For I had realized, earlier, that I'd known it on a gut level for a day or so now. Maybe more. The little things, I reflected. I found my voice. "Little things you said. When you heard Sarah screaming, you stepped out of your room to find Ad standing in the hallway. Another time you said you knocked on his door, and he was waking up from a nap. A small inconsistency, true, but it made me wonder. And that nonsense about Sarah being part of the fight the morning that Ivan and Leah had. You were forgetting things, slipping up, and so you rambled, threw stories out, helpless, trying to push me away. You were forgetting what you'd told me. What you'd told the cops."

A thin smile. "There was never a reason for me to rehearse a story."

"Until I arrived. Until Leah came back home."

She shuddered. "A seductive hoyden, that one."

"Tell me."

"I never knew anything." She refused to look at me, her voice dipping.

I broke in, angry. "Of course, you did. Molly, you're lying to me."

A long pause, the rattling of the cup. "He's my grandson. My favorite boy. The one blessing to this family."

"I wondered about the boys in the back room. I grant you that. Something always bothered me. In all the stories Ad was different. Under Levi Pinsky's moralistic instruction, he frowned on the others teasing about Leah, though I gather he once did so and Ivan yelled at him. That deadly conversation he had with Jacob on the porch. The day before the murder. The failed rabbinical student, a lark for a moment, intrigued by Levi's stories, but he saw himself as chivalric, the one who had a rarefied view of women. Levi's insidious gift to him. It explained his long, unfulfilled engagement to Minna. So many times he saw himself as a hero. The clay hero, or mud, saving others. A little thing, but maybe not."

Molly shook her head. "Maybe. Maybe not. But even when he was a small boy, he had a boyish crush on Leah. His best friend's mother. A beautiful woman who teased him then. He became a little… protective…" A sigh. "The hero nobody needed."

"Or possessive."

Bitterness in her tone. "That fight Ivan had with Leah. That morning. Adolph hated Ivan—so many times, hearing them fight, he—seethed. Adolph with his hot temper. Back to when that man hurt poor Minna—shattered that poor girl. Adolph stepped in, sorry for her. Always the knight hungry for a—a battle to show off. Adolph didn't want to marry her—he wanted to *defend* her."

She stopped talking, her eyes watching the doorway.

"Go on, Molly."

She breathed in. "That morning he wanted to go there—to *fight* Ivan. He was afraid for Leah. 'I got to help her. That…that bastard!' The way Ivan smacked Jacob the day before—hated his own son, mocked him. Adolph, the protector. Adolph, the savior."

"But you left, went to Maxwell Street."

"I made him go shopping with me—to get him away. But I could see the fury in his face. His eyes—so…crazy. I lied and told everyone we were together the whole day, as if we'd never left each other's sides. And we were—most of that day. The truth. But later on, back home, I napped in my room. I heard screaming. Sarah screaming." For a second she closed her eyes. "You know, I'd heard Adolph running up the stairs a short time before, out of breath, sobbing, slamming into his room. It woke me up. No, Adolph wasn't in the hallway. When he came out after I called him, he was scared. Shaking. His hands shook. I *knew*. But what could I say? My boy. Adolph. Everyone calls him Ad. Everyone loves him—a good boy. Edna, he never found his way. He's an unfinished boy."

"A scared man." I waited a second. "You never asked him?"

"How could I, Edna? How?"

"And he let Leah take the blame."

She didn't answer except to say, "He changed after that day. I could see it. He'd stare, he'd get white in the face, he'd get that faraway look in his eyes. He lost…ambition. Minna pursued him, got him—but what did she get? A shell, a vacant-eyed wanderer, lost in this house, on the streets. A thousand jobs."

"But Leah…"

She raised her voice. "Leah was sent to a home. Not a prison. I could see how he thought that saved everyone, like Leah was visiting out-of-state relatives. He stopped thinking about it. I doted on him, but he'd see me watching him because he knew I *knew*. The way he looked that day when I came out of my room. And now and then he'd spot me staring at him, something in my eyes that he saw there. I don't know. At those moments I saw fear, a look that said: Don't tell, help me, don't tell help me I don't know what I did help help help me. Like words strung together without a breath between."

"But he watched Jacob have a breakdown. Jacob, filled with his own self-doubt. Jacob, blaming himself, Jacob willing himself to die."

A sob escaped her throat. "You saw how Jacob drew apart from Adolph lately, no? Adolph was baffled. Your doing, Edna. You put that doubt into Jacob's head, and he obsessed about it and somehow wondered about Adolph. A suspicion, maybe, the way Adolph acted. Back then."

I agreed. "That's what got me thinking about him, Molly. God knows how Jacob's mind worked, but something triggered such thoughts. He sent me a poem, asking me to be nice to him, but talking about a 'comrade song.' Something that made no sense. What 'comrade song' did he have? Only one. Written on the back of an old poem about the boys watching his mother. He must have known Ad's attitude toward Leah. I wondered about that. And his last conversation with Ad—something about it being time. 'Don't you know it's time?' His best friend, he realized—and it was time to come clean. Time!"

Molly's face was tear-streaked. "How Adolph hated Ivan." She shuddered. "And adored Leah."

"Ad on a moral crusade, starting in that back room."

"A good boy…"

"Somehow when it came together for Jacob, he couldn't be around Ad. It bothered him. It ate at him."

"You scared me at Leah's this afternoon, Edna. You made me wonder. What does Edna know? Did I miss something? It made no sense, but I couldn't take a chance. A whole part of me knew there was nothing in that back room—how could there be? why would there be?—but I couldn't sleep. I'm an old lady—confused. Fifteen years—of course nothing, though Morrie left it cluttered, untouched. I had to *be* there. I couldn't *ask* Adolph."

"And so you headed there."

"The evidence still there? Impossible. Fifteen years. But that news about the break-in that same night. I never heard that before. Never. A locked back door—broken into. It frightened me. I could see Adolph doing that. I thought—yes, I thought—yes, hide something. Hide a knife. Adolph broke in, hid the knife and bloody clothing so that the police would blame Morrie."

"I don't think the police even considered…"

A sharp look. "That's why I thought… maybe…"

"But there's no evidence. I never believed there was any."

A dusky chuckle. "Which is why Adolph went to the movies. He knows there's nothing there. And anybody else hearing you today. Everybody else but…but me." She eyed me. "You knew I would do something. That news about the break-in that same night. You probably saw my face." A sickly smile, those ivory-blue false teeth. "The only hope you had was—me."

I shook my head. "I didn't know. But there was no other way to prove my theory. Too many years have gone by. Who would believe me? What proof? The only way was to get the only other person I suspected who knew what happened that day to…to go there."

"Me." She could barely get the word out. "An addled old lady. Adolph believed he was safe."

"You didn't."

Her voice broke. "I *had* to go there."

"And so did I." I sighed. "Molly, I swear I didn't want to see you there, but there was no one else who would come. The only person who might come—you."

Her laugh broke at the end. "So in walks this little old lady, crippled, banging away with her cane." She saluted me with her teacup. "I was pan-icky. Yes, that's the way he thinks. Blame Morrie.

Stupid Morrie—the philanderer." She locked eyes with mine. "The idea drove me—*crazy*. But, you see, I couldn't take a chance."

My voice trembled. "I'm sorry for you, Molly. Of course, I am. For your family. For Ad. You are people I care about. You have to believe that. But I'm not sorry for what I did. Leah had to have that black stain taken off her."

"Leah! Temptress. Look what she did to Adolph."

I stared back, stupefied. "Look what *he* did to her, Molly."

Footsteps in the hallway, a door slammed, an ebullient Ad bursting in, giving Molly a peck on the cheek. She held up her hand.

"What?" he demanded. "The two of you are so serious…"

Molly took his hand in hers, held it, squeezed it. "I've told Edna." She started to cry.

He knew then, he had to.

His jaw dropped. He spun around, mad-dened, glanced toward the back door. A coward, I thought—a callow man, a bounder. Worse…a killer.

"But…no." He yelled out the word. It sailed across the kitchen.

"It's over, my Adolph. I'm old and I'm tired."

"What?"

She reached for his hand, but he pulled it away. "Edna knows what you did."

"No."

"I told her."

"No."

"Sit down, Ad." I pointed to a chair. He debated what to do, but finally he did, hunched over. "Now tell me."

For a moment there was a flash of anger and resentment, of utter dislike, but it passed. What surfaced was the little boy, the town bully who hopes you'll pity him, console, forgive. *My excuse is weakness, frailty, I'm all too human. I didn't know… Forgive me. Love me. It wasn't my fault. It was an accident.*

Believe me. I—

So he blubbered, ugly, but I reached over and gripped his arm. Steely-eyed, I demanded, "Tell me."

"He made fun of me."

Molly patted the back of his wrist. "Adolph, my Adolph."

He refused to look at her. "That day, yes, but it wasn't the first time. He was a hard man—cruel. What he did to Jacob. To me. 'You look at my wife, you lousy creep.' He struck me once. I never told you that—I was so ashamed. And that morning, the fight. Horrible. Leah crying and crying—the sobs carrying across the yards. I was so afraid he'd hurt her. So when we got back from shopping, I snuck over."

Molly frowned, "You didn't have to, Adolph. I stopped you that morning, but that's all you talked about with me. You got so crazy." A sigh. "Always a *hitsiger*, my boy." A hothead.

"I had to. You were napping. I heard Leah crying on the back porch, and then I saw her go into the back garden. She was sobbing in her garden. Pitiful." His voice became a whine. "When I walked in the front door, he was there—on the sofa. He laughed at me. Again." He swallowed. "He's sick and irritated and…and…I snapped. He was doubled over, but suddenly he reached out and pushed me. I snapped. I had the dumb pocketknife I always carried. Lord, we all carried them, and I pulled it out, opened it. I waved it at him. He laughed and laughed, tears in his eyes. 'That little knife. You'll never be a butcher if you use a knife like that. Oh, you'll never be nothing.' I don't remember what happened. I don't. But all of a sudden that knife was in his neck, a vein, and all this blood was gushing out, and he was choking, gagging. One loud shout, I remember, and then this gurgling sound, desperate. His hands pulled at his neck—all the blood. It was awful. Awful. I folded the knife, covered with blood, and tucked it into my pocket. I rolled up my sleeves, soaked with his blood. I wrapped my handkerchief around my fingers. I got out of there."

"Adolph." Panic in Molly's voice. "Adolph."

Ad watched his grandmother. "Yeah, you heard me running up the stairs. I knew that. That ruined everything. You saw what a mess I was—I could see the question in your eyes. That *hurt* me."

"So Jacob suspected you? He avoided you."

He nodded. "I was stupid. Crazy, he said to me, 'A knife. There was no knife.' And I said that maybe the killer took it with him. 'Yeah, running out the door with a cleaver?' But I said—maybe a small knife, a pocket knife.' A blunder, really. We both carried pocketknives, and he gave me the strangest look. It chilled me."

"What did he say?"

"Nothing. He walked away. But I thought— Christ, trouble."

"Ad," I began, "why didn't you speak up when it happened? Years ago?"

He ignored that. He was still staring at his grandmother, his eyes moist. "I haven't been happy since that day."

"Happy?" I screamed. "Ad, no…sense of honor…or proportion. Ad, do you hear yourself?"

Surprised, mouth twitching, growl of barely

suppressed anger. "You shouldn't have come here, Edna."

"No, Ad…"

Suddenly he stood, so abruptly I started. His fingertips rapped the table nervously. "I need air."

"Sit down, Ad," I told him.

He shook his head, his eyes white with panic. "This kitchen is too hot. It's too damn hot. No one ever opens the goddamn windows here. You can't breathe in here. No one can breathe in this house. What's the matter with you people? How do you expect a man to breathe in this house?"

"Sit down, Ad," I repeated. "We have to talk to the police in the morning…"

He started. "No."

"We have no choice."

Molly made a choking sound. "No, Edna, all the years."

"No." My voice firm. "It's over, Ad."

He looked down at his grandmother and mouthed the word—over.

"Over," he said out loud. Then, in a small, tinny voice he rambled, sputtered nonsense, but dark, frightening. At one point he mouthed the name Jacob—"Oh Jacob, Jacob"—and he sobbed. Then, his eyes weepy, he said, "I always knew my story would have a bad ending."

He bumped into the cabinet, banged his fist

on the sink top. Blindly, furiously, he stared out the window at the black night.

He rushed to the door, though Molly screamed, "No, no. Don't go."

"Not this way," I pleaded. "No, Adolph."

But he was gone, the door slamming behind him.

Molly had her eyes closed. When she opened them—when she caught my eye—it was as if she'd seen a ghost. Her hands flew to her neck as she struggled for breath. Her fingers rubbed the right side of her face—the sagging jaw from her stoke—and she rocked in her chair.

The look we shared was horrible. In that moment we both understood that there would be a dreadful knock on the door the next morning.

Her face was ravaged now, ancient, the map of wrinkles deeply rutted, a dull purple. She tried to stand, reaching for the cane, but her elbow knocked it away, and it clattered to the linoleum floor. She stared absently at it but made no effort to bend for it. With one foot, jerking out, she kicked it across the room. It banged against the stove, a thud, the white enamel chipped. "Good."

"You did a horrible thing, Molly."

She spat out her words, an epitaph. "My own grandson, Edna." She sighed. "*A mane hot oygen fun gloz.*" A mother has glass eyes.

I shook my head. "No, Molly. You can't close your eyes to this."

"Edna…"

"You let an innocent woman suffer for fifteen years. You condemned her to ridicule and exile and shame and…"

She pounded a fist on the table. The teacup slid off, crashing to the floor. A ragged voice, icy. "And I didn't suffer all these years, Edna? You don't think I suffered? Every waking moment of these years has been my hell. Tell me I haven't suffered, Edna. You can't, can you?" She started to cry, thin, breathless gasps. "You can't. You can't."

To receive a free catalog of Poisoned Pen Press titles, please provide your name, address, and email address in one of the following ways:

Phone: 1-800-421-3976
Facsimile: 1-480-949-1707
Email: info@poisonedpenpress.com
Website: www.poisonedpenpress.com

Poisoned Pen Press
6962 E. First Ave. Ste 103
Scottsdale, AZ 85251

CPSIA information can be obtained
at www.ICGtesting.com
Printed in the USA
BVOW03s1921100217
475896BV00001B/28/P